PRAISE FOR STELLA RIMINGTON AND
ILLEGAL ACTION

"Stella Rimington bids to join the ranks of such secret-agent authors as W. Somerset Maugham, Graham Greene, John le Carré and Charles McCarry."   —*The Wall Street Journal*

"The details are rich."   —*The Arizona Republic*

"Several former spies have tried their hand at espionage fiction with great success . . . but Dame Rimington trumps all. . . . Her storytelling abilities are a welcome and delightful surprise."
—*The Baltimore Sun*

"Frighteningly authentic."   —*Chicago Tribune*

"An ideal beach read."   —*Booklist*

STELLA RIMINGTON

ILLEGAL ACTION

Stella Rimington joined Britain's Security Service (MI5) in 1969. During her nearly thirty-year career she worked in all the main fields of the Service's responsibilities—counter-subversion, counter-espionage, and counter-terrorism—and successively became Director of all three branches. Appointed Director General of MI5 in 1992, she was the first woman to hold the post and the first Director General whose name was publicly announced on appointment. Following her retirement from MI5 in 1996, she became a nonexecutive director of Marks & Spencer and published her autobiography, *Open Secret*, in the United Kingdom. She is also the author of *At Risk*, the first Liz Carlyle novel. Rimington lives in London.

ILLEGAL ACTION

ILLEGAL ACTION

STELLA RIMINGTON

Vintage Crime/Black Lizard
Vintage Books
A Division of Random House, Inc.
New York

FIRST VINTAGE CRIME/BLACK LIZARD EDITION, JUNE 2009

Copyright © 2007 by Stella Rimington

All rights reserved. Published in the United States by Vintage Books, a division of Random House, Inc., New York. Originally published in Great Britain by Hutchinson, an imprint of the Random House Group Limited, London, in 2007, and subsequently published by arrangement with Hutchinson in hardcover in the United States by Alfred A. Knopf, a division of Random House, Inc., New York, in 2008.

Vintage is a registered trademark and Vintage Crime/Black Lizard and colophon are trademarks of Random House, Inc.

The Library of Congress has cataloged the Knopf edition as follows:
Rimington, Stella.
Illegal action / by Stella Rimington.—1st U.S. ed.
p. cm.
Originally published: Great Britain: Hutchinson, 2007.
1. Women Intelligence officers—Fiction. 2. Russians—England—London—Fiction. 3. Spies—England—London—Fiction. 4. London (England)—Fiction. I. Title.
PR6118.I44I45 2008
823'.92—dc22 2008004148

Vintage ISBN: 978-0-307-38906-0

Book design by Soonyoung Kwon

www.vintagebooks.com

Printed in the United States of America
10 9 8 7 6 5 4 3 2 1

To
Brian and Christine

ILLEGAL ACTION

1

NOVEMBER

For once Alvin Jackson had made the wrong choice.

Usually he had an unerring eye for a soft target. It wasn't about size—once a man built like a nightclub bouncer had cried when Jackson showed him the knife. No, it was something less tangible, a kind of passivity that Jackson could sniff out, the way a sniffer dog smells contraband.

Not that he expected much resistance from anyone in this part of London. He stood against the iron railings in one of the squares that run off the side streets below Kensington High Street. The night was moonless, and a mass of grey cloud hung over the city like a dirty blanket. Earlier in the evening it had rained: now the tyres of passing cars hissed as they splashed through the puddles, and the pavements were the colour of dark sodden sponges. Jackson had picked a corner where two of the street lights were out. He'd already checked carefully for patrolling policemen and traffic wardens. There weren't any.

The woman walking towards Jackson along the opposite pavement was well into her thirties—not young enough to be foolish and too affluent to be streetwise. She wore a smartly cut black overcoat, her hair was coiffed back, doubtless from a fancy salon, and her heels went *clack-clack-clack* on the pavement. There was a bag hooked over her right shoulder, one of those trendy leather bags with floppy handles. That's where her purse would be, Jackson decided.

He waited against the railings until she was about fifteen feet away, then sauntered casually across the road and stood on the pavement, blocking her path.

She stopped, and he was pleased to see she looked a little startled. "Hello," he said softly, and her eyes widened slightly. She had a delicate, pretty face, he thought. "I like your bag," he said now, pointing at it with one extended arm.

"Thank you," she said crisply, which surprised him, since most of the women were too scared to speak. Funny how reactions differed. Maybe she was foreign.

With his other hand he showed her the knife. It was a seven-inch blade, with a sweeping crescent curve that ended in a honed point. The Americans called them bowie knives—Jackson liked the name. He said, "Give me the bag."

The woman didn't panic. That was a relief; the last thing he wanted was for her to scream. She just nodded, then reached with her left arm and unhooked the bag from her shoulder. She held the bag's handles with one hand, and he started to reach forward to take it, then realised she was rummaging in it with the other. "Just hand it over," he was saying as the woman withdrew her hand. It suddenly shot out straight towards him, and something glinted in the dark.

He felt an agonising pain in his left arm, right below his shoulder. "*Jesus!*" he shouted, wincing. What had she just done to him? He looked and saw blood spurting from his arm. The pain was excruciating. I'm going to cut you, bitch, he thought, full of rage. He began to move forward, but the metal implement she held glinted again and jabbed him sharply in the middle of his chest. Once, then twice, each time causing him to flinch.

He was in agony, and when Jackson saw the woman's hand move again, he turned and ran as fast as he could. He reached the corner, clutching his wounded arm, and thought, Who the hell was that? Whoever she was, Jackson decided, as blood continued to ooze through his fingers, he'd picked the wrong lady.

Looking around her carefully, she saw that there was no one else in the square. Good. Calmly, she took a tissue out and wiped the end of the Stanley knife, sticky from her assailant's blood, then retracted the blade. Normally she would never have resisted a street robbery, but there had been no way she was going to give the man her bag.

A light went on outside one of the houses and a curtain was drawn back, so she moved away quickly, still holding the Stanley knife, in case the man was waiting for her, ready to have another go. But leaving the square, she saw no one on the pavement ahead of her. A taxi passed by; it held a couple, necking in the back. At the corner she turned into a small side street which ended in a cul-de-sac. She stopped at the entrance to a large mansion block, let herself in, then climbed to the second floor. Here she unlocked a door and entered a flat, turning on a light in the small sitting room. The place was sparsely furnished by the landlord, gloomy in its bareness. But it didn't matter to her. She wasn't staying long—she only rented for a month at a time, and this was her third place. She knew that once her orders came she would be living far more comfortably.

She went to the bedroom where two computer bags sat in the corner, and carried them both to the pine desk in the sitting room. One bag held a small black machine that resembled a sleek sort of CD player; the other was a laptop computer. Connecting the two with a USB cable, she pressed a button on the black machine, and watched as it transferred to the laptop data that it had recorded in her absence. On the computer she then ran a software routine that filled the screen with numbers.

Sitting down in front of the desk, she reached into her own bag, the one the man had tried to take from her, and took out a large, hardcover book. It was a novel, well thumbed—*An Instance of the Fingerpost*. She wondered idly if she would ever read it.

She opened the book, flicked through it and finding the page she wanted carefully put it down next to the computer and drew up a chair.

Twenty minutes later she was finished. On a scratch pad she had a list of numbers, each with an accompanying word she had written down. She stood up now, and took the single page of Russian text to the lavatory, where she ripped it into small pieces before flushing it away. She put the black machine and the laptop into their respective carrying bags, then returned them to the bedroom.

Finally, she came back to the desk. She decided to allow herself a cigarette, and fished in her bag for a pack of Marlboros. What she really craved was a Sobranie. Presumably one of the fancy tobacconists in London, like Davidoff's, would sell them.

But Marlboros would have to do, she thought, as she lit her cigarette. *Always remember*, they had drilled her again and again, *it's
the little things you think don't matter that can give you away.*
She had memorised the message on the single page of text and
now she ran over it in her mind, focusing on the key instruction.

You should begin now.

2

I suppose it all went as well as could be expected." Charles Wetherby was standing by the window of his office, looking down at the Thames, where the little waves bristled, sawtoothed in the late November wind. A tourist cruising boat moved jerkily in the chop, its decks empty, the few passengers sitting snugly in the cabin below.

"Thank goodness it was no worse," said Liz Carlyle from her chair in front of Wetherby's desk.

She had given evidence to the inquiry for over three hours; Wetherby had been there a day and a half. Now he looked tired, strained, and, unusually for him, made no effort to disguise it. Sighing, he rubbed a palm against his cheekbone thoughtfully, then turned and faced Liz. "DG says you did very well. Not that you ever had anything to worry about."

She nodded, wishing she shared his confidence. The fallout from that last operation had not yet subsided. The discovery of a mole in MI5, who had been intent on undermining the Service, was likely to reverberate for years to come. As the Home Secretary had taken to saying, with the monotony of a mantra, "If the Security Service isn't fit for purpose, how the hell can we win the war on terrorism?"

The same Home Secretary had insisted on an inquiry into the whole sorry business. Fortunately he'd eventually grasped that a public inquiry would be a disaster, so it had been held in closed session, chaired by a former Cabinet secretary, assisted by a judge and a trusted businessman. No prying press, no trial by headline; no MPs posturing in some parliamentary committee room for the benefit of the cameras. The report when it came had been a model of Whitehall-ese, beautifully expressed, utterly undramatic, no blame, reasonably fair.

"What will happen now?" asked Liz.

Wetherby moved back to his desk, sitting down and picking up a pencil. He tapped distractedly on a pile of papers. "There'll be a review of recruitment, enhanced vetting procedures . . . other things. But as I say, you've got nothing to worry about."

"Have you, Charles?" she asked. It had been Wetherby himself who had predicted heads would roll after the near debacle and the Thames House rumour mill had suggested Wetherby's would be one.

He shrugged, leaning back in his chair. He was not as engaged as usual, which alarmed Liz. What else could he be thinking about? Finally he said, "I'd like to think it will be all right for me as well. But who knows? I've learnt these things are hard to predict. Anyway, I won't be here for the aftermath. I'm taking some leave."

"Oh," she said.

He heard the question in her voice. She was wondering whether this was voluntary. "It's my choice, Liz." Wetherby looked at her. "I'm entitled to a sabbatical and I've decided I should spend some time at home." He gestured with a quick motion of his head at a framed photograph of his wife and sons.

Liz nodded. This was why he seemed so subdued. Joanne Wetherby had been seriously ill for as long as Liz had known Charles—over five years. It could not have been easy, juggling his job with his role as the husband of an invalid and the father of two boys. She was sure he would miss the challenge, the excitement and the colleagues. And her, Liz wondered, would he miss her?

Liz asked, "How long will you be away?"

Wetherby shrugged and flicked a non-existent piece of fluff off his suit jacket. "I'm not sure. Perhaps three months, something like that. We'll have to see how things go. While I'm away, Michael Binding will run the branch."

Oh God, thought Liz, not that condescending oaf. They'd crossed swords more than once. She tried her best to mask her reaction, but Wetherby gave her an ironic smile. "Don't worry. He won't be telling you what to do."

"Won't he?"

"No. You're being posted. DG and I have discussed it, and we want you to move to Counter-Espionage."

"What?" she asked bluntly, unable to contain her surprise. Nor her dismay. During the Cold War, Counter-Espionage had been the plum assignment, the *primus inter pares* of the Service's various branches. But in a post-9/11 world, its light was dimmer, overshadowed by Counter-Terrorism. Counter-Espionage was something of a backwater now.

"You need a change. You know that."

"I don't need a demotion, Charles. That's what it is. I feel as though I'm being pushed out." She paused, realising that her hurt was showing, and bit her lip.

Charles looked at her gravely. "That's not it at all," he said. "We just want to broaden your experience. People think espionage is no longer a problem. Well, they're wrong. There are more foreign intelligence officers in London now than before the fall of the Berlin Wall. The Russians are back in force, the Chinese are more active than ever. So are some of the Middle Eastern countries. And the game's changed, you know. It used to be all about political and military intelligence—all about winning the Cold War and the fighting war that never happened. Deadly enough, but strictly for professionals. Now there's money, big money in it. We wouldn't be posting you there if there wasn't a job for you to do."

"Who will I report to?" she asked.

"To Brian Ackers," said Charles. "You'll be in the Russian Section and he's the assistant director. He's also acting director of the whole Counter-Espionage Branch for the time being."

Liz raised her eyebrows. Brian Ackers was a Cold War veteran who hadn't moved on. Prickly, touchy, a man who resented the displacement of counter-espionage as the Service's highest priority.

"I know he's not the easiest man to work for," Wetherby continued, "but he's got enormous experience. You could learn a lot from him. After all, that's where the whole intelligence game started and where many of the real skills still are."

Liz nodded. "Yes, Charles," she said, trying not to sound as disappointed as she felt.

"Brian won't be there forever, Liz," said Charles encouragingly. "He'll retire in two years." He looked at her meaningfully. "There may be opportunities after that."

She tried to take this in. Was he suggesting she might replace Brian Ackers one day? Become an assistant director? She was flattered, but she still found the prospect of a move to Counter-Espionage uninspiring. "When do I start?" she asked.

"Next week. Peggy Kinsolving is going with you."

So, thought Liz, they're moving everyone closely involved with the mole investigation. But this was good news. Peggy had been seconded by MI6 in the previous year, then opted to stay on in MI5. She was a desk officer, with boundless energy and an almost unique ability to ferret out facts. If Wetherby and DG were offering her to Liz, she was more than happy to accept the gift.

"Anyway, I'm off next week, so I'll say goodbye now. Good luck in the new post," said Wetherby, and Liz took her cue and stood up. He held out his hand and grasped hers. Suddenly he said, in an awkward, tentative voice, "Do me one favour, please."

"Of course," she said, suddenly near tears.

"Stay in touch." He said this shyly, then quickly looked down at the papers on his desk.

And turning to go, Liz saw through the window the tour boat returning from its quick jaunt upriver, moving more smoothly, travelling with the receding tide. Dusk was turning to dark. As the windows lit up in the offices and flats on the far bank, the river became quite quickly a gleaming black flood, flecked with gold.

3

LATE MARCH

That morning spring was at its most capricious. The sun shone from a bright blue sky, but the wind came from the north, and its gusts were strong and biting. Walking up into this remote part of Hampstead Heath, Simmons recognised the familiar bench—but not the man sitting on it. He was about to walk on when the man called out. "Jerry," he said, and lifted an arm in greeting.

Simmons hesitated, hearing his name. "Who are you?" he asked, cautiously coming a little closer.

"Your new contact," the man said. He tapped the seat sharply. "Sit down."

The bench was in the shelter of a ring of ancient oaks,

bounded by iron railings, on the top of a hill. There was no one on this part of the heath except a few dog walkers in the distance below. Slowly Jerry Simmons moved to the bench and sat down at the far end. "What happened to Andrei?" he asked, keeping his eyes on the heath.

"He's gone," said the man tersely. "I'm Vladimir."

Jerry turned his head slowly and inspected the Russian. He wore a belted raincoat, polished brogues, and a checked cloth cap. He might almost have passed for English, but his accent and high Slavic cheekbones gave him away.

He seemed on edge, which in turn made Jerry anxious. I'm losing my nerve, he thought, remembering his army days, when only ice water had run through his veins. When Jerry had passed the final SAS interview (something he dreaded far more than the forced march, the mock interrogations, any of the physical stuff he was so good at) the sergeant had told him: "You're not the sharpest knife in the box, Simmons, but we liked your cool. And your size counts. Don't rely on it, that's all."

Now he said to the man, "When I left the hotel I told Andrei that I was finished working for you guys."

Vladimir shrugged. "Of course you did. But situations change, don't they?"

Not for me, thought Jerry. When he had left the army he'd been delighted to find the security job at the Dorchester. Sure the money wasn't terrific, but it was a famous hotel, superbly run, and he'd been well treated. The only injury he'd suffered in his time there had been a bruised knee when he'd slipped on a freshly mopped bathroom floor. It certainly beat four-man night patrols in southern Afghanistan.

His problem had been Carly, wife number three. Now divorced. Three in chronological order, that is, but number one for greed. So it had been a blessing when Andrei had turned up. The job had been a doddle. Just tittle-tattle, names and addresses, comings and goings at the hotel, what the occasional sheikh got up to (gambling, usually, and girls; sometimes gambling and boys). It had been money for jam, even if Carly got most of it.

He'd had a pretty good idea who Andrei was. Organised crime he'd thought at first, but he'd recognised a certain military touch—official, he'd decided. Jerry had never had the slightest fear he was doing anything that might harm Britain. Though by the time he had left the employ of the hotel, lured by a security firm with the promise of better pay and better hours, he was relieved to put his days moonlighting for Andrei behind him.

"I'm not at the Dorchester any more," Jerry said, trying to sound conclusive, though he was not so naïve as to think Vladimir didn't know this already.

"I know. Congratulations. You're working for a very wealthy man."

Jerry shrugged. He'd never heard of his present employer until he'd become his "driver"—which meant his bodyguard behind the wheel. "Maybe he is," he said. "I just take him where he wants to go and look after him. That's all I know."

"You know more than you think," said Vladimir.

"What do you mean?" said Jerry. His heart was starting to sink. Vladimir didn't seem edgy any longer.

"Your new employer is a countryman of mine. I'm very interested in him."

They sat in silence for a moment. The wind had picked up again, and Jerry stirred uneasily on the bench, feeling cold. Why did I have to get a job with a Russian? he wondered sourly as he waited in vain for Vladimir to break the silence.

At last Jerry sighed. "What are you looking for?" he asked quietly, trying to make it clear he hadn't agreed to do anything.

"Same as the Dorchester," said the man on the bench. "And this time there's only one 'guest' to keep an eye on."

"But this guy doesn't get up to anything," Jerry protested. "He doesn't do nightclubs, doesn't even go out much to restaurants. A new girlfriend's around, and he spends most of his spare time with her. Their idea of a big night is ordering a takeaway and watching a DVD."

Vladimir shook his head knowingly. "But people come to see him on business; sometimes he goes to see people. In his large chauffeur-driven Bentley automobile," he added pointedly.

Jerry sensed he had already given away too much ground. He looked out at the slope below them, where a man in a green anorak was walking a large frisky Doberman through a patch of yellowed grass. "Most of the people he sees are Russians. I can't tell one name from another. And I can't understand a word they say."

Vladimir snorted. "We're not asking you for transcripts," he said caustically.

"What do you want to know?" Jerry demanded. "I'm not a traitor, you know."

Vladimir did not answer him directly, but said, "It's a purely Russian affair. Nothing to do with the queen." Vladimir waved his hand expansively.

Jerry shook his head. "But what if I won't play ball?"

An expression Vladimir must have been familiar with, for he said, "That is your choice." He paused, and his eyes were cold slits as he stared at Jerry. "As it would be ours to discuss your former activities on our behalf with the firm that placed you in your post."

I should have seen this coming, thought Jerry, way back

when he'd first met Andrei, that evening in the Dorchester, when the Russian said he was locked out of his room and Jerry had been sent up to let him in again. Andrei had given him a bottle of champagne from the minibar as thanks, which Jerry—strictly against the rules—had accepted, hiding it in his locker deep in the bowels of the hotel.

Then the next night he had bumped into Andrei in the pub on South Audley Street where Jerry liked to unwind after working hours. And on the night after that. They'd become friends, which meant Andrei paid for all the drinks, the odd meal they'd had together, once even for a girl. When Andrei had made his offer of a cash retainer in return for information that was not much more than hotel staff gossip, it seemed a natural extension of his generosity.

Yet now, three years later, it was coming home to roost. "Of course you must decide," said the Russian Vladimir, with apparent indifference and no pretence of friendly persuasion.

Jerry considered his options. There weren't any. Brigadier Cartwright wouldn't give him five minutes to clear his desk if he discovered he'd been taking cash on the side—even if it had been before Jerry joined the firm. Particularly when he discovered it was cash from a foreign government. With a black mark from the brigadier, Jerry would never find a cushy job again. He'd enter middle age reduced to being cheap hired "muscle." As a bouncer in a nightclub if he was lucky. More likely in a pub somewhere, throwing out the drunks.

"Okay," he said at last, reluctantly. "But the money had better be good."

"Meet me here again in a week," declared Vladimir. "The same time. I will give you your orders then."

"And the first payment," said Jerry trying to extract some small satisfaction.

4

Liz pulled the duvet up to her chin, stretched out her legs and reached out to switch on the eight o'clock news. She briefly wondered whether to get up and make a cup of coffee, and just as quickly decided against it. In all the years she had worked with Charles in Counter-Terrorism, she had never really relaxed, even on a Saturday morning. Counter-Terrorism operations came up suddenly out of the blue and needed a fast response. She was usually home late, often away from home altogether, but the sudden excitement, the tension, were what she had loved about the job.

Admittedly her private life had become a mess. Her small flat in Kentish Town, once much loved, had become dowdy.

Things broke down and she never had time to fix them; the tide of muddle had advanced inexorably. In the four months since she'd moved to Counter-Espionage everything had changed. The job wasn't without interest, but the pace was slower, more nine to five.

She had used her unaccustomed spare time to get her life in order. The peeling wallpaper in the bathroom had been replaced with tiles. The whole flat had been repainted and a smart new stainless steel washer-dryer had replaced the stuttering old thing she had inherited when she bought the flat. The goose-down duvet she was cuddling was bought on a whim, but was the most satisfactory of all her improvements.

Now from the comfort of her bed, she contemplated the elegant new bedroom curtains and the uncluttered carpet and thought about the weekend ahead.

Most of it would be spent with Piet. He was Dutch, an investment banker with Lehman's in Amsterdam. Every third Friday he came to London for a meeting in Canary Wharf and he would stay in London for the weekend. Friday night he went out to dinner with his colleagues but at lunchtime on Saturday he would appear at the basement door in Kentish Town, clutching champagne or a bottle of perfume he had bought on his way through the airport, and he and Liz would spend the rest of the weekend together. This was an arrangement which suited them both perfectly. It was warm and happy and undemanding.

If Piet knew what Liz did (and she suspected he did as she had met him at a colleague's Christmas party), he never asked. It wasn't that kind of relationship. They laughed a lot and ate good food. They talked about music and plays and the state of the world, and everything except work. Today they were going to a late-afternoon concert at St. John's Smith Square. Then they'd have dinner somewhere and Piet would come back and share the goose-down duvet. Liz curled her toes in anticipation. They would stay in bed late in the morning and then after a pub lunch, Piet would make for the airport and back to Amsterdam.

All in all, a heavenly prospect. Thank goodness for counter-espionage, she thought, though still there in a small corner of her mind was her first love, counter-terrorism and working with Charles. She hoped all was well with him. And Joanne, she mentally added—conscientiously.

5

Wally Woods was too tired to sleep. He'd worked seven shifts in four days, which would have been beyond a joke in the old days. They'd been camped out in South Kensington for the last two weeks, trailing an Iranian who specialised in late-night partying. Dennis Rudge had come down with flu and there hadn't been any option but to stand in for him.

Rudge had struggled back at last that morning, looking like death and blowing his nose, so Wally had gone home. He drove, dazed with fatigue, up to Crouch End, where he'd found a bad-tempered note from his wife, who had already gone to work. "Dear Stranger" it began, which didn't sound too good. He caught three hours' kip only to wake up, groggy, to find Molly, his dog, licking his face and whimpering for a walk.

There was nothing for it. He'd never get back to sleep. So he showered and shaved and dressed, then took Molly in the car and drove down here, to Hampstead Heath, where there was plenty of room, even for a Doberman with energy.

He liked to walk on the heath. It was a natural, uninhabited space, which had only one thing in common with North London around it—anything could happen there, and did. Its different areas—woodland, rough meadow, a string of ponds, Parliament Hill with its panoramic views of the City of London—afforded constant variety to his walks. Parking in The Grove, opposite a row of elegant Georgian mansions, he put on his anorak, and walked down a tree-lined lane, with Molly on her lead. The wind was picking up and the sun was obscured by cloud. Where *is* spring? he wondered, still feeling stiff after so many hours on duty, sitting in a parked car.

When they reached the bottom by the boating pond, where the heath began, he let Molly go. And it was as he watched the dog lope off—funny how unthreatening a Doberman's trot was, considering the fear they inspired in people—that he saw the man. Trudging past the men's pond, then turning and heading up the hill along a path much favoured by dog walkers and joggers, his back to Wally—which paradoxically was what gave him away.

It sounded strange, as Wally knew from trying to explain to his wife, but after twelve years of following people for a living, the way they looked from behind did for Wally just what fingerprints did for a forensic technician. The traits were just as individual, just as telltale. So when he saw that slow gait, like that of a man walking to get married to someone he didn't love, Wally knew at once he'd watched that back before.

And who it belonged to: Vladimir Rykov, trade attaché at the Russian Embassy. Wally had followed him before—to a restaurant in Charlotte Street, to a meeting at the Institute of Directors in Pall Mall, once on a Saturday to an Arsenal match in their last season at the old Highbury ground.

But what was Rykov doing here in the middle of a working day? Steady on, he told himself, he's probably going for a walk, just like you are, only without a dog. After all, the Russian Trade Delegation was only a few hundred yards away, perched on Highgate West Hill above the heath, a gruesome fenced-off compound of sixties modules.

But there was something deliberate about Rykov's progress. He was going somewhere, with a purpose, Wally told himself after following him for less than a minute. As he climbed the path, Rykov veered right, and walked across the rough grass towards a group of trees, known locally as Boadicea's Tomb. A stand of large oaks backed by towering pines, planted in a circle and ringed by iron railings. High up, the tomb was impossible to approach unseen. There was a bench on its north side where the Russian now sat down.

Wally turned away, calling to Molly. He fussed with her for a while, keeping his head down. Two minutes later, he stole a quick glance up the hill and saw that a man had joined Rykov on the bench.

In another part of the heath, nearer the men's pond, it might have been a cruising encounter, but not here—and besides, the men sat far apart on the bench. Rykov seemed to be doing the talking, though from this distance it was hard to tell. But it was a meeting, not some chance encounter; of that Wally was sure. Why in such a remote place? Because Rykov didn't want to be seen—presumably neither did the other man.

He'd loitered enough. There were other dog walkers around,

but people didn't forget a Doberman, so Wally followed Molly along the same path Rykov had climbed. He only stopped walking when he was sheltered by a dip from the view of the bench. He waited for what seemed an eternity, stamping his feet to keep his circulation flowing in the sharp wind, letting the dog sniff rabbit holes. He was rewarded for his patience when Rykov came into view descending the hill, followed thirty seconds later by the other man.

Wally didn't hesitate. There was no point in following Rykov—he could find him any time. But who was this other man? He was six feet or so, short back and sides, and wore a windcheater that highlighted a powerful build. Unlike Rykov, he didn't look foreign—not at this distance at any rate—but there was something distinctive about the man. Ex-army, thought Wally. And he quickly put Molly back on her lead, then moved down the field, trying to act like just any other dog owner who had finished the morning's exercise.

Ahead, Rykov disappeared towards the path between the dog pond and the men's pond in the direction of the Trade Delegation. The other man went right, skirting the pond, heading towards the low green grass of Parliament Hill. Wally picked up the pace, though careful to keep a good 200 yards between them. The tennis courts and buildings of a sixth-form college loomed ahead, but the man swerved left suddenly and Wally half-sprinted to catch up. He reached the road just in time to see the man emerge from a crowd of teenagers, sprint across the road and hop on to a double-decker bus. It chugged away in a swirl of black exhaust. Cursing, Wally looked around hopelessly for a cab.

Then London Transport came to the rescue, in the form of another bus, right on the heels of the earlier one. Wally ran to the stop, the bus pulled up, and he had both feet on and was reaching for change to pay his fare when the driver started shaking his head. "Not on my bus, mon," he said, in indisputable Jamaican tones. The driver pointed an accusing finger at Molly.

"I can bring a dog on the bus," Wally protested.

"Not that dog and not my bus. No way."

"She won't do any harm," Wally said, grabbing the dog's lead tight. He could see passengers staring at him and the dog.

"That's what you say," said the driver, keeping a careful eye on the Doberman. "But that's no Seeing Eye dog for sure. Them's dangerous. You get off now, mon, or I'm not starting."

He pointed to the pavement fiercely and when Wally tried to argue, simply shook his head. Molly, who disliked arguments, uttered a noise somewhere between a yawn and a yelp, then licked her lips. A drop of saliva fell on the platform. Some of the passengers muttered and Wally, recognising a lost battle, got down, groaning with frustration. The bus moved off.

The leading bus had by now long disappeared in the direction of central London. There was still no taxi in sight. "Come on, Molly," said Wally, "let's go home." But who the hell was the man?

6

Brian Ackers looks knackered this morning, thought Liz. Normally he was almost zealously energetic.

"Bad news," he announced to start the weekly meeting of the Counter-Espionage Branch. That's motivating, thought Liz caustically. The third-floor conference room was too large for the twenty intelligence officers present, bunched together at one end of the room.

In the Cold War, there had been specialised teams of investigators and agent runners, focusing on different aspects of the espionage threat from the Soviet Union and its allies. With the Cold War over and terrorism now the priority, the Counter-Espionage Branch had been reduced to two largish sections—

one directed at Russia and one at everywhere else. As well as being acting director, Brian Ackers was directly in charge of the Russia Section, agent runners and investigators working together.

Now, next to Liz, Peggy Kinsolving was scrabbling in her briefcase. She was leaving the meeting early to attend a European conference on the current threat from the Russian intelligence services.

"The Foreign Office has come back to me," announced Ackers. He always spoke loudly at these meetings, as if a booming voice could somehow bring back the days when the sixty-odd seats in this room would all have been occupied. He was a gaunt, thin-faced man with pale grey eyes. Today he wore an old tweed jacket and a narrow club tie of some kind that had seen better days.

Propping her chin in her hand, Liz gazed at him with an expressionless face. She was thinking how typical it was of a certain kind of male to cover up an unshakeable conviction with a nondescript appearance. Of his conviction there was no doubt— Liz was impressed as well as slightly amused by Ackers's insistent denial that the world had changed irrevocably with the end of the Cold War. To Ackers, the Russians remained Enemy Number One, and Liz knew that he regarded the relegation of the Russians in MI5's ranking of threats as deeply misguided. The Red menace might have changed, Ackers would grudgingly concede. It was no longer red, but it was still a menace.

He said now, "They've accepted that we have the right man, and the proof of unacceptable activities." He paused to heighten the effect. "But they refuse to take any action against him."

Liz was not altogether surprised, though she shared Ackers's disappointment. For the last three months she had been involved in the case in question. A government scientist named Maples had reported an approach from a member of the Russian Embassy he had met at a defence exhibition in Cardiff. The Russian had wasted no time in offering Maples money in return for information about the plans for the renewal of Trident.

Once informed, MI5 had moved in. Liz had become case officer for the scientist, Maples, whom she had told to play along with the diplomat, a young man named Sergei Nysenko. After several meetings in London suburbs, Maples had pretended to agree to Nysenko's proposals, and four days later in Kew Gardens had given Nysenko an attaché case containing a fabricated government policy paper classified Secret. In return, Nysenko (surreptitiously photographed by A4 surveillance officers) had handed over £40,000 in cash.

Once UK officialdom would not have hesitated: Sergei Nysenko would have been on the first flight home. But the British attitude had changed, as Brian Ackers was now explaining. "The FCO says they'll have a word with the Russian ambassador, and suggest Nysenko confine himself to more conventional activities in future." He shook his head. "The SVR will be laughing at us."

"Why won't they expel him, Brian? It was an attempt to suborn a British official. He's an undercover intelligence officer. He'll go on being a problem for us." The question came from Michael Fane, a recent MI5 recruit who had joined the branch only a month before, after an initial year in Protective Security. He was quick-witted, keen, and seemed—to Liz—very, very young. He was a bit of an oddity in the Service, since his father, Geoffrey Fane, was a senior controller in MI6. Liz had got to know Geoffrey Fane when she was working with Charles Wetherby in Counter-Terrorism; the two men were opposite numbers. Geoffrey was a smooth operator in the labyrinthine politics of interdepartmental relations, and a man to be wary of.

"All the usual reasons," Brian said with a sigh. He picked glumly at his tie. "The prime minister has plans to go to Moscow next month and they don't want to rock the boat right before his trip, or risk reciprocal action against the embassy there. Expelling Nysenko would jeopardise the 'new cooperation' between us in the fight against terrorism." He looked angrily out the window of the conference room at the plane trees lining the pavement, as if even they should share his low opinion of this "new cooperation."

"These fellows in Eastern Department nowadays have no idea how to deal with the Russians. They've only been involved with them since the Cold War ended and we became so-called allies. They can't seem to see that if we show any weakness at all, they'll be all over us."

Liz spoke up. "Surely the operation has done some good, Brian. It tells the Russians that we haven't gone to sleep, and that we know what they're up to."

"Perhaps," said Ackers, and rested his gaze on Liz. "Though why should they worry if we can't act?"

There wasn't a good answer to this, thought Liz, and she couldn't help sympathising with Ackers. Charles Wetherby had been right—there were more Russian intelligence officers in London than ever before. The day she'd arrived on the third floor Ackers had briefed her on the extent of SVR activity known to MI5, and she'd been in his office most of the afternoon.

The difference now lay in the targets of Russian espionage. In the Cold War they'd been largely British: the combat-readiness of British troops in Germany, high-tech programmes and British firms, even the views and character of British politicians. Now the targets were just as often not British. London's international community and its rise as the world's financial hub meant there wasn't a country of importance that wasn't doing business on British shores. London was an excellent listening post for one of the world's most aggressive intelligence services. Particularly if MI5 had one hand tied behind its back.

The meeting moved on. An old hand named Hadley explained that, now the Nysenko episode was over, A4 were beginning random surveillance on other identified intelligence officers in the embassy.

"How much coverage have we got?" asked Brian.

Hadley shrugged. "With the resource we get," he said pointedly, "not much." He inspected his notes. "We're focusing on the economic and trade people for now. Our friends Kaspovitch, Svitchenko and Rykov."

Brian Ackers's eyes glinted, and it was clear to Liz that after thirty years of hunting Russian spies he still lived for the chase, even if today's terrorist priorities meant he was hobbled. Liz couldn't help but respect his commitment.

With the Nysenko case concluded, Liz herself was taking a look at the wave of Russian oligarchs who had been establishing themselves in the UK. Peggy Kinsolving called them the "New Arabs," and there was truth to the sobriquet. London hadn't seen anything like this burst of new money since the arrival of oil-rich Arabs in the seventies. The Russian billionaires were rapidly buying up large country houses, whole blocks of Knightsbridge flats, the occasional football team and most of the masterpieces sold at high-class art auctions. The Bentley and Rolls-Royce dealers hadn't had it so good since the days of the Indian maharajahs.

With the billionaires came some unsavoury connections to the Russian mafia, which were more the concern of the new Serious and Organised Crime Agency than MI5. But the presence in the UK of so many characters of dubious origin with so much

Russian money, a number of them openly hostile to the regime in Moscow, was bound to interest the Russian intelligence officers in London. And that, as Brian Ackers insisted, was in turn interesting to the Counter-Espionage Branch.

Liz felt a tap on her arm and Peggy pushed across a note. "Got to go" it read. She nodded, and Peggy slipped out as Brian Ackers asked for other reports. Liz's mind began to wander. She wondered what was happening in Counter-Terrorism and how they were getting on without Charles. She was jolted back to the meeting by the sound of people beginning to stir in their chairs, sensing the meeting was coming to an end. But Ackers wasn't finished yet. "If we could go back to Nysenko for a moment," he said, and Liz thought she heard a small groan from Michael Fane.

"I have to say, the approach to Maples strikes me as very poorly executed. Almost amateurish, in fact," Ackers mused, and it struck Liz that he was almost feeling let down by the incompetence of his old adversaries.

He looked over at Hadley. "Nysenko's very young, isn't he?"

Hadley nodded. "In his twenties."

"So he's green," said Ackers. "Too green. I'm puzzled. They needed an experienced officer for that kind of operation. Someone who'd have taken more time to sound out Maples before making his approach."

Michael Fane spoke up. "Maybe Nysenko was the best they've got in London."

"I don't believe that for a minute. We know they've got some much more senior officers here." Ackers didn't look at Fane, and Liz sensed he was thinking out loud. "Unless," he said, his eyes slowly widening, "the whole thing was intended as a distraction. From something more important."

No one said a word. Brian Ackers's pale eyes swept across his audience, as if daring anyone to challenge his reasoning. "That certainly could be the answer," he declared firmly, with an unmistakable note of elation. "Yes. There could well be something else going on that we don't know anything about. That's the worrying part."

But if he were worried, thought Liz, he didn't sound it. Brian Ackers was scenting the enemy and that made him a happy man once more.

7

Geoffrey Fane was not a modest man, but neither was he ostentatious. He moved quietly and unobtrusively among a wide group of acquaintances in various overlapping circles at the upper end of London society. He knew the inside of most of the embassy dining rooms, and all of the St. James's clubs, but Rupert's Club, where he had been invited to meet Sir Victor Adler, was virgin territory.

As he lifted the knocker on the front door of the small Georgian town house in a quiet street on the west side of Berkeley Square, he allowed himself to wonder for a moment what he would find inside.

Adler was a man he had known for a very long time—

socially they had met at the occasional dinner party and embassy function—but their contact was mainly professional. Adler had for years supplied MI6 with what was perhaps little more than gossip which he had picked up on his regular visits to the Soviet Union and now to Russia. When Fane, who kept a close eye on these things, knew that Adler had returned from a visit, he would invite him to MI6's headquarters at Vauxhall Cross for a chat. The contact was low-key, very civilised and understood by everyone, including the Russians. Fane was curious to know what had caused Adler to break the pattern and initiate a meeting.

The front door was opened silently by a short, frog-eyed man in a tailcoat. To Fane's enquiry for Sir Victor, he inclined his head, and without speaking motioned towards an inner room where about a dozen men and a few women sat in groups in high-backed, well-padded armchairs. Conversation stopped for a moment as Fane walked in, and eyes were raised as quick assessments of the newcomer were made. Victor rose from his seat in a corner and indicated the chair opposite him.

As Fane sat down, he looked around. The room was highly decorated, overdecorated in fact, almost vulgar to Fane's ascetic eye. On the high ceiling were painted scenes of nymphs and swags of flowers, the walls were hung with gilt mirrors and every available inch was covered with assorted pictures in gold frames. The curtains were heavy brocade with tasselled tie-backs and the side tables were fruitwood. It was quite obvious from the general air of opulence that to become a member of Rupert's Club a man could be tall or short, fat or thin, Christian or (as with Adler) Jew, but the one inflexible requirement was that he be rich.

Which Adler indisputably was. He had social cachet from birth, since his mother came from one of the earliest Sephardic families in Britain. Any residual doubts about their Englishness had long been assuaged by a series of canny marital alliances made over the course of several centuries—including, a century before, marriage to a Curzon.

But it was from Adler's father's side that Victor had inherited the cash that supported the cachet. The Adler clan descended from a single banking patriarch who, like the original Warburg and the early Rothschilds, had come to London from Germany in the 1840s—as if sensing a hundred years ahead of time that it was better for a Jew not to stick around in Frankfurt.

Sir Victor Adler himself had never shown the slightest interest in joining the family bank, but then, thought Fane, why should he have? He owned enough of it to finance his other, far greater interest. From adolescence, curiously perhaps considering his own Germanic antecedents, Victor was deeply, passionately interested in Russia. Its art, literature, music, food and particularly its politics.

Adler was one of a small elite band of international figures who wielded "influence," that strange, difficult-to-define commodity, which if examined too closely, seemed to dissolve into thin air like a djinn. But it was real to those who believed in it, and there were many such believers who sought Adler's advice— companies doing business with Russia, banks investing there and, of course, politicians. Fane was not one of the believers, but he knew that Adler talked to people he and his colleagues were interested in. And that was enough for him.

Now he looked at his host and waited for him to speak. A heavy cut-glass tumbler of whisky materialised on the table by Fane's arm. Victor pushed across the jug of water, then leant back in his chair, crossing his well-padded legs at the ankles. "Let me tell you why I wanted to see you. As you will know, I returned from a short visit to Russia a few days ago. I was there for a week, seeing mainly old acquaintances. Some of it was social, some political, some business; most of it all three." He smiled briefly. "Then the day before I left I had a message at my hotel from someone I have known for years. He said he had something of the utmost importance to tell me. I was curious, so we met in the morning before I left for the airport." Victor paused and leant forward almost imperceptibly in his chair. He didn't whisper but spoke in a low voice that Fane had to struggle to hear. "I am sure you know the name Leonid Tarkov?"

Fane nodded. "One of the oil ministers."

"That's right," said Adler, and chuckled. "That's part of his problem—that he is *still* a minister. Do you remember when the Russians nationalised Yukos Oil?"

"Of course." How could he forget? It was a notorious act of expropriation which seemed to reverse the trend towards privatisation begun under Yeltsin, and warned that the Russian state could still bare its autocratic Communist teeth whenever it wished.

"Tarkov was slated to become a senior official in the new nationalised company. After twenty years in the Kremlin, he was looking forward to working somewhere else—and to the perks of the job. At the last minute, Putin gave the post to someone else. Who knows why? But it served to alienate Tarkov from Putin. He still has a government position but is no longer on the inside track. Which may explain what he told me."

Fane could see Adler was enjoying himself, so he took a sip of his drink and leant back. There was no point in trying to rush the old boy.

"Last summer, Tarkov attended a wedding, at a dacha outside Moscow. It was a lavish affair—the groom's father had made a fortune in platinum during Yeltsin's time, I believe—

attended by many senior political figures and businessmen. There was a lot to drink—perhaps you have been to a Russian wedding—and towards the end of the evening Tarkov found himself sharing a bottle of vodka with a colleague named Stanislav Stakhov."

Fane nodded. Stakhov was one of the few senior Yeltsin aides who had managed to prosper under Putin.

"He and Tarkov have known each other since they were boys. They grew up together in Minsk; they even joined the Party in the same year. Yet, Tarkov told me, he was careful when they talked, since Stakhov is a Putin man and always much in favour. Tarkov says he didn't grumble about the president or about his own fall from grace, though I take that with a grain of salt since the man seems incapable of opening his mouth without complaining."

Fane smiled. He had long ago learnt that Victor Adler performed best before an appreciative audience. Adler continued, "However, according to Tarkov, the drunker Stakhov got, the more he became critical of Putin. He said Putin was starting to act erratically, power was going to his head. He was growing insecure, almost paranoid."

Fane nodded, not entirely surprised. It was almost an axiom in his experience that the greater the accumulation of power, the greater the fear of losing it. One had only to look at Stalin, without a challenger to his authority in sight, yet obsessed with conspiracy phobias by the time he died. Fane asked quietly, "Any particular people he's paranoid about?"

"That is the odd thing." Adler paused and took a sip of whisky. "Apparently, he's not worried by the Russian mafia—most of them are on his side anyway—and internal political opposition is negligible. What seems to concern Putin are the new oligarchs."

"But they're utterly dependent on him. He can ruin any one of them just by nationalising their company."

"Indeed, so. But it's the oligarchs who've *left* Russia that he's scared of."

"Most of them are here," said Fane. There were said to be thirty Russian billionaires living in London alone.

"Exactly. Putin is terribly uneasy that so many are in one place."

Fane frowned. "What does he think, they'll form a government in exile?" he asked. "That's just the old Bolshevik neurosis about émigrés, like the White Russians congregating in Paris before the war. They never stood the slightest chance of toppling the Communists."

The little man in tails reappeared, and placed a bowl of macadamia nuts on the table next to them. Adler offered them first to Fane, who shook his head, then took a handful himself, with a large hairy hand, munching thoughtfully for a moment. Then he said, "I doubt it's anything that extreme. Stakhov can be a little dramatic."

"I know Putin a little," Adler continued, and Fane knew this was true. "I don't view him as paranoid. Stakhov might call him that, but I think the appropriate word would be 'careful.' He can see a threat before anyone else can even imagine it. Of course on a personal level, Putin despises these expatriate oligarchs because he thinks they are decadent. He is, after all, ex-KGB. But their money makes them powerful. They don't like him and some of them have become quite vocal. They could help fund opposition to him within Russia and certainly on Russia's borders. That's what concerns Putin."

Though President Putin's concerns were interesting, Fane didn't imagine for a moment that Victor Adler would have asked him here just to relay high-level Kremlin gossip emanating from a late-night session with a vodka bottle. He waited patiently, looking as if he had all the time in the world. No one would have guessed he had a dinner to go to.

"Tarkov claims he didn't react when Stakhov started spouting about Putin. He just waited to see what would come next. It seems that Stakhov thought he didn't believe him. It was then he told Tarkov about the plot."

Fane raised an eyebrow and crossed one leg languidly across the other. Only those who knew him very well would realise this indicated a sudden raised interest. "Plot?" he asked mildly.

Adler nodded vigorously. For the first time, he looked around the room, which was slowly emptying as its occupants moved to the dining room or left for engagements elsewhere. He leant forward and spoke again in a lowered voice. "It has been decided to make a pre-emptive strike against the oligarchs. One of them is going to be silenced, *pour encourager les autres*. By removing one thorn in its side, the government intends to convey a very strong warning."

" 'Silenced'? " asked Fane.

Adler merely shrugged in reply. They both knew what it meant.

"Here in England?" Fane asked casually, as if it happened all the time.

"Apparently."

"Which oligarch has been selected for this privilege?" He kept his tone light, but he was watching Adler intently.

"That Tarkov couldn't tell me. Not because he didn't want to, but because he didn't know. He said he had the distinct impression the plan hadn't been finalised yet."

"Would he be able to find out?"

Adler looked doubtful. "Probably not. He told me he phoned Stakhov a week later to ask him to lunch, but Stakhov didn't take his call."

Fane was thinking hard. "Wouldn't they try and lure their target back to Russia? Surely, he'd be easier to deal with there than here."

"Of course. But then it would lose its symbolic power. If they're hoping to show that no enemy of the state is safe, wherever they live, it will happen abroad."

"God knows it's happened often enough before," said Fane grimly. The Kremlin's assassination of opponents overseas had a pedigree dating back to Trotsky's murder. In Mexico, of all places. But then, thought Fane, the story might be nothing more than a rumour, inflated into certainty by too much vodka, relayed to Sir Victor for some Byzantine Muscovite motive, as impenetrable to British observers as tarot cards. And what about Sir Victor himself? He was not exactly a spring chicken, thought Fane, taking the last sip of his whisky. Might he not be mistaking some tittle-tattle for a state secret, out of some inflated sense of self-importance perhaps, or even incipient dottiness?

"Did he have any more specific information about this plot?"

"He said he had told me all he knew," said Adler, and his dark, sad eyes were unwavering.

"If Tarkov attended this wedding in the summer, then he's waited long enough to tell anyone."

"I know. But I think it was only this autumn that Tarkov's hopes of a job in the private sector were extinguished. After that, he decided to approach me." Adler reached down and scooped up another handful of nuts. But he paused before popping them into his mouth. "I think Tarkov is intent on an old-fashioned act of revenge. Not professional perhaps, but perfectly understandable in personal terms. That's why I believe him."

Fane nodded. It made sense. He looked around the room and realised that he and Sir Victor were alone. "So," Adler said shortly, "I was asked to communicate this to the appropriate person—someone who would know who should be informed. You and I have seen each other over the years, and I knew I could trust both your discretion and your judgement."

The flattery was wasted on Fane, for already he was thinking about what to do with this interesting piece of information. "But I mustn't keep you from your dinner," said Adler, now lighthearted. The implication was clear: he'd done his bit.

8

The plane was an hour late taking off from Charles de Gaulle. With security at the same high level on both sides of the Channel, Peggy knew she would have been better off on the Eurostar, right from the middle of Paris to Waterloo, just across the river from Thames House.

But there was something about the prospect of those fifteen minutes deep under the sea which put Peggy off. Even the thought of it brought her mild claustrophobia bubbling to the surface. She knew aeroplanes affected some people in the same way, but to her air travel seemed open—nothing around you except sky.

She didn't know why she suffered from claustrophobia. She

had had it mildly since she was a child, a shy, serious child with freckles and round spectacles, who was much happier with her head stuck in a book than out with friends or playing games. It had troubled her much more in her first year at Oxford, preventing her from going to crowded parties or even to concerts where she might be stuck in the middle of a row. But after she settled down at Oxford and began to be successful, it largely disappeared, only to return again in her first unsatisfactory job in a private library in Manchester, working with a middle-aged librarian who barely exchanged a word with her.

Peggy was not one to give in to weakness, which was how she regarded claustrophobia. She had fought against it, but she had learnt to win her battles in life bit by bit, opportunity by opportunity and very patiently. Since she had joined MI6 as a researcher and was seconded to MI5 to work with Liz on the mole investigation, it had gone away almost entirely. Avoiding the Channel Tunnel was, she hoped, its dying twitch.

Peggy felt tired now. She had spent a day and a half in a hot, airless room, in the basement of the headquarters of the Direction de la Surveillance du Territoire on rue Nélaton. Even in France, smoking was now forbidden inside government buildings, but she'd had the misfortune to sit next to Monsieur Drollot, the French official from the Renseignements Généraux, who at every coffee break rushed outside and chain-smoked Gitanes. Now, tilting her chair back as the seat-belt sign went off at last, the memory of the Frenchman's stale aroma made her feel slightly sick.

She had seen nothing of Paris and would have regretted not adding a day off to her schedule—enough time anyway to see at least one museum, dawdle over coffee in one café—had she not felt she must get back to Thames House urgently. Because towards the end of the meeting, she'd learnt something startling.

She had not expected any surprises. The meeting had been an assembly of "friends," security services from Western Europe with a long history of close cooperation, along with a Polish representative, the lone emissary from the old Iron Curtain countries. The Scandinavians had been there—a stereotypically gloomy man from Sweden and a reserved, soft-spoken woman from Norway known only as Miss Karlsson.

The delegates had convened round a large oval table in the basement meeting room. Peggy had felt a secret thrill, sitting for the very first time behind a card marked "United Kingdom" and a little Union Jack. She had looked around her, taking everything in. A team of interpreters sat in a glassed-in gallery, providing simultaneous translation to the twenty or so intelligence officers sitting below them, each putting on and taking off their headphones, depending on the language being used. Most people in the room knew each other, if not by appearance, at least by name, because they communicated from their head offices, sharing information regularly by secure phone and fax.

The interpreters too were part of the charmed circle of intelligence professionals. They spent their days, when they were not interpreting at conferences, listening to intercepted telephone calls in various languages or straining to hear what was said on concealed microphones in buildings all over Europe. They too knew most people in the room—and their linguistic foibles. The Spanish major, for example, who insisted on speaking French, with an accent so thick that he was almost incomprehensible, even though there was a very competent Spanish interpreter present, or Miss Karlsson, who spoke beautiful, almost unaccented English, but in a voice so quiet that the interpreters were continuously on edge to catch her words.

The discussion was wide-ranging. The breakdown of the old East-West divide had produced new players on the espionage scene and an ever increasing targeting of the advanced economies of Western Europe. A lively debate developed during the first morning session about espionage versus commercial secrets. Peggy found herself in an argument with her neighbour at the table, the smoky M. Drollot, when she said that companies must look after their own security. When the Spanish major chipped in to make a point in his fractured French, even M. Drollot looked confused and put on his headphones to pick up the English translation, only to hear the interpreter unprofessionally muttering, "At least I think that's what he said."

Peggy wasn't used to public disagreement, though she held her end up with M. Drollot, and was glad when in the afternoon the discussion moved on to the less controversial theme of the activities of the intelligence officers in the Russian embassies in the capital cities of Europe. All agreed that they were back to something approaching their pre–Cold War strength.

When it was Peggy's turn to speak, she listed the intelligence officers she had identified in London and their roles. Her mention of Vladimir Rykov, an SVR officer fairly recently posted from Germany to the Russian Trade Delegation in Highgate, produced a loud guffaw from Herr Beckendorf. "Well, you won't have too much trouble with that one," he announced. "He has two left feet. When he was in Dusseldorf we knew exactly what he was doing. I can't think how they thought he was up to a posting to London."

But it was something else Herr Beckendorf said, on the second day, that riveted Peggy. It emerged at the very end of the morning from a joint presentation by Beckendorf and Miss Karlsson. Beckendorf, a grey-haired veteran of the old West German security service, was a tall, dour man, who wore a sleeveless jumper under his jacket and comfortable shoes. Like Brian Ackers, he had spent his career combating the efforts of Iron

Curtain spies, and he seemed just as sceptical that anything had changed. This would be the last presentation of the meeting before they broke up after lunch, and as Beckendorf began to speak, several delegates were looking bored and struggling to suppress yawns. But as he got into his stride, there was a stirring of interest.

"The new world of espionage we have been hearing so much about is undoubtedly very exciting," Herr Beckendorf began, and listening to the voice of the interpreter, it took Peggy a moment to grasp the sarcastic edge to his words. "But I would like to raise the renewed presence of an old kind of threat. Miss Karlsson and I have observed activity which we believe indicates the Russian SVR is once again actively planting *Illegale.*"

There was a pause in the translation and the interpreter said tentatively, "Illegals."

Most of the audience were long-time intelligence officers who understood, but Signor Scusi, a young Italian army officer, new to his service, asked in broken English, "Illegals? What are they?"

"Ah," said Beckendorf. "For those of you new to the phenomenon, Illegals are officers of an intelligence service who live outside the embassy. They assume a false nationality and identity to cover their presence."

Beckendorf was warming to his theme. "The Russians long ago recognised that for the most secret work an intelligence officer under a completely false identity was much more likely to escape the attentions of the security service in the country where he was living, than an intelligence officer inside the embassy. As you all know the intelligence component of the embassy is called the 'Legal Residency.' So those outside it are 'Illegals.'

"An Illegal is supported by an officer in the embassy but he is not supposed to have any direct contact with him, except in an extreme emergency. He gets his instructions by direct communication with his controllers at home. But an Illegal is never documented as a national of the country he is infiltrating. They are carefully trained to pose as foreigners. Obviously if they wanted to infiltrate the United States, it would be far too risky for their officer to pretend to be American: such an impersonation would be virtually impossible to sustain. So instead he would present himself as something different altogether—as a Brazilian, say, who has come to live in the U.S. This 'third nationality' has always made Illegals extremely hard to detect. And the damage they have caused in the past has been proved to be immense."

"One of the most famous cases," chipped in Peggy—in her usual thorough way she had researched the recent history of Russian espionage—"was in England. There were two spies at the Admiralty in the fifties, called Harry Houghton and Ethel Gee, and they were controlled by Colonel Molody of the KGB, who was documented as a Canadian businessman called Gordon Lonsdale." Peggy stopped abruptly, realising that she had stolen some of Herr Beckendorf's thunder.

"Quite," said Beckendorf, taking back the initiative. "Some people," he said, making clear this did not include himself, "have gone so far as to think that this phenomenon has disappeared altogether. But they are wrong. It is with us again."

By now he had his audience's full attention. Peggy herself found the history of Illegals intriguing, but it had always seemed to her just that—history. Another aspect of the Cold War passed and gone. Surprised by the dramatic start to Beckendorf's talk, she began taking careful notes.

"For the last three years the BfV has been keeping an eye on Igor Ivanov, an economic attaché at the Russian Embassy in Berlin. We learnt some time ago from a defector to a friendly country"—America, thought most of the delegates—"that he is an Illegal support officer. He travels frequently in Germany, which is understandable, given his official duties. What has interested us very much are his regular trips to Norway. It seemed curious. After all, there is a Russian Embassy in Oslo, with a good number of SVR officers in it."

"Twelve," interjected Miss Karlsson quietly.

"After his third trip, I asked Miss Karlsson and her colleagues if, on the next occasion Ivanov travelled to Norway, they would keep an eye on him."

The Norwegian woman flicked the switch on the microphone on her desk. "After arriving in Oslo, Ivanov took a train the next day to Bergen, then returned the following afternoon and went back to Germany. Six weeks later, he visited Norway again, and this time we followed him to Bergen. His anti-surveillance measures are excellent and unfortunately, once there he managed to lose our surveillance. He went to extraordinary pains to do so, though we do not think he knew we were there."

Beckendorf resumed. "We thought perhaps Ivanov had personal business in Bergen. Possibly even a mistress." He allowed himself a fleeting smile. "But then why not fly direct to Bergen? Why take a slow train, unless you were trying to cover your tracks even more carefully than a straying husband? And why leave the hotel in Bergen? Is it not hotels where these sorts of assignments are conducted?" he asked rhetorically.

He must have said "assignations," thought Peggy, amused by the first slip in the translator's otherwise flawless English.

"Excuse me," interjected Scusi, speaking in his heavily accented English and looking confused. "You say he *wasn't* assigning anyone?"

"On the contrary," said Beckendorf, sticking to German. "I am certain he was. But not a lover. I think it was an altogether different type of person. An Illegal. As I have said, a support officer hardly ever actually meets with the Illegal—it's far too risky because he himself will most likely be known to the security agencies. He may just have been leaving something the Illegal needed. But in my view they met; that would explain why Ivanov travelled so far and went to such trouble to be unobserved."

"We decided to mount full-scale surveillance on Ivanov if he returned to Bergen," said Miss Karlsson. "With any luck, we would discover who he was meeting; then we would investigate this person."

Peggy and the others waited, caught up in the chase. Beckendorf gave a shrug, and said, "It never happened. He did not go to Norway again." Peggy noticed with a start that Miss Karlsson and Herr Beckendorf seemed to be looking at her.

"But," said Beckendorf, "we have just learnt that he is intending to visit London. We believe that may mean the Illegal has moved to London."

9

Just before three the same day, as Peggy was waiting impatiently at Charles de Gaulle airport, Geoffrey Fane was stalking confidently along the corridors of the Foreign Office on his way to see Henry Pennington, head of Eastern Department.

Fane regarded Pennington with scorn. The two men had known each other for years and much earlier in their careers; when they were young men, they had served together in the British High Commission in New Delhi, Pennington as a second secretary and Fane undercover as a press attaché. They had never got on. Pennington thought Fane was deeply unreliable and Fane regarded Pennington as a panicker, with a tendency to paralysis in a crisis. Even if events hadn't amply demonstrated this, it would, Fane secretly thought, have been evident enough from his peaked face with its large nose and his jerky hand movements. He would rather have been dealing with almost anyone else in the Foreign Office than Henry Pennington, but the man was responsible for relations with Russia, so it was with him Fane had to share what Victor Adler had related.

The nose hasn't got any smaller, thought Fane, as Pennington rose from behind a massive mahogany desk. The room had a high ceiling with an elaborate white cornice, a marble fireplace and windows overlooking St. James's Park. Propped upright beside the fireplace was a violin, its presence proclaiming that this was the office of a highly cultured man. Fane thought the conceit pathetic.

Without much more than the briefest of courtesies, Fane recounted his conversation with Victor Adler the night before. He watched as Pennington's expression moved gradually from cautious curiosity to anxiety and his hands began to clutch each other jerkily, suggesting, to Fane's experienced eye, the beginnings of panic.

"Didn't Adler have any idea *who* they might target?" asked Pennington plaintively.

"No. He had the impression that there has been a decision, but who and how may not have been settled yet."

"Why should we think they'll do it in the UK?"

"Most of the oligarchs live here," said Fane mildly, "so London seems rather more likely than, say, Peru."

"Christ!" Pennington exclaimed. "This is the last thing we need. We've got the PM due to go to Moscow, the counter-terrorist liaison is rocky and the press will go mad if there's another Litvinenko."

"Quite," said Fane, trying to look sympathetic.

"Well, what can we do to prevent it?"

"I've spoken to Head of Station in Moscow, and we'll try and talk to Tarkov. But frankly, I think this was a bit of a fluke. Even if Tarkov's willing to help, I'm not sure he's well placed to find out anything more. We'll try other contacts, of course, but I can't promise anything. We'll have to bring in MI5, but I thought I'd tell you about it first."

"Bloody Brian Ackers," said Pennington with undisguised bitterness. "That will only make things worse. And right before the PM's trip to Moscow."

"Oh, I don't know," said Fane easily. "Brian's no fool. He's been around. He knows a thing or two about the Russians."

Pennington shook his head. "*Cha!* He's just another spook who can't accept the Cold War's over and we have to get on with the Russians," he declared, seeming to forget his listener's own vocation. "He's always wanting to take action."

Fane decided not even to pretend to take offence. "I tell you what," he said brightly. "I know the Thames House people pretty well, so why don't I talk things over with some of them informally? We're going to have to work in tandem on this one in any case. Let me have a word before you speak to Brian Ackers."

"Would you?" asked Pennington, looking grateful.

"Happy to," said Fane shortly, and stood up. "If the Russians are still in the planning stage, we've got a little time. Leave it to me for now."

10

Liz was just beginning to think about going home when she looked up from the papers on her desk to find Peggy Kinsolving standing in the doorway of her office, with a carry-on bag in one hand and her briefcase in the other. Her hair was up in a severe bun, and she was dressed in a smart rose-coloured suit. The effect was to make her look older, but there was something youthfully eager about the excited expression on her face.

"Hello there," said Liz. "Have a good trip?"

"Can I talk to you for a minute?"

"Come on in," said Liz.

Still holding her cases, Peggy advanced into the room. "The Germans and the Norwegians think there's been a Russian

Illegal in Norway. They've followed the support officer there from Germany and now he's coming to London, so they think the Illegal's moved here," she said breathlessly.

"Why don't you put your bags down?" said Liz gently. "Take a seat, and tell me all about it."

When ten minutes later Peggy finished recounting Beckendorf's and Karlsson's story, she looked at Liz and asked, "What do you think?"

Liz tapped the desktop pensively. Then she said, "It seems a bit thin. It's based on a lot of assumptions. Have they tried to detect any communications to or from this Illegal? I thought in the Cold War it was radio transmissions that pinpointed the existence of Illegals. Even though we couldn't read what the messages said, didn't we know where they were coming from and broadly where they were directed to?"

"Herr Beckendorf is a complete expert on this," Peggy replied. "He was working on it for years during the Cold War and he says they're using encrypted computer messages now. They bounce them through countless network nodes so it's very difficult to detect the ultimate destination."

"All right," said Liz, now into full investigative mode and not noticing that Peggy's face had fallen at her sceptical reception of this news. "But why does he think this Ivanov kept going to Norway at all? The whole point of Illegals surely was that they never met their support officer."

"I wondered about that too," said Peggy. "Perhaps the Illegal needed something that he couldn't get for himself. Documents perhaps. Or maybe his communications had broken down and he needed a spare part," she added desperately, looking increasingly troubled by Liz's lack of enthusiasm.

"Maybe," said Liz thoughtfully.

"Whatever it's about," said Peggy, "if Ivanov's going to visit here, don't we have to follow it up?" She seemed troubled by Liz's lack of reaction.

"Of course we do," said Liz. "What else came up?"

"Oh just that the Germans think Rykov, that SVR officer in the Trade Delegation here, is a complete incompetent."

"Rykov?" exclaimed Liz. "That's interesting. Just a few minutes ago Wally Woods from A4 came in to tell me he'd seen Rykov meeting someone on Hampstead Heath. I've asked him to write a detailed report." She paused and looked out the window for a moment. "Do you remember, at the meeting Brian was saying that he thought it was odd that the Maples case had been handled by someone as inexperienced as Nysenko? Now we're being told Rykov's no good."

"That's what Herr Beckendorf said," interrupted Peggy. "I'm sure he knows what he's talking about."

"I'm sure he does too," replied Liz thoughtfully. "Hampstead Heath's a pretty obvious place to have a covert meeting in broad daylight, isn't it?" She stopped again and gazed at Peggy. "Maybe all this adds up somehow—but differently from the way it looks. After all, the Russians are professionals. They've been at this game for years and they're in a league the terrorists can't dream of. Well," she concluded, standing up and starting to put away her papers, "at least they're making us think!"

11

Wally Woods of A4 had been proud of his discovery of Rykov, apparently having a covert meeting on Hampstead Heath, but the wind was quite taken out of his sails when Liz told him that the Germans thought Rykov's tradecraft was pathetic. Now, this Wednesday morning, out with his surveillance team following Rykov, Wally found himself having to agree with the Germans.

Liz had decided that to try to identify Rykov's contact A4 should follow him exactly two weeks after the meeting that Wally had observed. If Rykov was as incompetent as the Germans judged, he would stick to a predictable meeting pattern and two weeks was a typical interval. On the first occasion nothing had happened. So, a week later, when she found that a couple of A4 teams were unexpectedly available, she decided to have another go. Now one team was staking out the bench on Hampstead Heath, while Wally and his team followed Rykov, code name Chelsea 1, through his morning agenda.

Peggy Kinsolving had been doing some research into Rykov's activities and had discovered that whatever actual intelligence work he was doing seemed to come second to a voracious appetite for food and drink. All his meetings, and there were many, were in ritzy bars and expensive restaurants. He made no effort to conceal any of this and there was no sign that he either knew or cared that MI5 might be aware of his activities.

So, thought Liz, as she looked in on the A4 Operations Room in the early afternoon, what did that say about the man on the bench? Why had their meeting been so different from the usual pattern? She hoped to find out today.

Reggie Purvis, in charge in the Ops Room, brought Liz up-to-date. After a long lunch at Kensington Place with a journalist from the *International Herald Tribune*, Rykov was walking slowly up Kensington Church Street, stopping to examine the windows of the antiques shops, with Wally and two A4 colleagues on either side of the road behind and in front of him. Others in cars were nearby. Suddenly, with a crackle of static, Liz heard Wally announce, "Chelsea 1 has hailed a cab. Heading north." Liz sat down on the worn leather sofa that was provided for visiting case officers to the Operations Room.

On Notting Hill Gate, Maureen Hayes, parked at a meter outside an estate agent's, put down the *Evening Standard* and turned the ignition of her grey ten-year-old BMW 318i estate. "Ready and waiting," she said.

As the taxi emerged from the top of Kensington Church Street and turned right, Maureen gave it five seconds, then sidled out into the traffic and took up a position two cars behind. Various other anonymous vehicles pulled out from their parking places and slotted into the traffic. Rykov, sitting in the back of the taxi, was reading a newspaper, giving no sign at all that he was alert to possible surveillance.

He must just be going home to the Trade Delegation in Highgate, mused Liz to herself, as the taxi proceeded up Albany Street, through Camden Town and Kentish Town to the bottom of Highgate West Hill.

"Bravo team alert," called Reggie Purvis over the microphone, "Chelsea 1 is coming your way."

Nothing obvious changed on Hampstead Heath, but a scruffy young man sitting beside the boating pond shifted position imperceptibly and higher up the hill, from a small plantation of trees, a couple strolled out towards the open ground.

At the foot of Highgate West Hill, where the buses turn round, Rykov's taxi stopped and he emerged and walked slowly on to the heath and up the hill towards the bench, under close scrutiny from the A4 team. At almost the same time, a tall, powerfully built young man in a windcheater emerged from the trees and started walking down the hill.

"Chelsea 2 is here and about to make contact," came over the loudspeaker in the Ops Room.

"Tell them to stick with him and leave Rykov alone," said Liz to Reggie Purvis.

The instruction was radioed out. "Roger that," came back from the heath.

For fifteen minutes there was silence in the Ops Room, then the radio crackled. "Targets are moving. We're taking on Chelsea 2."

And for the next ten minutes radio messages went back and forth as the unknown man repeated his movements of two weeks before, leaving the heath on the south side. Again he waited at the bus stop, until a C2 bus appeared. As he got on and walked towards the stairs leading to the upper deck, he passed A4's Dennis Rudge, already on the bus, sitting downstairs by the window at the front. The bus itself was followed patiently by Maureen and her A4 colleagues in their nondescript cars, as it worked its way south, down into London's West End.

When Chelsea 2 got off the bus outside Liberty on Regent Street, along with half a dozen other passengers, Dennis Rudge stayed on board, watching as the young man crossed Regent Street and cut down a side street, followed by three A4 colleagues who had emerged from nearby cars. By the time the procession entered Berkeley Square, Maureen in the BMW was parked at yet another meter, and she had a clear view as their target walked to the southern end of the square, entered a large office block and disappeared.

"Can they find out which floor he goes to?" asked Liz, by now warming to the chase.

Purvis relayed the request. "I'll have a go," said Maureen.

Liz and Reggie waited tensely, sitting silently, for almost five minutes until Maureen's voice came through the speaker on the table.

"Fifth or sixth," she declared. "Multiple occupants and a security guard on the desk."

"Okay. Leave it now," said Liz. "We'll sort it from there. Please say thanks to everyone."

"Stand down all teams. Well done," said Purvis.

"Roger. Out," came back from the heath and Berkeley Square.

12

By the standards of his earlier career, it was not an exotic view. On Geoffrey Fane's first posting abroad, in Syria twenty years ago, his office had overlooked the souk, noisy with its milling crowds, quiet only at prayers. Later, in New Delhi, he had watched labourers arrive on bicycles, wearing flip-flops and shorts as they went to work in the liquid heat, erecting a flamboyant new Middle Eastern embassy building across the road.

Here in Vauxhall Cross, high in the office block that sat like a postmodernist Buddha on the south bank, there was nothing so dramatic. Just the heavy, comforting presence of the Thames as it swept from Vauxhall down to the Houses of Parliament. He

liked to think its colour reflected the changing seasons—or was
it just his mood? Today at low tide the water was steely grey, the
colour of old flint.

There was a tap at the door and his secretary stuck her head
in. "Liz Carlyle is downstairs. Shall I go and collect her?"

"Please," he said. He checked the knot of his tie and
brushed his jacket lapel automatically. He cared about his
appearance; his ex-wife, Adele, had accused him of vanity, but
that had been just before they separated, when she'd accused
him of a lot of things. It was Adele who had insisted on his buying only Hermès ties. It was she who wanted people to think he
was important, and she who had taken all too literally his offhand remark, made over a second Armagnac in a Burgundy
restaurant many years before and subsequently much regretted,
that if all went well one day she might be Lady Fane.

Adele had never accepted that in his line of work any success
had to be private—fame for someone like Fane was an infallible
indicator of failure. His reward came from knowing his work
was important, rather than from public recognition.

When he'd left his meeting with Pennington at the Foreign
Office, he had considered carefully who to approach at MI5. If
he stuck to Service etiquette, Brian Ackers should be his first
port of call, but the problem there was simple: Ackers instinctively distrusted MI6, considering its officers louche individuals
who at best were soft on Communism, at worst were secret sympathisers to the Islamist cause. This meant he would view Fane's
approach with distrust and reject any suggestion about how to
proceed in what Fane already thought of as the "Adler Plot."
And though Fane didn't think he could entirely control the
investigation, he was damn well going to keep a strong, guiding
hand on it. The last thing he wanted was MI5 running amok,
pursuing Brian Ackers's anachronistic obsessions and creating

the kind of diplomatic "incident" Henry Pennington was so scared of.

If only Charles Wetherby were the director in Counter-Espionage rather than Counter-Terrorism: they had worked together well enough in the past. But it wouldn't have mattered anyway, since Wetherby's wife was reportedly terminally ill and he was on extended leave.

It was then he had thought of Elizabeth Carlyle, Wetherby's talented junior, and remembered that she had been moved to Counter-Espionage after the mole affair. She had poached that young researcher, Peggy Something or Other, whom he had lent to them, but he could only muster a superficial resentment at this, since he knew that in her shoes he would have done the same.

Theirs was not an altogether happy history—there had been an episode in Norfolk Fane would sooner forget—but he determined now to enlist her in sorting out the truth of Victor Adler's story. Whatever small resentment she might still be nursing, he was sure she could get over it. Elizabeth Carlyle had impressed him in the past with her professionalism. She was intelligent, without needing to demonstrate it, and decisive when it mattered. What's more, she seemed tactful and discreet. Right now those were the qualities he needed most.

The door opened again and she came in, a woman in her mid-thirties, with light brown hair in a neat bob and a slim figure, which made her look taller than she was. There was a calm watchfulness about her, but her grey-green eyes were striking and alert. As always, Fane found her attractive, the more so because she didn't make a show of it. She was dressed simply, in a blue skirt and pearl satin blouse. How unlike Adele, he thought, remembering his ex-wife's weekly trips to that extremely expensive hairdresser in Knightsbridge, and its showy results. As well as her countless shopping expeditions to Harvey Nichols.

"Elizabeth," he said, standing up and coming out from behind his large desk to shake her hand. He motioned her to sit on the sofa on the other side of the room and himself took the armchair opposite. "How very nice to see you."

She declined tea or coffee while he made small talk. "Congratulations on your new position," he said. "I hope you're enjoying it."

"I am, thank you," she replied, "though it's only a lateral move."

"I wouldn't be so sure," he protested, then stopped. He'd always sensed the resolute independence that accompanied her unflappable, professional façade. The last thing to do was to patronise her. "I was sorry to hear about Charles's situation," he said, changing the subject. "It must be grim for him."

"Yes," she said simply, gazing back at him with a level expression.

He changed tack. "How's that young woman getting on?" he asked. "I wasn't very happy to lose her, you know."

Liz acknowledged this with the faintest hint of a smile. "Peggy's been transferred to Counter-Espionage as well."

"Ah. I'm sure she'll prosper there." He paused a beat, then said casually, "You've got my boy working for you too now, haven't you?"

"That's right," she said.

He waited, toying with a cufflink, but she said nothing beyond this, and something in her expression made him feel unable to ask anything else. He wished for once she could let down her guard. She's wary of me, he thought, and decided to move to business. He leant forward in his chair. "Well, let me explain why I wanted to see you. Does the name Victor Adler mean anything to you?"

"Only vaguely," she said. "Banking?"

"Among many other things," said Fane, rubbing his palms together gently.

As he talked, he sensed that Liz was watching him intently. His own eyes strayed occasionally towards the window as he gave a précis of Adler's story. From time to time he looked straight at her but it was impossible to gauge the effect his account was having. He found her inscrutability intriguing. And slightly irritating.

When he finished he sat back again. "I hope that makes sense."

"I think so. But why are the Russians so worried about a bunch of London émigrés, however rich they are? Surely there's not much harm they can do from here. Why would they risk killing one of them in London? Not after the Litvinenko business. The press would have a field day and if it was known to be an official operation, the political fallout would be immense."

"Yes," agreed Fane, "you're right. But they've done it so often before. They regard assassination as an acceptable form of defence." He thought of Markov, the Bulgarian exile, stabbed by a stranger's umbrella on Waterloo Bridge in 1978. Even at the time, the height of the Cold War, his claim he'd been attacked had seemed fantastic. But then Markov had died from ricin poisoning and it had emerged that the umbrella had injected him with a poisoned pellet. All because he was criticising the Bulgarian president.

"I can't see it myself," said Liz. "The criticism would be worldwide, worse than Litvinenko. At least he was an ex-KGB officer, so he was seen as, in a sense, all part of the murky world. But as far as I know these oligarchs aren't. They're just men who got very rich in rather dubious ways."

"And yet . . . ," said Fane, looking out his window thoughtfully, "don't forget they recently introduced a new law allowing their security services to kill Russia's enemies abroad without court authorisation."

Earlier in the morning, mist had hung over the Thames like bonfire smoke, then it had suddenly cleared, though dense cloud still covered the sky. In the distance Vauxhall Bridge Road stretched monotonously north towards the office blocks of Victoria. "And now we have this story of Adler's. His information has always been A1 in the past."

"Maybe. But from what you say his source admitted he didn't know the full facts. He may have got hold of the wrong end of the stick. Or maybe there isn't a stick at all and the Russians are just using him for some purpose of their own."

"Of course," agreed Fane. "Even Adler would admit the story was vague. But why spread it around? What's the object? All it's done so far is cause alarm."

To his surprise, Liz gave a light spontaneous laugh. "Are you alarmed?" she asked.

"I'm never alarmed," he said with false gravity, then laughed too. "But I can't say the same of the Foreign Office. Do you know Henry Pennington?"

"Only by name," she said.

He nodded, amused by the rare pleasure which lay in store for her. "Well, Henry *is* alarmed. In fact," he went on, thinking of Pennington's anxious twittering, "I would say he's absolutely panicked."

"Really," said Liz noncommittally.

He admired her calm. Brian Ackers would be pacing the room by now, he thought. He was pleased that he'd decided to approach Liz first. If he could interest her in this, he was confident Ackers would let her take the case. "I'm tempted to say that as a rule the Foreign Office opposes anything happening at all, but in fairness, I think they're worried that an incident would damage our joint efforts to combat terrorism."

Liz nodded. So far, so good, thought Fane, but here comes the tricky bit. There was no point trying to disguise it. "And that, Elizabeth, is where you come in."

"Me?"

Her surprise seemed entirely genuine. "Yes," he said firmly, "the FCO wants to be certain that this plot never gets off the ground. They want us to find out what is being planned, and then to make sure it doesn't happen. I already have half our Moscow Station trying to find out more."

He spoke with assurance, keen to make it all seem obvious. But he saw that Liz was having none of it. "Wait a second, please," she said, and he groaned inwardly. "Why isn't the FCO talking to us directly, since we're talking about an incident that's supposed to take place on British soil?"

"Oh, that's simple," said Fane. "I offered to be the intermediary in the first instance as I was the one who received the information." Which was partly the truth, he reassured himself.

"All right," she said, her tone making it clear she wasn't sure it was. He sensed she was digging her heels in. "But why are you talking to me? Shouldn't you first be talking with someone more senior? Brian Ackers, if not DG?"

Fane shrugged. "Think of this as a strictly unofficial chat." He continued confidently, "You and I have worked together in the past. You see, I need somebody who can get things done *discreetly*."

He paused, wondering how *in*discreet he could afford to be. To hell with it, he thought; this Carlyle woman played such a straight bat that he might as well level with her. If she baulked, he could always revert to the orthodox channels. There seemed nothing to lose. "Look," he said, though not aggressively, "if I brief Brian Ackers first, chances are he'll go charging in and try and get someone arrested or expelled. And then all hell will break loose. That's exactly the kind of diplomatic fiasco the FCO wants to avoid." He looked at her almost beseechingly. "You do see that, don't you?" he said.

And watching her, he could tell that she did—no flies on her. But he also sensed that she was never going to criticise her own boss in front of him. So he waved what he hoped was an understanding hand. "I know, I know. You can't possibly comment. I'll speak with Brian, of course. So will Pennington. But I wanted to forewarn you that we're both going to ask that you be the one to deal with this."

"How thoughtful of you," she said expressionlessly. He shrugged, controlling his annoyance. Didn't she appreciate the opportunity she was being offered? If she sorted this out, she would have the eternal gratitude of the FCO and MI6. Well, not perhaps eternal. She thinks she's being set up, Fane decided, but then conceded to himself that in one sense she was absolutely right. For it was not normal practice for an MI6 officer to choose which MI5 officer was going to work with him. Or to try (and this he fervently hoped wasn't so obvious) to control what should be, at the very least, a joint operation.

"I wish we had a little more to go on," said Liz finally. "There are at least thirty oligarchs in London who could be targets." She thought for a moment. "If they're focusing on someone politically active, that helps to narrow things down. But we still have at least half a dozen possibles. Matrayev—he says they've already tried—Obukhov, Morozov, Rostrokov, Brunovsky, Meltzer, Pertsev . . . I'm sure there're several others who could be eligible."

Fane nodded sagely, but inwardly he was pleased to see her already at work on the problem they faced. She can't help herself, he thought, and he knew he was just the same. What had

Adele said the first time she'd left him? "When your job takes you over, I might as well not be here. So I won't be."

"Anyway," said Liz, "I'll wait to hear from Brian about this." She glanced at her watch. "If that's all, please excuse me. I should get back."

Fane was slightly irked by the suggestion she had more pressing things to do, but realised that this was all he could expect at this stage. He stood up to shake her hand, saying, "You and I will need to work together on this."

She nodded—was it reluctantly? He hoped not. "I'll ring you," she said. "That is, if Brian gives me the case."

"Never fear, Elizabeth," he said lightly, hoping to end the meeting on a friendly note. But he suddenly realised she was cross.

"It's Liz," she said sharply. "People call me Liz."

"I beg your pardon," he said, annoyed that he felt it necessary to apologise. God, he thought as she went out of the door, she is prickly.

But at least she had a sense of humour, unlike so many of her po-faced colleagues in Thames House. And Fane found himself looking forward to her phone call, and to working with her. When he glanced out the window, he saw that the sun was shining, the tide was coming in and the river held a hint—just a hint—of blue.

13

As he approached the house in Belgravia, a beautiful white stuccoed mansion just off Eaton Square, Jerry Simmons kept his eyes peeled, which was what he was paid to do. But there was nothing unusual on the street.

A month before there'd been a man sitting in an electric blue Audi saloon car, two days in a row, within view of the house. Each day he'd disappeared by mid-morning, though once Jerry thought he'd spotted the car, further down the street, at dusk.

Jerry reckoned that the man had been there on Rykov's orders, probably to confirm where Jerry worked. Certainly since then there'd been nothing unusual, although Tamara, the PA, had been jittery lately. But then she'd always struck Jerry as highly strung, neurotic even. One day she'd grilled him after a substitute postman had made the delivery. Had he seen him? Did he look genuine?

Jerry's daily routine was straightforward. He'd come out from the Underground in his standard blue chauffeur's suit, do up his tie and walk across the park in time to reach the house by eight o'clock. There he'd collect a mug of tea from Mrs. Grimby in the vast basement kitchen, then retreat to the Bentley Arnage, and wait, reading the *Mirror* he'd brought along with him on the Tube. By eight-thirty the Russian would come out and get into the back seat, and Jerry would drive him to the gym, an expensive place with a pool down near Chelsea Harbour. Then on to any appointments, and perhaps a restaurant for lunch, after which the Russian liked to be in his house.

On those mornings when Brunovsky stayed in, Jerry might go out and top the car up with petrol, get it washed or take it for its quarterly service; otherwise, he killed time by waxing and polishing the car until it gleamed, by making himself useful around the house (he was good at DIY) or just by reading.

It could be a long day sometimes, especially when there was an evening engagement, but his weekends were usually free, since Brunovsky liked to spend them in the country where he kept a Range Rover which he drove himself. And the money was good enough, so he wasn't complaining, especially now that he had the generous top-up from Rykov.

He had had two more meetings with Rykov, though they had been brief. He'd given accounts of his employer's comings and goings, and supplied what little information he had about where the man might be going next. It had seemed skimpy even to Simmons, but Rykov had not complained. And he'd paid him well.

Still, it violated what Simmons knew should be his professional code: a man had one employer, and therefore one loyalty;

less clearly, it also stirred some unease, since Jerry was well disposed to the Russian and it seemed obvious that Rykov's close interest in him was a threat of some sort.

Not that he knew his employer very well. He was small and wiry, but seemed a cheerful bloke. His English was excellent, and he always said hello to Jerry in the morning and asked how he was. He would apologise if his schedule changed unexpectedly, or if he had to go out suddenly in the evening. But they didn't have much other conversation, and when he was on his mobile, which seemed most of the time, or Tamara was with him, he spoke in Russian.

Tamara was not so friendly. Frosty, fortyish, dyed blonde hair, she spoke English with an accent that got on his nerves, though that was nothing compared to her manners, which were high-handed and officious. She wasn't Russian herself, but from some country Jerry could not identify. Macedonia? Montenegro? Something like that, though you would think she had been born on Park Lane the way she behaved. Her demeanour suggested that although she too worked for the Russian, she was not a mere employee—which someone like Jerry, who was a mere employee, should not forget.

Yet she was the only unpleasant note in the household, which had a sizeable retinue—Mrs. Grimby the cook, a housekeeper named Warburton who didn't say much but was friendly enough, a series of temps who helped Tamara when she found typing beneath her, a young maid, two gardeners and Monica, Brunovsky's girlfriend. She was nice, Monica—a looker of course, but not stuck up. He was sometimes asked to chauffeur her on shopping expeditions, though most of the time she seemed happy to drive herself. Who wouldn't, given an Audi 6 coupé and licence to knock up as many parking fines as they wanted?

This morning he was collecting his tea from Mrs. Grimby

when he heard voices in the corridor upstairs, speaking in Russian. He was used to the voices of Tamara and the boss, and today there was a strain to their exchanges, which Jerry could detect without understanding a word.

"Is he going to the gym today?" he whispered to Mrs. Grimby. Stout and white-haired, she wore an apron around her ample waist and was opening a canister of flour.

"I don't know," she said equably, "though he's here for lunch. But I think something's upset him." She raised her eyes; upstairs, voices continued in an agitated staccato of Russian. Suddenly he heard the noise of clacking heels come down the stairs, and Tamara swept into the kitchen.

"Jerry," she said shortly, "when did you get here?"

"Just a minute ago," he said. She looked even tenser than usual. "Is something wrong?"

Tamara ignored his question and turned on her heel. Leaving the kitchen to go upstairs, she called back over her shoulder, "Sir will be down shortly."

Sir, thought Jerry sarcastically, who was happy enough to address his employer that way, but was buggered if he'd use the expression when the man wasn't even there. He looked at Mrs. Grimby. She and her late husband had run a pub in South London, then a boarding house in Poole; Jerry couldn't believe she hadn't seen a thing or two. "What's got into her?" he asked.

"Takes all sorts," said Mrs. Grimby philosophically, starting to sift some flour.

Jerry picked up his mug, then went outside, where the car sat in a narrow cul-de-sac, next to the small garden between the back of the house and a mews house which the Russian also owned. It was going to be a fine day, he thought, watching as the sun began to eat up the early-morning haze, and the dew on the close-cropped lawn began to dry.

Ten minutes later, he had worked his way to the sports page when Brunovsky came out. Jerry put the paper down, got out and opened the back door. "Morning," said his boss. Usually he was openly cheerful, even expansive if the day was fine. But this morning he looked preoccupied, and got into the car quickly.

Jerry had just backed up the car to turn around and leave, when there was a sudden exclamation from the back seat. "*Bozhe moi!*"

"Sir?" said Jerry tentatively, stopping the car.

The Russian had his computer open on his lap and had opened a copy of the *FT*. He raised both hands to his head in a parody of despair. "I've left my folder."

"Shall I run in and get it, sir?"

"Please do." Brunovsky gestured to his lap and made a gesture of helplessness. "It's right on the desk in my study."

Jerry turned off the engine and got out. In the kitchen Mrs. Grimby was rolling out pastry on a butcher's block. Jerry went straight through and climbed the stairs to the ground floor, two at a time. In the front hall, two storeys high and boasting a splendid curved staircase to the upstairs bedrooms, he turned and strode down a thin corridor lined with watercolours of Russian landscapes.

At the back of the house he found the door of Tamara's office open. He walked through it into the study where his boss worked, a cosy room with vivid scarlet wallpaper, two floor-to-ceiling bookshelves at one end and a small sofa and TV at the other. Between the bookshelves hung a large oil painting of a Cossack bestride a horse—normally, that is, for now the Cossack picture was on the floor, leaning upright against the wall. In its space was a square wall safe, its door wide open.

Jerry stared at the safe for a moment, then, overcome with curiosity, took two steps closer and peered inside. He saw a couple of large envelopes and a leather jewellery case. Not unexpected, nor was the existence of the safe—a man as rich as Brunovsky must have plenty of valuables he'd want to protect. What did take Jerry aback though was the sight of a small handgun, lying flat on the safe floor.

He turned quickly and went towards the large partner's desk in front of the window overlooking the back garden, where he saw the file and picked it up. He was about to turn to leave when Tamara suddenly came into the room. "What are you doing here?" she demanded, almost shouting. Her eyes shifted towards the safe, then moved back, blazing, to Jerry.

He calmly waved the file, deliberately keeping his gaze on her, well away from the open safe door. "Mr. Brunovsky left this behind. He asked me to fetch it for him."

There was nothing she could object to in this. "Go on then," she ordered, and Jerry nodded and left the room. Christ, he thought, as he made his way downstairs and returned to the car. What sort of bloke am I working for? He could understand Brunovsky's having a gun, but it was the type of gun that shook him. The Izhmekh MP 451 packed the punch of a .38, and was the weapon of choice for Russian detectives and intelligence officers wanting a compact weapon with maximum firepower. So lethal was this gun that private citizens there were not allowed to own them.

Damn, thought Jerry, for he had grown to like his peaceful chauffeur's routine, and had almost forgotten that he was also being paid to protect his boss. Not peaceful any more, he thought, suddenly alert, recognising that if Brunovsky felt he needed an MP 451, then there must be something to protect him from.

14

"ouldn't we just show the photograph to the people at reception?" complained Michael Fane, drawing up a chair next to Peggy Kinsolving in the open-plan office. He held a sheet of paper in his hand, and flapped it irritably. "This is like searching for a needle in a haystack, when we could easily blow all the hay away. *Whoosh!*" He blew air like a mechanical leaf-blower.

Peggy shook her head. Michael must be my age, she thought, yet sometimes he acted like an undergraduate. He certainly looked like a student, with a boy's thin build and unruly hair. There was no doubting his cleverness—not with a Double First from Cambridge—but he was also impatient and quick to criticise, even when what he took for stupidity was actually something he didn't fully understand.

Peggy said, "Come on, get real. If we start asking around, somebody in the building will talk. We've got to try it this way." She pointed to her laptop, where the most recent Google search showed thirty-seven hits.

"Safer maybe," grumbled Michael, "but pretty slow."

So far, Peggy had to concede, Michael had a point. She looked at her list of the tenants in the building in Berkeley Square. She'd trawled through the register from Companies House and found three-quarters of the tenants; now she hoped Google would further illuminate the nature of their businesses.

But how could one tell whether the man A4 had followed had entered the offices of Stringer Fund Management or Piccolo Mundi, importers of fine Italian foodstuffs? Or gone into McBain, Sweeney and White, an up-and-coming ad agency, or Shostas and Newton, lawyers specialising in intellectual property law?

She looked at the next name on the list and typed "The Cartwright Agency" into the Google query box, then sighed. Doubtless another advertising firm, or a casting agency for films.

Almost a minute later, Michael Fane finally broke the silence. "What's the matter, Peggy?" he asked, noticing she was staring at the screen.

He leant over and read:

The Cartwright Agency is a new consultancy but with veteran credentials, specialising in providing advice and other forms of assistance on matters of corporate and individual security.

"Where are you going?" he said, for Peggy was on her feet and already moving fast.

"I'm going to see Liz," she called back over her shoulder. "I think we may have found our mystery man."

Her appointment was at noon, and when Liz Carlyle emerged from the Underground at Green Park she had half an hour to spare. After a week of steady drizzle, the sky had suddenly brightened and the temperature was in the mid-sixties.

Mayfair must be one of the nicest places in the world to kill time, she decided as she strolled along New Bond Street looking in the shop windows. It was interesting to have the occasional glimpse into a world of people where money seemed to mean nothing (or was it everything?), but Liz had neither the time nor the inclination to follow fashion or to know who was who among the famous designer names in the shop windows. It was not that she had a puritan's aversion to a life where what was fashionable mattered; she simply didn't have the time—or the money.

Maybe, she thought, this was her chance to find something for a wedding she was going to in May, but a quick foray into Burberry on the corner of Conduit Street unearthed nothing under £500. So she decided she would do as she usually did and look in the little dress shop in Stockbridge, which she passed on her way down to her mother's Wiltshire house. Cutting down towards Berkeley Square, her thoughts turned to her impending appointment.

Liz was using her operational cover name of Jane Falconer. She had her hair tied back and she wore a conservative grey suit, for from his CV, the man she was going to meet, Brigadier Walter Cartwright, was unmistakably traditional: Wellington, Sandhurst, four tours in Northern Ireland, active duty during the Falklands campaign, followed by command of a tank regiment during Operation Desert Storm in the first Iraq War.

He had resigned from the army soon after the Gulf campaign and begun a second career in a risk analysis/security firm of international repute. After five years he had struck out on his own, forming his eponymous consultancy. Such companies tended to divide between the cerebral, specialising in "risk analysis," and those at the sharper end, who provided protection—for multinational corporations worried about the kidnapping of their chief executives and sometimes for people rich enough to pay someone to create an illusion of risk.

From Peggy's briefing to Liz, it was clear the Cartwright consultancy was in the heavy category, with most of its staff ex-military. Yet it managed to mask the muscular aspects of its business by having peers of the realm among its nonexecutive directors and by situating its headquarters in the smartest part of London.

On the sixth floor of the modern block at the south end of Berkeley Square, Walter Cartwright greeted Liz with a firm handshake and a slow smile. He looked younger than his fifty or so years. He was on the near side of six feet, and wore a suit of rumpled gabardine. Only the erect way he held himself gave any indication of his military past; that, and the square outline to his shoulders.

His office overlooked Berkeley Square, though at this height the view was obscured by the early leaves on the square's perimeter trees. The sound of the traffic was dulled and the noise of birdsong came through the window, melodious and clear. "Lovely, isn't it?" said Cartwright. "That's a blackbird. Not many nightingales in Berkeley Square nowadays."

Liz pointed to a pair of watercolours on the wall, each depicting a black Labrador retrieving pheasants at a shoot. "They're rather fine," she said.

Cartwright chuckled. "You're either being very polite or you've been well briefed. I painted them myself."

They sat down and Cartwright looked at her with friendly curiosity. "Miss Falconer, you said you're from the Home Office?"

"I'm actually from the Security Service."

"Ah. MI5. I thought so. I had some contact with you chaps when I was in Ireland. Is Michael Binding still around?"

"Absolutely," she said, hoping the brigadier didn't share Michael Binding's opinion of women's professional abilities.

"And there was another man." The brigadier scratched an eyebrow thoughtfully. "Ricky something. Nice fellow."

"Ricky Perrins. I'm afraid he was killed in a car accident."

"Oh I'm sorry," said the brigadier with genuine regret, and Liz found herself warming to him. "I'd better not go on about Ireland," he said, "or we'll be here all day. You said you wanted to speak with me about one of our employees. Which one?"

Liz didn't have the faintest idea of her quarry's name, so she extracted a 10x8 black-and-white photograph from her briefcase, and handed it across the desk to the brigadier. It had been taken by A4 with a telephoto lens, enlarged and cropped to show only the mystery man on the bench.

Cartwright studied it carefully, while Liz wondered what she would do if he said he'd never seen the man before.

"Simmons," said the brigadier, to Liz's relief. "Jerry Simmons."

"He works here?"

"Yes. Is this work-related?" His tone was slightly sharper.

"We don't know yet," admitted Liz. "That's why I wanted to talk to you."

"Has he done something wrong?"

"We're not sure. We had a surveillance operation on a foreign national and saw what looked like a covert meeting with

Simmons." She pointed to the photograph. "That was taken in a remote part of Hampstead Heath."

"Is this a hostile foreign national?"

Liz spoke carefully. "Let's just say his country used to be hostile; its present status is unclear. We're concerned enough to be following this man, and curious as to why he's meeting with your employee. Can you tell me something about Simmons?"

"Of course. I'll get his file." Cartwright walked over to a filing cabinet in the corner of the room and pulled out a folder. "He's from Lancashire. He left school and signed up—he was in the Paras for six years, then the SAS. Left five years ago. He seems to have made the transition to civilian life without any problems—and believe me, not all of them do. He used to be in security at the Dorchester Hotel. The people there weren't very pleased when we lured him away, but they gave him a good reference. As far as we're concerned, he's worked out very well. He's reliable, very competent." He added, without malice, "If not precisely a mastermind."

"What does he do for you?"

"He's a driver and bodyguard."

"For many different clients?"

"No," said Cartwright with a quick shake of the head. "Our contracts are strictly long term. He's working for a Russian named Nikita Brunovsky."

"Why does Mr. Brunovsky need a bodyguard?"

Cartwright shrugged. "He's one of the oligarchs. Having protection is part of their way of life. Brunovsky is comparatively restrained. Some of them have teams of people, but he relies mainly on Jerry Simmons. He doubles as chauffeur and protection."

"Is there anything about Simmons that particularly stands out? Anything unusual?"

Cartwright reflected for a moment. "One's always tempted to find *something*. Simmons has been married three times, but is that remarkable these days? I'm sure one of the reasons he left the Dorchester to come here was the money—it's a lot better, and I had the feeling he needed it. But other than that, I can't think of anything out of the ordinary about him."

Then why, thought Liz, was he meeting a Russian diplomat in a remote corner of Hampstead Heath? It must have something to do with Brunovsky. "We'll need to talk to him."

Cartwright nodded and said, "During the day, of course, he's usually with Brunovsky. There's a house in Belgravia, and an estate in Sussex. But I'd rather you didn't bother him on the job. I'll give you Jerry's home address and telephone. Perhaps you can take it from there."

"Actually, I was wondering if it would be possible to meet him here. I don't want to cause alarm before we speak to him. Or upset his family."

"Not sure if he's still got one," said Cartwright, then looked again at Liz. "Would it help if I found a pretext to get him in here?"

"That would be ideal."

"Right. Personnel can say there's been a mix-up with his National Insurance. Something like that. Just tell me when."

"It should be in the next few days." Liz stood up to leave. "It will be one of my colleagues who talks to him. I'd be grateful if you wouldn't mention my visit to anyone, especially Simmons."

"Of course," he said simply, and then as if to emphasise that her presence would be wiped from memory, exclaimed, "Listen to that!" Now there were two blackbirds singing, high up in the trees, creating a rich brocade of alternating song.

Let's hope Simmons sings as well, thought Liz. She felt a

sense of measured optimism, like someone starting out on an enormous jigsaw puzzle who makes unexpected progress early on, though it was only corner pieces of the puzzle that had come her way. She had no idea what the larger picture would look like when it emerged. If it ever did.

15

This is a Fragonard," declared Nikita Brunovsky, pointing delightedly at a beautiful young woman in a flower-filled garden.

"Marvellous," said Henry Pennington of the FCO, in an unctuous voice which was beginning to grate on Liz.

Brunovsky had already shown them a small Cézanne, a Bonnard, a Picasso sketch from his Blue Period and a Rembrandt drawing. Liz felt she was back at university, paging through an illustrated textbook on art history. Only none of these were reproductions.

Now Brunovsky stopped in front of the marble fireplace and pointed to a large abstract in a gleaming steel frame above the mantelpiece. Dark purple waves of paint met ebony swirls in a circle of orange fire. "Who do you think painted this?" the Russian asked.

Liz wasn't going to venture a guess.

"Howard Hodgkin?" asked Pennington.

The Russian laughed gleefully. He was a small man with tousled hair, a sharp nose and dark, dancing eyes. "It is the work of my sister," he replied, and cackled again.

The grim-faced blonde woman who had escorted Liz and Henry Pennington upstairs had introduced them and disappeared. Brunovsky had greeted them enthusiastically without asking their business. Now, as Pennington tried to match Brunovsky in affability, Liz looked around her.

The previous year she had treated herself to membership of the National Trust and had become a keen visitor to stately homes. But this first-floor Belgravia drawing room was like nothing she had ever seen. The large high-ceilinged room had six long, elegant windows overlooking the square at the front and the garden at the rear. The delicate duck egg blue brocade on the walls served as a subtle backdrop for the art collection hanging there.

But what Liz found startling was the bewildering mixture of furniture crammed into the room. Eighteenth-century English pieces jostled with heavy, ornate Russian cabinets and sideboards. On a corner table there was a large glass model, half castle, half fort, with intricate onion minarets and towers reproduced in exquisite detail. It seemed oddly familiar, until Liz realised it was a replica of the Kremlin.

Above all this, two vast fountain chandeliers glittered like tinsel festooning a Christmas tree. Looking towards the windows, Liz recognised a Regency pier table with a marble top and ornate legs that was similar to the cherished family heirloom her mother kept in her cottage in Wiltshire. Then Liz noticed there were five of them, one between each window.

"Come," Brunovsky said abruptly, and Liz and Pennington obediently followed the slight, wiry figure out of the room and down a passageway. His high spirits struck Liz as slightly artificial. He was presenting himself to his visitors as disarmingly impetuous, and slightly mischievous as well, like a charming small boy, Liz reflected. There was nothing boyish about his clothes, though: Brunovsky wore an elegant blue blazer with four gold buttons on each sleeve, a well-cut striped shirt, silk tie, flannel trousers and tan Gucci loafers.

Opening a door, he ushered them into a dining room, which had in its centre an elegant burred walnut table. The classical effect was spoiled by the set of chairs surrounding it—Russian monstrosities of oak, each built like a throne, upholstered in gaudy red plush. More paintings hung in clusters on the walls, though these were modern oil paintings.

"My Russian collection," Brunovsky announced with an expansive sweep of his hand.

Liz noticed that on the far wall there was an empty space in the middle of a group of still lifes. Brunovsky smiled, "You see the missing one, no?"

"Is it on loan somewhere?" Given the quality of what she was being shown, Liz would not be surprised if museums were lining up to borrow Brunovsky's holdings for their own exhibitions.

"No," said Brunovsky, shaking his head. "It is not mine to loan," he added playfully. He walked to a sideboard at one end of the room, and picked up a sale catalogue sitting on top of a stack. Flipping through its pages he stopped at one and handed the catalogue to Liz.

She looked at the page, which was dominated by a colour

reproduction of an abstract, its mass of darkish blue broken by a slash of yellow paint. The guide price, she noticed, was £4 million.

"You like it?" demanded Brunovsky.

"It's very interesting," said Liz diplomatically.

"Lovely," said Pennington, peering at the catalogue over Liz's shoulder. "When are you selling it?"

"*Selling* it?" asked Brunovsky. "I am not selling it, I am buying it. I would *never* sell a Pashko." There was genuine outrage to his voice.

"Of course, of course," Pennington said soothingly.

Liz pointed to the space on the wall, and said, "To go there?"

"Yes!" declared Brunovsky, pleased to see she understood. "It will be the crown of my collection. To me, Pashko is a god. The Russian Picasso. Now let's go downstairs."

This time he led them to his study at the back of the house. Motioning them to a sofa in one corner, Brunovsky sat down on a leather chair on casters, on which he began to roll around gently like a restless schoolboy. "So," he said and grinned, though Liz noticed his eyes darted nervously, "what is it I can do for you?"

Liz let Pennington make the running. After all it was at his instigation that they were there. As soon as Brian Ackers had been told of Victor Adler's information, true to form, he had decided that something must be done. Much against Pennington's wishes, Special Branch had been brought in. They were to warn each of the oligarchs of a heightened risk to them from Russia, though without any specific mention of the Adler information.

Pennington, who regarded the police as chronic leakers, had sulkily predicted that as soon as they were involved the whole thing would be on the front page of the *Evening Standard* within twenty-four hours. When he heard that Rykov had recruited a source in Brunovsky's household, he had leapt to the conclusion that the plot was already under way and had insisted on visiting Brunovsky himself, to warn him to avoid any public criticism of Moscow. Brian Ackers, whose opinion of Pennington matched Geoffrey Fane's, had asked Liz to go too, to report back on what was said. After a show of reluctance, Pennington had agreed to her accompanying him, though when he discovered that Liz would be using the alias of Jane Falconer, he had huffed about spooks and their unnecessarily secretive ways.

As Pennington delivered what seemed to Liz an especially long-winded warning, her eyes moved discreetly round the room. It was the only room in the house that didn't look like a museum. Here in his study, she thought, Brunovsky was for once not showing off.

Their host had stopped sliding his chair around and was listening intently. When Pennington had finished, he nodded, still taking it in. "*Tak*," he declared at last, his expression now serious, his lips taut. "And you think it is me the Kremlin plans to move against?"

"We can't be certain," said Liz, "but you're an obvious candidate."

He nodded again and leant back in his chair, then shrugged. "I am not surprised. All of us living here know our government keeps an eye on us. What do you want me to do?"

Pennington adopted a thoughtful expression. "Your views about the present Russian government are well known. It occurred to us that perhaps for a little while you might want to curtail your public pronouncements about President Putin. Just until the alarm is over."

"Curtail?" Brunovsky raised an eyebrow. "You mean you want me to shut up." He laughed but his eyes were steely.

"We thought," said Pennington, moving on hastily, "that you might want to take extra security measures, or have us take them for you."

"I have a bodyguard already. From one of your country's most reputable firms. I don't need another one."

Liz looked at Pennington, as if to say, now what? He was looking at Brunovsky, with the sympathetic expression of a parent counselling a wayward child. "I can certainly understand that," he said carefully. "But perhaps there's an alternative."

Like what? thought Liz, suddenly alert.

"Perhaps we could assign someone to . . . ," Pennington paused, searching for the right phrase, "be around. Someone who wouldn't get in the way, but who would keep an eye open on your behalf, be able to recognise if there was anything to be concerned about and be in a position to . . . respond if you needed any kind of help."

Brunovsky looked puzzled. "Would this person be armed?"

"No," said Liz quickly, wondering what the hell Pennington was talking about. He now also shook his head, but rather more slowly.

"What are we talking about then?" asked the Russian, sounding puzzled.

Don't ask me, thought Liz, still mystified. She was going to have to speak to Brian Ackers right away, she decided.

Pennington spoke more slowly, almost ponderously, as if this would somehow give greater weight to his words, "Let's just say it would be someone very experienced in recognising and handling potentially threatening situations."

"Aha," Brunovsky said with sudden enlightenment. "Someone from your famous intelligence agencies." When Pennington didn't react, the Russian scratched his head and seemed to think about this. Suddenly he gave a sharp nod of assent. "I like that. I like that very much."

"Why don't you think it over?" said Liz, infuriated by what was happening and trying to leave space for the withdrawal of Pennington's impulsive offer.

"Okay," said Brunovsky, but before Liz could relax he pointed at Pennington. "I will telephone you tomorrow."

As they said their goodbyes Liz just managed to contain her anger but when the door closed behind them and they descended to the pavement, she rounded fiercely on the Foreign Office official. "What on earth was that about?" she demanded.

"I don't know what you mean," said Pennington. He refused to meet her stare, making a show of looking around for a taxi.

"You know perfectly well this isn't something for the intelligence services. If Brunovsky's in danger, he needs protection from Special Branch, not a babysitter from Thames House."

"You saw yourself he wasn't keen on having another bodyguard."

"Then you should have insisted. You can't just offer MI5's services."

A taxi braked sharply and its window descended. Pennington leant in to speak to the driver as Liz opened the back door, determined to continue the argument on the way back to Westminster. "Sorry," said Pennington, still avoiding Liz's eyes. "You'll have to get another cab. I'm going the other way."

As he drove off, Liz stared after him with unconcealed fury. Wait until Ackers hears what you've done, she thought, starting to walk towards Green Park Underground station. He'll have an absolute fit.

16

But it was Liz who almost had the fit. "I'm supposed to be *what*?" she demanded. Outside, low clouds piled up like dark balls of wool. It had been threatening to rain all day.

"Considering Brunovsky's art interests, it seemed apt. We couldn't have you posing as a platinum expert, could we?"

"I'd rather not be posing as anything, thank you very much. The whole thing's preposterous."

Ackers looked taken aback, and fidgeted uncomfortably in his chair. Liz realised he was unused to his staff arguing back. Hadley, his right-hand man, was a classic yes-man; sometimes it seemed he even yawned at the same time Ackers did. Liz sensed that her boss wasn't altogether happy with the new blood that had arrived in his department almost simultaneously: Michael Fane, Peggy Kinsolving and Liz—especially Liz. She looked at Brian and could see him thinking, "Difficult woman."

He said reluctantly, "If you must know, Brunovsky himself asked for you."

"Am I supposed to be flattered?"

Brian didn't reply so Liz continued, "And you say I'm going to pretend to be a 'mature student' who's studying Pashko?"

"Yes. That was also Brunovsky's idea."

"Brian," she said patiently, trying not to show her annoyance, "I read history at university, art history only just came into it. When Nikita Brunovsky showed me the painting he's planning to buy at Northam's I could no more have told you who painted it than I can tell you how to make a nuclear bomb."

"We thought as much," Brian said, and Liz wondered who this "we" was. Geoffrey Fane, doubtless. "It's been decided you should have a quick brush-up on art history, and some intensive tutorials into this Pashko." He enunciated the name carefully. "You're not going to be posing as an expert, never fear. Just an enthusiast—someone doing a diploma or whatever, who's writing a short thesis about him. Only what's needed to justify your presence in Brunovsky's household."

"Where am I going to have these intensive tutorials? At the Courtauld?" she added, unable to suppress her sarcasm.

"No," said Brian measuredly. "But it's probably just as good. You're to spend a week in Cambridge. There's a woman there, a don at Newnham, though I gather she's retired. She is an expert on Pashko." He added as an afterthought, "And she's a Russian."

"Whose idea was this?" asked Liz, thinking, I bet it's bloody Geoffrey Fane again. She glanced out towards the Thames and noticed that the first spits of rain were streaking the windows.

. . .

Liz was still fuming as she left Thames House to go home. Her mood was not helped by the rain, by now sheeting down and being blown erratically sideways by a gusty westerly wind. The umbrella her mother had given her last Christmas, while handily compact when folded in her handbag, was completely useless against these conditions. By the time she got to Westminster Tube station she was soaked from head to toe and her navy blue suede shoes, chosen more for visiting Brunovsky than for wet pavement walking, were squelching hopelessly.

The rain had let up a bit by the time she emerged from the Underground system, still soaking wet, at Kentish Town and she wondered briefly whether to ring Dave Armstrong, her old colleague and friend from Counter-Terrorist days, and entice him out for a pizza and a moan about Brian Ackers. But remembering this was one of Piet's weekends, she decided instead to stop at the Threshers wine shop, open late as usual on a Thursday, and indulge herself with a bottle of the New Zealand Sauvignon they kept in their fridge, and a hot bath, before tidying up the flat.

As she opened the front door she saw the flashing red light of her answerphone reflected in the glass pane. Mother, she thought guiltily. She had been meaning to ring her for days, but hadn't. Ever since her father had died, Liz had felt responsible for her mother. Not enough to persuade her to agree to give up her "dangerous" job and her life in the "squalor" of Kentish Town and come back home to share the running of the garden centre and marry a nice steady young man. But enough to make her drive the long journey down to Wiltshire every month and to keep regularly in touch by phone.

Susan Carlyle lived at South Lodge, the house in the Nadder

Valley where Liz had grown up. When Liz was a child the pretty octagonal lodge had guarded the entrance to the Bowerbridge sporting estate, where her father had been the manager. But Jack Carlyle had died and so had the estate's owner. Bowerbridge's woods and coppices had been sold off, and its gardens had become a specialist plantsman's nursery. Pressed for money, Susan had started work there; now she ran the place. Last year she and Liz had had a scare when a lump Susan had detected had turned out to be malignant. Thankfully, surgery seemed to have been successful, though who could be sure, and she was back working just as before in the nursery.

Unfortunately the illness had coincided with the investigation of the mole in MI5 and Liz still felt guilty that she had not been able to be more available.

So, shedding her wet clothes in a heap on the bathroom floor, wrapping herself in her dressing gown and pouring herself a glass of wine, she dialled her mother's number, bracing herself for a long chat.

Her mother answered on the second ring. "Hello, darling. I'm so glad you rang. I wanted to ask you a favour."

What on earth is this going to be? wondered Liz, noticing her mother's unusually bright and brisk tone.

"I've been asked to the theatre on Saturday evening and I wondered if I could come and stay with you."

"Well, of course you can," said Liz immediately, trying to disguise her amazement. Her mother had never once expressed any interest in coming to London since Liz had lived there. Quite the opposite. She had always given the impression that she thought London a sink of iniquity. "Who are you going with?" asked Liz.

"No one you know, dear. I met him when I was ill. He's got some tickets for that play with Judi Dench in at the Haymarket, on Saturday evening. So if that's fine with you I'll catch a mid-morning train and get a taxi from the station. Be with you about two o'clock."

"All right, Mother," said Liz, hardly able to believe what she was hearing. "Shall I come and meet you at the station?"

"No need, darling," came the reply, "I've got your address and I'm sure the taxi man will find it. Must dash now. See you Saturday."

Liz sat down and drained her glass of wine. What on earth was going on? Her mother, with a boyfriend. Is that what it was? It sounded like it. She couldn't believe it and she felt a flash of resentment. All those weekends she'd forced herself to drive down to Wiltshire when she would much rather have stayed in London. Now there was her mother happily paired up while she still had no close boyfriend.

What could he be like? She hoped he was suitable. What if he was a fortune hunter? How ridiculous you are being, she said to herself. Mother hasn't got a fortune. But though she tried to laugh herself out of it, she went on feeling faintly uneasy and disturbed at this totally unexpected turn of events.

As she sat and brooded, she suddenly remembered Piet. He was expecting to come on Saturday. She would have to put him off. She did not want Piet sharing her bed whilst her mother was in the spare room next door, so feeling very confused and thoroughly disappointed at the ruining of her weekend she rang Piet.

At the end of that conversation she felt worse. When she'd explained what had happened, Piet had replied that he was about to ring her. His meetings in Canary Wharf had been discontinued and he would not be coming to London so often. He had in any case been meaning to tell her that he had met someone in Amsterdam whom he was now seeing regularly, so he thought it best if they stopped seeing each other. He added charmingly that he would miss her and the jolly weekends they had spent together and he wished her the best of luck, before ringing off.

So, thought Liz, that's that. Well at least she couldn't blame the job for the end of that relationship. But as she sat in the bath in her bright, freshly tiled bathroom, she reflected that everyone's life seemed to be improving except hers. And now she was stuck with this ridiculous scheme dreamt up by Brian Ackers and Geoffrey Fane and was going to have to spend a week in Cambridge with some mad old Russian bat.

17

She had been trained to deal with any crisis, if necessary with violence, just as she'd dealt with that mugger the other month. In her lengthy training, they had made her kill. They took convicts out of the prisons—those who'd been sentenced to death—and put the trainees up against them. At the beginning they'd intervened to make sure the trainees survived. But later in the course, it was a free contest. No one interfered; it was a fight to the death. She had been determined that whoever died, it would not be her. She had surprised herself with the ease with which she killed—stuck the knife in or pulled tight the garrotte—and they had noticed too, the instructors, those hard-eyed, expressionless men whose job it was to turn out graduates of their courses who could survive in the most extreme situations. So she was chosen for assignments where violence was likely, though she had not expected to have to use it so early in this job, and not on the streets of London.

But, as she sat in her latest apartment off Victoria Street, it was not the possibility of violence that was causing her concern. It was something completely unexpected—the intrusion on the scene of British Intelligence. What, she wondered, had brought them buzzing around Brunovsky like flies? There must have been a leak, or why else would they have suddenly turned up? And why had he encouraged them? How much did they know and how best to deal with the situation?

Unzipping the computer bags, she took out the laptop and its small black companion, that would, she hoped, provide her with the answers, and laid them out on the dining table. Half an hour later, she leant back in her chair with a satisfied grunt and, looking out of the window at Westminster Cathedral, glowing pink in the setting sun, she imagined her message bouncing around the world, disguising itself as it moved from server to server, on its way to its eventual destination, a desk in a Moscow office building. A government office building.

18

He knew it was crucial to show you were in charge from the start. On the training course they had taught him that if you began with an iron fist you could lighten up later on, but that it never worked the other way around.

Michael Fane ignored the butterflies fluttering in his stomach. This was his chance to show what he could do. He looked out of the thin window at the trees above Berkeley Square. The weather had reverted: after a glorious early morning, a sepia trail of cloud moved in with the easterly wind like ominous writing in the sky.

He sat down but found he couldn't sit still. The people here at the agency had given him their interviewing room, which was small and square, down the hall from Brigadier Cartwright's spacious office. When Liz Carlyle announced she'd be away for a week and asked him to do the interview in her place, he was thrilled. You had to belly up to the bar sometime, he told himself, using the cowboy lingo of the westerns he loved. His father had been contemptuous of those movies, implying that he knew about the real thing. He probably did, Michael thought crossly, and doubtless this forthcoming interview would be beneath him. Geoffrey must have recruited countless agents in his time—in much more difficult circumstances. What else could he have been doing all those years abroad? Even the teenage Michael Fane had known enough to understand his father wasn't really a cultural attaché.

Not that he'd seen much of him. There was the occasional outing—a day at Lord's, watching the Australians in the Test; lunch at the Traveller's Club when Michael turned sixteen—as if his father, suddenly remembering he had a son, had dutifully decided to try and "bond." When his mother at last grew fed up with Geoffrey's absences, always excused as a matter of work, and her patience had finally snapped, Michael didn't blame her. Now she lived in Paris, remarried to Arnaud, an international lawyer—the kind of stable *haut bourgeois* she should have married in the first place.

Michael had applied to join MI5 wanting to outplay his father at his own game—but from the safe distance of a rival service. He had had a letter from him, suggesting lunch, just two weeks before he joined. At first Michael had accepted, then, when the day came, he'd left a message that he was ill. There'd been no communication since, which, thought Michael, suited him just fine.

He looked at the dossier Peggy Kinsolving had helped him put together. He'd spent the last hour practising his set recital, checking the pictures for the umpteenth time and arranging the chairs. Instead of the sofa and low table near the door, used for more informal chats, he opted to stay behind the desk at one end of the room. That should give him an air of authority.

He wished he didn't look so young. Even the photos he'd seen of his father as a young man made Geoffrey Fane seem at twenty confident, commanding. No one had ever called his father lacking in maturity. The phrase used by Michael's girlfriend Anna to explain why she was breaking up with him. The memory still rankled.

There was a sharp knock and the door opened. The brigadier marched in, looking stern, followed by the tall leggy woman from HR. Behind them, standing in the doorway, stood a man in a blue chauffeur's suit. Simmons. He looked confused.

"Here he is," announced the brigadier to Michael. "Shout if you need me." He and the woman went out, shutting the door firmly behind them.

"Sit down, Mr. Simmons," Michael said, pointing to the chair he'd placed in front of the desk. "My name is Magnusson," he added mechanically, as if he'd said this countless times before.

Simmons sat down and hunched forward, his legs apart, arms hanging down between his knees. He clasped his hands loosely together and looked at Michael, his face an open anxious book.

"Can I see your passport please?" Michael asked crisply, holding out his hand.

Simmons hesitated, then slowly passed it across the desk. He had been instructed to bring it with him. "What's all this about?"

Ignoring the question, Michael leafed through the pages. There weren't many stamps, but passports were no real guide nowadays—Morocco, and Cyprus twice. Holiday locations. "Have you ever been to Russia?"

"Russia?" Simmons seemed caught off guard. "No. Never. Why?"

Michael shrugged and made a show of examining the passport some more. He flipped it down on to the desktop, where it spun briefly then stopped, well short of Simmons's reach. "Have you ever known any Russians?"

"Well I don't know about 'known,' " said Jerry. "When I worked at the Dorchester loads of foreigners stayed there and some of them were Russians. And I work for a Russian now, you must know that, and he's got lots of Russian friends. What's all this about?"

"I work in the Security Service. We've had reason to mount a surveillance operation recently, on a member of the Russian Embassy. We followed him to a number of meetings with people, some open and public, some clandestine. One of them was with you."

"You must be confusing me with someone else," said Jerry. But there was colour in his cheeks, and he was clasping his hands tightly now.

"Possibly," Michael said, "though they say the camera never lies." He opened his dossier, lifted out two of the prints and slid them across the desk.

Jerry made a show of carefully inspecting them. "When were these taken?" he asked, as if they might be snaps from a holiday so long ago he couldn't remember it.

"Recently," said Michael.

"I talk to a lot of people," said Jerry. "There's nothing wrong with that."

"Of course there isn't." Michael smiled fleetingly, though now there was a cutting edge to his voice. "But what are we supposed to think when we find you meeting a Russian intelligence officer? Old friends talking about old times? I don't think so."

"I work for a Russian, for Christ's sakes. I know a lot of Russians. I told you that."

"I bet you do, and we're going to talk about every one of them. But it's this Russian"—and he stabbed his finger at the photo—"I'm interested in now."

"Does the brigadier know why you're talking to me?" Simmons asked. He looked to be flailing, like someone pushed out of a boat, trying to determine how deep the water was and whether there was any chance of swimming to shore.

Michael regarded Simmons knowingly. "What do you think?"

Simmons groaned, then put his head in his hands.

"However," Michael announced, "he might overlook it. If we asked him."

There was resignation rather than hope in Simmons's eyes as he lifted his head. "If?" he said.

"Excuse me?" asked Fane.

"I said *if*. There's always an 'if.' You'll get Cartwright to keep me on *if* I do what you say."

"Sure."

"And when you're through with me, what happens then? Do I keep my job?"

"That's between you and the brigadier. Now why don't you tell me when you first met Rykov?"

"Who's Rykov?" asked Simmons, and Michael realised his bafflement was genuine. Damn, he thought, annoyed with himself for letting the name slip out. He pointed at the photo.

"Oh, Vladimir," said Simmons with a dull nod.

"Go on. How did he first contact you?"

And twenty minutes later he had heard all about it: Rykov's

approach, the meetings with his predecessor, Andrei, during Jerry's days at the Dorchester, what they'd wanted to know, and what Simmons was getting paid. He first denied receiving any money at all, then seemed to realise this made him look even worse.

Throughout, Michael Fane took careful notes. He did not want Jerry to know he was recording everything on a tape deck in the top desk drawer. And in any case he wasn't sure it would capture Simmons's low monotone.

Finished at last, Simmons looked tired.

"Good," Fane said, doling out a titbit of praise. "Was Andrei your only other contact?"

Simmons nodded quickly, but Michael remembered Brian Ackers's maxim that for spies, truth was an abstract notion better not put into practice. "Have another think," he ordered. "Who knows what you might remember?"

Simmons stared back at him, but coldly now, the earlier dead look to his eyes replaced by ice. For a second Michael felt uneasy. There was something unnerving about this man, he thought, as if pressure was building inside that quiet shell, just waiting to explode. But Michael knew he mustn't back off.

"Tell me, why do you think Vladimir is so interested in Brunovsky?" he asked.

"How should I know?" replied Simmons with a shrug.

"Are you the only one watching Brunovsky?"

Simmons's eyes widened slightly. "What do you mean?"

"Has Vladimir got anyone else keeping tabs on him?"

"Not as far as I know," said Simmons stiffly.

"All right," said Michael. "I'll want you to look at some more pictures next time to see if you can recognise anyone else."

"Next time?" A fatalistic note had returned to Simmons's voice.

"We'll meet in ten days."

"Where?" he demanded.

"Here." He hadn't checked, but he was sure the brigadier would allow it. "If anything else occurs to you in the meantime, you can call me on this number." He scribbled the number down and passed it over. "I already have yours."

Simmons pocketed the slip of paper without looking at it. "Is that all?" he said stonily.

"For now," said Michael Fane.

Simmons stood up abruptly and left without saying a word. As the door closed behind him, Michael felt a mix of relief and elation. In a minute he would go and see the brigadier, but he sat for a bit, savouring his feeling of accomplishment. He could see now why Liz Carlyle and Peggy Kinsolving, and yes, even his father, grew so involved with their work.

He thought again of Simmons. I've got him where I want him, thought Michael. He's not even going to try and lie to me.

As he left the building Jerry Simmons was seething. It was bad enough to have been found out—bloody Vladimir and his insistence on Hampstead Heath, he thought furiously. He might as well have chosen Piccadilly Circus.

Even worse was being played like a fish by this fresh-faced twerp. If his name's Magnusson, thought Jerry bitterly, mine's Marco Polo. He'd do what he had to do—"Magnusson" wasn't exactly leaving him a choice, no more than Rykov had. No, he wasn't going to tell the kid any lies. Yet as Jerry remembered the gun he'd seen in Brunovsky's safe, he didn't see any reason why he should tell the whole truth, either.

19

"Your turn," said the old lady, Sonia Warschawsky, encouragingly.

Liz took a step forward and peered at the painting. Once she would have said it was a picture of a horse and left it at that, but she knew better now. "Let's see. It's a modern painting but the expert handling of paint gives it a sensuousness that is very old-fashioned. It's full of references to earlier painters—the chiaroscuro light and shadow of the field is straight out of Vermeer." She stood back contemplatively. "And the anatomical precision of the horse is pure Stubbs."

"Excellent," said Sonia. "Give me another week and I'll make an art critic of you." She gave a high clear laugh that belied her years and elegant appearance. Sonia was tall and slim, remarkably upright for a woman in her eighties, with silver hair held back by an ivory cameo slide, startling blue eyes, a nose as sharp as a cutter's prow and that great asset called "bone structure"—in her case, high cheeks and a small but sturdy chin. She wore a green tweed suit that had certainly been purchased before Liz was born, but, having come originally from a Paris salon, found itself, forty years on, in fashion once more.

Born in the twenties into a wealthy French-Russian family, Sonia Warschawsky had in her young days moved easily through Europe, visiting members of her extended family in great houses and charming holiday villas, meeting artists and musicians, speaking fluent English, French and Russian, a child of aristocratic interwar Europe. She had been staying with her grandmother in the South of France when the Second World War was declared and suddenly privilege ended. In the panic of June 1940, she escaped to England with some of her young relatives on a Dutch merchant ship, probably the last ship to leave France for England. After the war, her formidable intelligence, her cultured background and her family influence had got her to Girton College, Cambridge, and in Cambridge she had remained, eventually becoming a don at Newnham, where even now she occasionally taught, still full of opinions, energetically and often tartly expressed.

"That's enough for now," Sonia declared. "Let's have some tea."

They left the gallery of the Fitzwilliam and went to the museum's café in a covered courtyard. This was Liz's first sortie out with Sonia since she had arrived in Cambridge three days before. She felt like a learner driver on an inaugural run with her instructor.

On the previous Thursday, a courier had rung the bell to her flat in Kentish Town, and while Liz was still blinking the sleep from her eyes he had handed over a large Jiffy bag. Inside she'd found three illustrated histories of art, and she had spent the weekend going slowly through their pages. On Monday, when she'd taken a taxi from the station and dropped her bags off at the Royal Cambridge Hotel, Liz not only knew when Gainsborough had been born, she could name half a dozen subjects of his portraits.

Sonia lived alone, ten minutes' walk from the city's central cluster of colleges, in a small Victorian house of yellow brick. It had a large bay window and a white wooden trellis by the front door, on which an iceberg rose was already beginning its spring-time climb.

She made it clear from the start that she knew Liz's line of work, though she accepted at face value that Liz was called Jane Falconer. "The brief I've had," she said on the first morning, as they sat down in her sitting room by the bay window, "is to give you a crash course in art history, with some special tuition on modern Russian painters, especially Pashko. Is that correct, Jane?"

Liz nodded. "Yes."

"And as I understand it," Sonia said with a sly smile, "it's not so much what you know that will be important, but what you *seem* to know."

Liz smiled. "*A Bluffer's Guide.*" They both laughed and the ice was broken.

They soon established their working routine. Sonia sat in one corner in a rocking chair, while Liz took over an old Knole sofa, surrounded by her books and notes. On the walls there were dozens of drawings and pictures, most landscapes of English scenes, but with the occasional Russian subject—a small portrait of Tsar Nicholas, an aquatint of the Hermitage.

Similarly, the many bibelots that dotted the side tables and mantelpiece were mostly English, but there was a black lacquer box, with a hand-painted scene in gold, which especially attracted Liz, and several miniature icons.

They worked chronologically, trying to cover a century a day. Sonia talked while Liz took voluminous notes. She was a spontaneous, gifted teacher, given to aphorisms that Liz could use:

"The Norwich School is Constable moved to Norfolk, and suffering in the journey"; "The thing to remember about Pissarro is that he is simply Cézanne without the genius"; "Turner is the first Impressionist. He prefigures Monet in two key respects: light—and more light!"

Every two hours or so, they took a break, retreating to the small kitchen at the back of the house, where Sonia would make tea, and they'd sit for a quarter of an hour at the small pine table and talk about anything but art history.

Sonia spoke freely and fascinatingly about Europe between the wars but about her life after she reached England in 1940 she was more reticent. She said she had spent the war near London, and gave just a hint that there might have been an intelligence connection—she mentioned Bletchley once as if she'd known the place. And that was all. Liz knew Sonia had married—Warschawsky was her married name—but she did not know what had happened to her husband and didn't want to press, especially as Sonia seemed to sense that Liz herself did not welcome many personal questions.

It was the Easter vacation, so the Fitzwilliam café was crowded with parents and children. Finding a corner table at last, Liz went to get tea and scones. "I've been admiring your ring," she said when she returned with a tray, pointing to the large oval emerald, set in silver on gold, and surrounded by old, dark petal-shaped diamonds.

"When my mother fled Russia in 1921, she left with the clothes on her back and this ring. She was so poor that she was going to have to sell it to pay her rent, but fortunately she met my father first." She gave a light laugh. "He was French—I spoke Russian and French before I knew English.

"But enough about the past," she said briskly, putting her cup down. "I was wondering, would you like to have supper at my house tomorrow night? I have some friends coming—they're Russian. Well, Anglo-Russian. Like me."

"I'd love to," said Liz.

Sonia nodded. "Good. Now perhaps we can have a look at the Monets. Don't look so worried—there are only four of them."

At her hotel on Trumpington Street, Liz went to reception to ask for her room key. Behind the counter the manager, a diminutive man with a red bow tie, smiled at her. "Did your friend find you?"

"Sorry? What friend?"

"There was a lady asking for you."

She'd told no one she was in Cambridge—not even her mother, since she could always reach Liz on her mobile. In Thames House, Brian Ackers knew, and Peggy Kinsolving and Michael Fane and possibly also DG. Geoffrey Fane in MI6 knew but that was all. Peggy was the only woman and certainly she would never call at the hotel.

"Hold on a minute," said the man when he saw the puzzled look on Liz's face and retreated into the back office. When he returned he was accompanied by a plump girl with hennaed hair and a silver stud adorning one side of her snub nose. She was chewing gum and looked distinctly put out. "Camilla spoke to the lady," said the manager.

"That's right," she said. "About an hour ago. I told her your room number and she went up to see if you were there but you were out."

"You didn't give her the key?"

"No. Of course not. We're not allowed to give keys out to anyone except the registered guest," said Camilla huffily. The manager nodded in confirmation.

"Did she leave a message?"

Camilla shook her head. "No." She looked quickly at her boss. "I offered but she said not to bother. She just wanted to know if you were in."

Liz said sharply, "What did this woman look like?"

Camilla seemed to think this an odd question. "Just normal," she said.

"Old or young? Tall or short?"

"She looked ordinary. Just, like, middling."

"Exactly what did she say? Can you remember?"

"She said, 'I'm looking for Miss Falk.' That's all."

"Falk? My name's Falconer."

The girl shook her head. "No. She said Falk. I'm positive." She added impatiently, "Because of the actor—you know, *Columbo*."

Liz looked at the man in the bow tie. He shrugged, helpless in the face of the gum-chewing girl's incoherence. "Is there a Miss Falk staying in the hotel?" she asked him quietly.

He went and consulted the screen on the counter. "No, there isn't. And you are the only lady on her own."

"Oh well," said Liz, since it was clear from the girl's glum face that she wasn't going to be of further help. "Doesn't matter."

She took her key and went up to her room. There was a thin line between alertness and paranoia, especially in Liz's line of work, and to stay sane it was important to keep on the right side of it. Gormless Camilla had been categorical that she had not handed out a key but nevertheless Liz opened the door cautiously and stood looking carefully at her room before going in. Nothing seemed to have been disturbed, so shrugging off her uneasiness, she went into the bathroom to get ready for the evening. It wasn't for a second or two that she noticed that her sponge bag, which she was sure she had left on the dressing table in the bedroom, was now on the bathroom shelf. All its contents had been taken out and arranged beside it in two neat rows. Except for one thing. A bottle of mouthwash had been dropped in the bath. It had formed an unpleasant red stain.

20

Like the guests, supper at Sonia's was an Anglo-Russian mix. They started with cold borscht that Sonia made a point of calling beetroot soup. "Delicious," said Misha Vadovsky. He was a slight figure who walked with a cane. When he spoke, in fruity tones redolent to Liz of the BBC of her childhood, his Adam's apple moved in and out like a pair of bellows.

His wife, Ludmilla, was a tiny woman who wore black orthopaedic shoes. She had been an undergraduate with Sonia at Girton—"About a millennium ago," her husband declared tartly.

The other couple were called Turgenev-Till, an Anglo-Russian alliance of surnames which Sonia seemed to find very amusing. "Oscar taught at the Courtauld for many years," she had told Liz that afternoon. There was a mischievous glint in her eye. "He is a descendant of the great writer, which his wife, Zara, will tell you before she gets her coat off. Though some have been unkind enough to remark that Oscar is a rather *remote* descendant."

For supper, they sat around a dark, round oak table in the small dining room. As the light of the spring day faded, Sonia lit two tall church candles in wooden candlesticks. Next to Liz was an empty place, which Sonia explained—"Dimitri rang. He's missed his train and will be a little late."

Liz reckoned that the combined ages of the assembled company added up to four centuries, but the conversation proved remarkably lively. They talked and reminisced and joked about subjects from Stravinsky to rap, about Russian writers Liz had never heard of, and about the comparative merits of Sancerre (which Sonia served with the main course) and Saumur. It was all so deeply cultured, thought Liz, but without the slightest affectation. The gentility of English intellectual life from a bygone era.

But there was something different about them too, Liz felt, something setting them apart from, say, her mother's intensely music-loving friends in Wiltshire. And she realised what it was— a persisting Russianness they seemed happy to retain. As if, in the melting pot the UK had offered these descendants of émigrés, part of them had refused to melt.

Misha Vadovsky mentioned a service he and Ludmilla had attended at a Russian Orthodox church in London. "They are ruining that church. I tell you, soon there will be a complete takeover. Sixty years members of my family have attended service there, but I predict not for much longer."

Oscar tried to joke with him. "You mean, you'll take your business elsewhere."

"Business is precisely the problem." He sounded bitter.

"The likes of Pertsev think a church is just another piece of real estate. The largest donor gets the title deed."

Ludmilla remonstrated. "Oh, Misha, don't be so serious." She turned to Liz and explained. "The oligarchs. Misha gets furious with them when they throw their money around. I think you just have to laugh. They have so much money and absolutely no idea what to do with it. In the next generation I'm sure they will establish foundations and do good works. But not yet." She giggled. "Now it's spend, spend, spend."

"It's disgusting," said her husband.

"Shush," Ludmilla reprimanded him. "Don't be a sourpuss. It gives the newspapers something to write about. Every week I read a new article on their excesses. Or their wives'. Diamond-studded mobile phones. Taps of real gold in the lavatory."

"I ran into Victor Adler in London," said Oscar. "He told me the most marvellous story."

"The man's as bad as those oligarchs," declared Misha crossly. "He may mock them behind their backs, but to their face he acts like a courtier at Versailles, sucking up to the king."

"Let Oscar tell his story," his wife said sharply.

"Victor is Victor," said Oscar, seeming to acknowledge Misha's complaint. "But it's still a funny story. Apparently one of these oligarchs wanted to buy a house in Eaton Square. He commissioned some estate agents but then forgot he had employed them. Being Russian he charged in and approached the owner directly, only to be told the house was under offer. 'How much?' he demanded. Seven million pounds. 'I'll give you £10 million.' Sold.

"Three days later Knight Frank ring and say they've lost the house. 'What house?' You know, the one in Eaton Square. We offered £7 million as you instructed, but some lunatic went and offered £10 million."

While they were laughing there must have been a knock at the front door, because Sonia suddenly stood up. "There's Dimitri," she said. Liz assumed this late guest would be another Anglo-Russian septuagenarian, so she was surprised when a moment later Sonia returned with a man no more than forty. He was tall, with a handsome face and a shaggy mop of black hair that he brushed back with an impatient hand. He wore a grey polo neck sweater, dark slacks and sharp-toed boots.

"Come and sit down next to Jane," said Sonia, "and let me get you some supper."

Immediately Liz found herself engaged in animated conversation with the new arrival. He looked exotically Russian: high Slavic cheekbones, black eyes and long eyelashes that would have seemed feminine if he had not been such a powerful-looking man. He spoke good English, with a strong guttural accent, and had the gift, rarely found among English men in Liz's experience, of making everything she said seem worth listening to. He talked without inhibition, but his bluntness was refreshing, and when he told Liz how pretty her dress was, the remark sounded genuine rather than smarmy or flirtatious.

"You are really very English," he said at one point admiringly, and Liz found herself blushing like a child complimented out of the blue.

"Not like us?" teased Ludmilla. She gestured at the rest of the table.

"Definitely not like you," Dimitri said. "You are Russian. Maybe, one century from now, your great-grandchildren will *think* they are English. But we know better. Russia never leaves the soul." He beat his chest like Tarzan.

It turned out that Dimitri, far from being an actor, or a member of the Moscow State Circus, was a curator at the Hermitage, a world authority on Fabergé and Russian expressionism. "Mix and match," he said puzzlingly of his two specialities, one of many English expressions he seized on without regard as to their precise meaning. He was in Cambridge as a visiting Fellow at King's, and explained to Liz that he had gone to the British Museum that day to talk about a forthcoming Russian exhibition.

How had she come to be at Sonia's? he asked. Liz explained that she was interested in Pashko. His face lit up. "The master," he said simply, but to Liz's relief, before he could pursue the subject, Sonia started talking about the influence of Fauvism on the cubists, or was it the other way round?

Eventually Misha Vadovsky yawned, his wife stirred, and the party broke up. When Sonia came out with Liz's coat, Dimitri appeared as well, wearing a leather jacket. "May I walk with you?"

At his insistence they avoided the middle of town and walked along the west side of the Backs. It had turned cool again after a warm cloudless day, and Liz wrapped herself up in her raincoat and wondered when they would turn towards the town to reach her hotel. Suddenly Dimitri took her elbow and, striding forward, led her across a small bridge spanning the Cam. In the dark she could hear the mild gurgle of the river, and saw looming ahead of them an elaborate iron gate, leading to an avenue of trees.

The gate was locked when Dimitri tried it. Now what? thought Liz, feeling cold and a little annoyed by this elaborate detour. "The privileges of a visiting Fellow," Dimitri announced, and produced a key.

A minute later they stood on the back lawn of the college, staring up at the looming shape of the chapel. Lights flickered on the massive stained-glass window and Liz, who had only seen the building in photographs, thought how beautiful it looked silhouetted against the night sky. When Dimitri moved closer, she thought, Please don't spoil it.

He didn't. "Lovely, yes?" is all he said, then led her through the college on to King's Parade. It was almost deserted and they walked in ghostly silence, broken only by the sharp staccato of their heels on the pavement. At her hotel, Dimitri stopped outside. "You are very nice to meet," he said.

"Likewise," said Liz.

"You go back to London soon?"

"The day after tomorrow."

"No doubt you are very busy until then."

"Well, I have work to do with Sonia."

"I would like to meet you in London, for dinner perhaps."

Touched by his seeming shyness, Liz agreed.

He smiled. His hair fell over his forehead, and he pushed it back abruptly. "Au revoir then."

On their last day together, Sonia talked exclusively about Russian art, and in the afternoon she concentrated on Pashko. "All his life he was moving towards the abstract—first abroad, when he lived in Ireland and Paris, then in Russia when he went home after the revolution. Always in his pictures I find there is something deeply Russian, even when he had left. You must have observed last night," she said wryly, "how Russia lives on in the people who have left her."

Later, as Liz was leaving, she tried to thank Sonia for her help, but the older woman shook her head. "The pleasure was mine," said Sonia. "You have a good eye and a clarity with words. I am not worried about that." She hesitated. "I am not aware of exactly what you're going to be doing, which is as it should be. But there is one thing I think it is important to say.

People sometimes become a little starry-eyed about Russians. They are a romantic people, with great souls and passionate intensity. Many of them are utterly charming. Like young Dimitri." She smiled mischievously, then grew serious again. "But deep down they are all *hard*. Please don't forget that."

21

As the Bentley nosed down New Bond Street in the early evening's light rain, Liz, sitting in the front seat, watched Jerry Simmons out of the corner of her eye. The cream leather driving seat was pushed far back to accommodate his long legs and his large, muscular frame amply filled it. His face was expressionless as he wove the big car through the traffic with calm confidence but his eyes were alert and she noticed that the rear-view mirror was angled so he could see the passengers in the back seat. Michael Fane had told her that Simmons was fully on board and Liz hoped he was right. If he was cooperating he could be very useful, and in a fight you would certainly want him on your side.

Nestled comfortably next to Brunovsky, his girlfriend, Monica Hetherington, was checking her make-up in her seat's vanity mirror. She was quite lovely to look at, with fair, flawless skin. She could have passed as Russian or Polish with her blonde good looks, and although her surname was English enough, there was a trace to her accent which suggested years spent abroad—South Africa or Australia, Liz guessed, rather than an Eastern European country. Introduced to Liz, she had been friendly and polite but she gave no hint of being interested in anyone much beyond herself.

Next to Monica, Brunovsky fidgeted, peering impatiently over the driver's shoulder to check their progress. He had greeted Liz like an old friend when she'd arrived at the Belgravia house, seeming to forget that her role as a Pashko enthusiast was a fabrication—and his own idea. "Tomorrow the gap in the dining-room wall will be filled," he had crowed, like a little boy on Christmas Eve. Now as they drew closer to the saleroom, his excitement was growing.

Across from him on a jump seat, his PA Tamara spoke briskly in Russian. Brunovsky glanced at his watch and shrugged. Unlike her boss, Tamara had been tight-lipped seeing Liz again, almost frosty. She flicked back a strand of corn-coloured hair now—dyed, Liz decided, her mocha brown eyebrows gave that away. She had on the barest hint of make-up, and her gaunt face looked pale, though not unattractive. She was wearing the same maroon jacket and skirt she'd had on all day, and her only jewellery was a thick gold ring on her middle finger.

"Stop here, Jerry," Brunovsky said, leaning forward to speak to the driver. The car slid effortlessly to the curb, and the chauffeur got out quickly and opened the back door.

Inside, the saleroom was already crowded and buzzing with

conversation. Most of the seats were occupied and people were standing in the aisles on either side of the long room. A television camera crew had set up near the rostrum, a complication that Liz had not expected—she had no wish to have her cover blown on TV—and she was relieved to see that the camera was focused on the rostrum set up on an elevated dais, rather than on the bidders.

Spotting Brunovsky, an attendant came up and led them to a row near the front, where seats had been held for them. Liz noticed that Tamara had disappeared. She found herself sitting between Monica and a stranger in horn-rimmed glasses who promptly introduced himself. "Harry Forbes," he said, extending a hand. "Hi, Nikita," he said loudly to the Russian, who was on the other side of Monica. Turning back to Liz, he said more quietly, "I'm Nikita's banker." Then added with a chuckle, "Or one of them."

Forbes wore the banker's uniform of grey pinstriped suit, and Liz caught the flash of red braces beneath his jacket. Chatting easily in his East Coast American drawl, he explained that he wasn't at the auction in a professional capacity but as an art lover in his own right. Learning that Liz was a recent acquaintance of Brunovsky's and new on the London art-auction scene, he began pointing out people in the crowd, most of them Russian—an Abramovich sidekick and Rostrokov, a political dissident, said to be worth £2 billion.

"See that fellow," Forbes said, gesturing towards a tall, lean figure with a shaved head and a stubbly beard who was sitting several seats along the row from them. His face was lined with deep grooves and he looked tense and uneasy. "That's Morozov. He likes to compete with Nikita. We might see some fireworks tonight as the bidding gets going."

Liz nodded. She'd heard of Morozov, but she was surprised

to see him at such a high-profile occasion. He had a reputation as a quiet family man; she'd read something in a newspaper recently about his son, though she couldn't remember offhand what it was. Her attention returned to the brightly lit, expectant room. She knew that it was not just the calibre of the painting that was attracting so much attention, but the fact it hadn't been seen for over sixty years. Called *Blue Field*, it had been painted by Pashko during the years before the Bolshevik Revolution when he lived in self-imposed exile in Dublin, with the Irish artist Mona O'Dwyer. When Pashko left Ireland to return to Russia after the Bolshevik Revolution in 1917, he left many of his paintings behind with her. On her death in 1981, they had gone to the Irish National Gallery.

With one exception. *Blue Field* was one of a pair, painted by Pashko in 1903. Its complementary picture, *Blue Mountain*, had been ruined by a burst water pipe in Pashko's Dublin flat. Nothing was heard of *Blue Field* for sixty years, then a young woman had walked into a Dublin art gallery. She'd inherited a picture from her great-aunt, she said, and wondered if it was of any value.

Now at the front of the saleroom, a tall, elegant grey-haired man strode on to the dais and stepped behind the rostrum. At once the audience was hushed and the sale began.

The Pashko was to be auctioned last and Liz sat patiently for almost an hour as the sale moved slowly through some seventy lots, mainly early Russian religious paintings. Bids slowly edged up from the low thousands to six figures for a full-sized portrait of Peter the Great.

"Ladies and gentlemen, we turn now to the final items of the evening, Russian paintings of the twentieth century. May we have Lot 71 please?"

The attendant held up a large canvas which Liz recognised

as a constructivist painting, a mechanical-looking assemblage of neat circles and squares ascribed to Vladimir Tatlin. After a gentle beginning, bids suddenly blossomed all around the room and the picture was sold for £320,000.

Things were heating up. Suddenly the mute conventions of a British auction—the nods, the lifted catalogues, the head shakes—were replaced by raised hands and loud voices. A Russian woman in a mink coat tried to bid after the hammer, and protested loudly when told by the suave auctioneer that it was too late. "You should see the sales in Moscow," said Harry with a laugh. "It's like a meat market."

Then suddenly, without any particular fuss, *Blue Field* was held aloft, and the auctioneer was saying "Lot 77, an early Pashko from 1903. We will start the bidding at £4 million. Do I hear £4 million?"

At first there was no reaction from the audience, because everyone was still looking at the canvas. It was medium-sized, with a rich background of blue-black paint that stretched in waves across its surface. Curiously, for an abstract painting, the sea of dark paint did look vaguely to Liz like a field; a short vertical slash of yellow could perhaps be taken for a distant tree. But who's kidding? thought Liz. If it had been called *Blue Water*, I'd see the sea.

The room was hushed, almost in homage, then an almost imperceptible movement in the front row caught the auctioneer's eye. "Four million pounds. Bids for £4.1 million." This time it was someone at the back of the room who caught his eye. Liz noticed Brunovsky hadn't moved.

In fact he did nothing until the price reached £6 million, when she saw him give a short sharp jerk with his chin. Almost at once the bidding reached £6.5 million.

Suddenly the early bidders fell away, like blue tits scared off by a magpie's arrival. It was now that Morozov, down the row from them, also made his move, signalling with jerky movements of his hand. Another nod from Brunovsky followed, then Morozov's hand waved again. Within sixty seconds the bidding reached £8 million.

The auctioneer looked over at the aisle, where an attendant stood against the wall, listening to a telephone and raising his hand in the air. Cupping the phone between his collarbone and chin, he used both hands to show nine fingers. Nine million pounds, Liz realised, and turned to Brunovsky to see how he would react to this jump in the bidding war. Almost imperceptibly he raised his catalogue.

Morozov waved excitedly, and suddenly the bidding had reached £10 million. The atmosphere in the room was now electric. When the bidder on the phone jumped by another million, Brunovsky looked distinctly annoyed. He seemed to hesitate, as if no longer so certain of his commitment. The auctioneer looked at him but Brunovsky refused to meet his eye. His face was impassive. Liz noticed that Morozov was leaning forward in his seat, his shaved head perspiring now and shining in the lights. He was watching Brunovsky anxiously. When the auctioneer's gaze swivelled towards Morozov, he chopped sharply at the air: £11.5 million.

The phone bidder must have been unimpressed, for the bidding moved swiftly to £12 million. Each move saw Morozov uneasily match the anonymous punter, while Brunovsky sat, unmoved. Finally, at £13 million Morozov faltered, and putting a hand to his forehead failed to match the latest bid.

"Ladies and gentlemen, do we have any addition to £13 million?" The auctioneer scanned the room carefully, but nothing stirred. *Bang!* went the hammer. The picture was sold to the anonymous bidder.

Liz looked over at Brunovsky to see how he took the result. You had to hand it to him—he'd seemed to have his heart set on buying the picture, but he was hiding his disappointment very well. When Monica took his hand in sympathy he even managed a smile.

Further down the row, Morozov stood up to leave. Liz noticed his face had relaxed and he was smiling, too, presumably to mask his own disappointment. She said to Harry Forbes, "Morozov must be very put out."

The American snorted, then said knowingly, "Look at him. Does he seem upset to you?" He didn't wait for an answer. "All he cared about was keeping Nikita from buying the Pashko. For Morozov, this wasn't about art. This was about power."

22

G ood evening, Mr. Brunovsky," gushed the beige-coated doorman, rushing forward to open the doors of the Bentley, as it drew up at the Hilton Hotel on Park Lane. Brunovsky and Monica swept into the foyer and as they stood waiting for the others to join them, Brunovsky's eye lit on the plate-glass window of a jewellery boutique just inside the door, glittering with a display of diamonds and emeralds. Taking Monica's elbow and heading towards the shop, he said over his shoulder to the others, "We'll meet you on the twenty-eighth floor."

Emerging from the lift into the Windows on the World restaurant, Liz caught her breath at the almost 360-degree panoramic view of London, the roofs of Mayfair in the near distance, the dark tree-filled expanse of Hyde Park on one side and further away the lights of Kensington and Chelsea and Westminster where the river snaked past the Eye and the Houses of Parliament.

I don't know what I'm doing here, thought Liz to herself, but I'm beginning to enjoy it.

By the time Brunovsky and Monica appeared, the waiters had opened two bottles of Krug.

"Look." Monica delightedly waved a beribboned package and produced from it a delicate diamond and emerald necklace.

"Just a little something to celebrate," said Brunovsky with a big smile, drinking down a large glass of fizzy water.

How very strange, thought Liz. Why is he so cheerful? He's just lost the painting of his dreams.

By the time the party moved to their table beside a floor-to-ceiling window overlooking Hyde Park, they had been joined by Harry Forbes and a Danish woman introduced as Greta Darnshof, editor of a glossy art magazine. Then Tamara appeared, looking out of breath.

"Here we all are," announced Brunovsky expansively. "And now a toast to the successful bidder."

"Hear hear," said Harry Forbes, lifting his champagne flute.

And then Liz understood: it had been Tamara bidding over the phone. No wonder Brunovsky wasn't upset. He had bought *Blue Field* after all.

"I'd love to see Morozov's face when he finds out," Forbes said as a waiter began serving their first course.

"I do not wish him to find out yet," Brunovsky declared, and he put a finger to his lips.

"Mum's the word," said Forbes, nodding vigorously.

Greta Darnshof, sitting directly across from Liz, was dressed elegantly in a black cocktail dress and a single strand of pearls, her thick honey-coloured hair swept back with a demure velvet headband. "I understand you are a Pashko expert," she said, leaning forward. "Which is your favourite period?"

"I suppose the years just after he returned to Russia," said Liz. She added quickly, "But I'm not an expert. Just an enthusiast—more of a student, really."

Greta eyed her knowingly. "Pashko is easy to fall for. When did your own romance begin?"

Liz took a bite of terrine, using the food as a distraction. "Oh, I don't know," she said easily, with a placid smile. "I suppose I liked his pictures even as an undergraduate."

"Where was that?"

"Bristol," said Liz.

"And how did you meet Nikita?"

"Through friends."

"Russians?"

"No," said Liz, with just a touch of astringency, wondering if this woman would ask for her CV next.

Suddenly Brunovsky let out a huge guffaw and Liz turned with some relief to his end of the table. He had just ended a story he had been telling Harry Forbes and catching Liz's eye he said, "Jane, you should hear this. I've just been telling Harry what Morozov did." He paused just long enough to take a draught of mineral water and went on, "He's got a son who can't speak. The hospital in Moscow did something wrong when he was born. He's at a special school. One day he didn't come home, no one knew where he was, and Morozov got the idea he'd been kidnapped—called out the police, made a big stink. It turned out he was at school all the time. Some other boys had locked him in the bog! So there's little Ivanovitch shitting himself while his dad's crying his eyes out in the police station. What a fool." He roared with laughter again.

Shocked by the crude unkindness of the story, Liz cast an eye round the table to see whether anyone else was thinking as she was. But they were all laughing with their host, though Greta had managed only a cold smile.

Brunovsky turned to say something to Monica, and Liz, seizing the moment, asked Harry Forbes quietly, "Who is this Morozov?"

"He's from St. Petersburg. He made millions in industrial diamonds, then tried to move into oil. It didn't work out, and he managed to fall out with the authorities about the same time Nikita did."

"Do they know each other well?" she asked.

Harry shrugged. "They go way back, but I don't know the ins and outs. You'd have to ask Nikita for the whole story. There's some history there."

As Brunovsky's attention swung back towards them, Harry Forbes said to him, "Nikita, what I can't understand is why it took so long for *Blue Field* to be found. You'd have thought someone would have spotted it during all those years."

Brunovsky laughed. "Perhaps the old lady who owned it did not like it. Maybe she kept it in her attic."

Greta spoke up. "Some people say that *Blue Mountain* may also be found one day."

"You mean," said Harry Forbes, "rumours of its death have been greatly exaggerated?" He laughed loudly, and Liz realised that she found the man irritating. His high spirits seemed fake.

Brunovsky shook his head. "It was destroyed. Mona O'Dwyer said so herself."

"Yes," said Greta. "So we are led to believe. But why don't we ask the view of our Pashko expert?"

Liz wondered momentarily which expert Greta was referring to, then realised with a start that she meant her. As the waiter arrived at the table to clear the plates, she stalled for time, thinking furiously what to say. Even if she handled this question okay, Liz sensed there would be many more to come from Greta. The woman seemed bent on testing her, and Liz worried that sooner or later she was going to face an exam she couldn't pass.

Rescue came from an unexpected quarter. "Honestly, Greta," said Monica Hetherington, "give the girl a break. She's only just got here." She pointed at Liz. "I just love your dress, Jane. Where did you get it?"

23

O f course Jerry will take you home," announced Brunovsky, as the party collected their coats at the end of the evening. "Where do you live?"

Liz had foreseen this problem and had insisted Brian Ackers authorise full operational backup, including a cover flat.

"Battersea," she said airily.

"Good. He can take us to Eaton Square and then drop you off."

The cover flat, in a mansion block just across Battersea Bridge, was something of an optical illusion. Though its exterior was comparatively smart, inside it was a typical MI5 safe house. Fondly known by the operational officers as "civilisation's dead ends," these houses were meant primarily for meetings with recruited sources, possibly for an operational officer to stay the odd night, when, like Liz tonight, they needed a cover address, but certainly not for entertaining visitors. The furnishings were sparse and usually ill-matched and had invariably seen better days in more elevated official surroundings.

Liz threw her coat on a chair, turned on the electric fire and sat down on a sagging sofa covered in faded chintz. At least this place has a view, she thought. The sitting-room window faced the Thames and through it, she could see the traffic on the Embankment on the other side. The glow of the street lights made the low line of eighteenth-century buildings on Cheyne Walk look like dolls' houses.

She reflected on the events of the evening. Sceptical ever since Brian Ackers had given her this assignment, she was becoming increasingly convinced she was on a wild goose chase. It seemed like a training exercise to Liz rather than anything real, made more artificial by the surreal quality of the world she had now entered.

She was not unfamiliar with the rich—her father had worked for the owner of a country estate after all, and in Wiltshire where she'd grown up there were plenty of City moguls-turned-landowners. But she had never come across such conspicuous consumption. It wasn't that Brunovsky boasted about it. It was just that he took for granted a style of life—chauffeured limousines, private jets, expensive restaurants, a Belgravia mansion and a country estate—which most people only encountered between the covers of a glossy magazine.

It wasn't as if he'd been brought up to it. His wealth had been acquired suddenly and unexpectedly, by sharp practice in the economic confusion following the end of the Cold War. Another strange thing about Brunovsky, reflected Liz, was the sense of security he exuded. Was it real or was it just a cover? Because in fact he was far from secure, if Victor Adler's information was correct. None of the oligarchs were.

Liz got up and, after a search in the kitchen cupboards, unearthed a packet of cocoa that was just in date, so she heated some milk on the old electric stove, then sat down again with her mug. It could be interesting, she supposed, to spend time with a man who literally could buy anything he desired, but she couldn't say her heart was in it.

I could use some company, she thought, suddenly feeling very alone. Used to living by herself, she rarely felt lonely; loneliness was something she'd feared for her mother, not herself. But her mother didn't seem to be lonely or indeed alone any more. That weekend when she'd visited London, she had astonished Liz by not coming back to the flat after the theatre on the Saturday. There had been a late-night phone call from some post-theatre restaurant, and a slightly giggled explanation to the effect that Liz should not stay up since "Edward" would be putting her up for the night. Liz had resisted the temptation to ask if Edward had a spare room. Who on earth was Edward anyway?

Oh well, she thought now, sipping her cocoa, it's her business. Of course her mother should have a boyfriend if she wanted to. It was just—well, just that the idea took some getting used to. Her world had suddenly been turned upside down. Accustomed to looking after her mother, Liz found her sudden independence unsettling. She felt like a parent whose teenage child finally flies the nest.

She shook her head to get rid of the disturbing comparison and stood up, pausing for a moment to look out of the window at the north bank of the river. That is my turf, she thought, feeling rootless on this side of the Thames. Funny how London divided itself this way. She wondered if this was always true of cities with rivers running through their centre. Parisians thought of themselves as Right and Left Bank people; did the inhabitants of other major cities think that way too? What about Moscow, or St. Petersburg, she wondered, thinking briefly of Dimitri. Probably, though she doubted she'd ever get to know any other city well enough to find out. Foreign postings were not a common part of MI5 life, and she couldn't see any other reason why she might live abroad.

Unless she met somebody, she supposed. Again she thought of Dimitri, wondering if he'd ring as he'd promised when they'd said goodbye in Cambridge. She hoped so, though she couldn't see how any relationship with him had a future. He was going back to St. Petersburg at the end of this term, and she couldn't envisage herself following him there. In any case he thought she was Jane Falconer, an art student. She smiled at the thought of being swept off her feet, impetuously resigning her job, explaining everything to Dimitri and going to live in Russia. What would her colleagues make of that? She tried to imagine herself wearing a beaver hat and muff during the icy winters, studying the language, learning to cook blinis and borscht, but she could not sustain the picture. It was not going to happen.

Her thoughts moved on, and she found herself wishing Charles were back. She wouldn't have been seeing him very often as he wasn't her boss any more—lunch in the canteen once in a while, maybe a chat in the lift when they coincided in the morning, the odd glimpse down a corridor. But it would be enough just to know he was there. Even if she wasn't working for him, his presence in the office would somehow give her solid ground. As things were, she felt very much on her own in this curious operation.

She had no confidence in Brian Ackers and from past experience she wouldn't be at all surprised to find out that Geoffrey

Fane had involved her in some Byzantine scheme of his own. She wondered what Charles would think of it all. Not much, she guessed, and she imagined his expressionless gaze resting on her as she told him what she was doing. "Exactly what are we hoping to get out of this, Liz?" he would have said. "What's the risk and what's the likely gain?" I wish I could answer either question, she thought.

Bedtime, she said to herself, before I get even more maudlin. She detested self-pity, it was the one character trait she could be harsh about in other people. So she was ashamed to have indulged in it now. I chose this, she told herself. There's no one to blame but me.

She turned off the sitting-room lights and put her mug by the tiny kitchen's sink. Moving through to the small room in the back, with its single rather rickety bed, she flicked the light switch by the door. In the middle of the room, the ceiling bulb flared then popped. I'll change it tomorrow, she thought wearily, and got undressed in the dark.

24

The woman sat at a table in the bar of a hotel just off the Strand, reading *The Times*. At eleven o'clock in the morning it was gloomily lit and almost deserted. She knew it would be. She left nothing to chance and she had already reconnoitred the bar. From her corner, she saw the man arrive before he saw her. Looks like a pimp, she thought, taking in his black Armani suit and white silk shirt. She had nothing but scorn for Italian men.

He looked around him, puzzled, and with a faint air of disgust. "Am I early? Why choose this place to meet? It won't impress your client."

"It's convenient. Sit down," she said, pointing to the Danish-style chairs grouped around the table in front of her.

He slid into one of the chairs and laughed. "We might as well have a drink while we wait," he said, looking around for a waiter. There was no one in sight.

"Not a good idea," she said.

"Is this a puritan you're bringing to see me then?"

"I'm not bringing anyone to see you, Marco. It's just the two of us."

He stared at her for a moment, then shook his head in irritation. "You might have rung and spared me the taxi ride. I've come all the way from Kensington."

"Don't worry," she said. She leant forward now, putting her hands on the table, with the fingers extended. Her bag was on the floor and she moved it closer with her foot until it edged against her leg. "There is plenty of business for us to conduct."

"Oh." Marco's face lit up. "He's authorised you to negotiate. He's interested in the friezes?"

"No. He hasn't," she said, and watched as bafflement re-entered the Italian's eyes. "And anyway, it's other antiquities I want to discuss."

"Meaning what exactly?" he demanded, in an assertive voice she sensed covered a sudden nervousness.

She reached down for her bag and extracted a slim folder. "Meaning this," she said, sliding the folder across the table to him.

He looked at it for a moment with a show of distaste, then he sighed, reached for the folder and picked it up. He continued to gaze at the contents longer than was necessary to read the two typed pages. By the time he looked up, his swarthy face had gone several shades paler and perspiration stood out on his upper lip. He threw the file down on the table, leant back and held both hands open in a classic Italian gesture. "So," he declared. "What are you trying to say? You can't prove any of this."

She shrugged, making it clear she wasn't interested in arguing. "I don't have to. Nikita can judge for himself."

Marco blanched. "You'd show this to Brunovsky?"

"Of course," she said. Her voice was matter-of-fact but now turned icy. "He would not like to think that those beautiful and rare objects you acquire for him might not be what they seem."

Marco looked increasingly agitated. For a brief moment, she thought he might snap. Would he attack her? She hoped he wouldn't be so stupid. Not because she had the slightest concern he could hurt her, but because it would derail her plan. She lowered one hand towards the bag under the table.

If that had been his plan, he seemed to think better of it. "What do you want from me?" he finally asked, his voice weak and shaky.

"To do as you're told," she said menacingly. "You won't find it difficult." Just more lies, she thought, the kind that got you into such a mess before.

25

L et's go through it one more time."

It was evening on Hampstead Heath and a few dog walkers were taking advantage of the lengthening days. The sun was dipping below a ridge of trees to the west of them, casting long shadows over the bench where Jerry Simmons and Rykov sat.

Jerry sighed. He was tired after an early start that morning. He had taken Brunovsky's girlfriend, Monica, to Heathrow at the crack of dawn—she was meeting a friend in Paris for a two-day shopping expedition. "I've told you. There's his assistant, Tamara, there's Mrs. Grimby, Mrs. Warburton—that's the housekeeper—and a maid. And most nights, Monica. There was a temp as well, but she's gone now. Lately his decorator's been around—his name's Tutti. Italian bloke. Poof too."

"Poof?" asked the Russian. Jerry flapped his hand exaggeratedly and he nodded. "And that is all?"

"I told you about the American, Forbes. He comes around a couple of times a week."

"Other visitors?"

"Lots of them. But nobody regular. Only some student interested in Brunovsky's Russian paintings."

"Student? You said nothing about a student."

"I don't think she'll be there for long," Jerry said.

"Who is this girl?"

"Jane somebody. And she's not a girl—she must be at least thirty. I drove her home one night. She's one of those mature students." Seeing the puzzled look on the Russian's face, he explained, "Somebody older who's gone back to college." He looked at Rykov sourly. "We do that sometimes, you know."

Vladimir ignored him. "I want to know more about this Jane. Let's begin with what she looks like. And then where she lives."

26

Ah, look at this mouse the cat has brought in." The voice was distinctly Italian, and belonged to a slim man who appeared in the doorway of the formal downstairs dining room. Here Liz had set up shop, since for now *Blue Field* was sitting in a bank vault in the City of London. The delay had been caused by the insurers, who were insisting on yet more security. Only then would the Pashko be allowed to hang in the smaller dining room upstairs.

"I am Marco," declared the man, walking into the room. He was about Liz's age, with a slim build, dark complexion and sharp-featured face. He wore his hair short, and had a small neatly trimmed goatee. His clothes were stylish and a touch flamboyant—a canary yellow polo neck, pressed white linen trousers and brown ankle boots. "Marco Tutti," he said, extending a hand.

"Nice to meet you," said Liz from her seat. "I'm Jane." She gestured at the papers on the long mahogany table, which could seat twenty-four with all its leaves in. Each morning the young maid waxed and polished it until its surface shone like glossy chocolate. "I'm doing some research for Mr. Brunovsky."

"On Pashko, I see," said Tutti, peering inquisitively over her shoulder. "*Blue Field* is a very beautiful painting," he said approvingly, then gave a small titter. "But expensive. Personally I would consider putting the painting here." He pointed to the wall above the room's marble fireplace, where a gilt mirror hung. "But Nicky insists it go upstairs." He sighed to suggest the unreasonableness of the Russian.

There were footsteps in the hall, and Brunovsky himself came in. He was dressed casually—a cashmere sweater and thick corduroys—very obviously just back from the country. "Marco," said Brunovsky briskly, "you are on time. How remarkable. You have met Jane?"

Tutti nodded, and Brunovsky turned and walked over to the windows. He reached out and roughly grabbed a handful of curtain. They were made of heavy cream-coloured damask, bordered with antique gold braid and with thick red silk tie-backs. Looking at Tutti, Brunovsky asked, "What is it she wants to replace these with?"

The Italian shrugged. "I am still showing her samples. Something more colourful."

"More colour," said Brunovsky dubiously. He looked now at Liz. "Do you like these?" he asked.

"They're lovely," said Liz sincerely. She'd noticed them at once.

"Monica doesn't think so," said Brunovsky, letting go of the material and shaking his head. He pointed at Liz. "She likes them," he said aggressively to Tutti.

"It doesn't really matter what I think," Liz protested, and Tutti nodded, intent on his commission.

"But you are English," Brunovsky said sharply, as if this were an infallible guarantee of good taste. "It is English style I want in this room."

"Monica is English too," Tutti insisted.

I'm not getting in the middle of this one, thought Liz, as Brunovsky pursed his lips. "She is back today," he announced. "I will talk with her this afternoon." He looked again at Liz, who made a point of staring at her computer screen. She was using a new laptop supplied by Technical Ted, the head computer boffin at Thames House. Password-protected, it was loaded with so much additional security that the keenest hacker would have trouble even logging on. As an extra precaution, Ted had made sure that the machine stored nothing to indicate it was anything but the working tool of an amateur student of art.

Liz had begun that week, spending half her working day in Belgravia, the rest at Thames House running her section. The division of labour was making her life complicated. She had to dry-clean herself each time she moved from one location to the other, to ensure she was not being followed. Though she did not think anyone in the Brunovsky household suspected her, she did not know enough about what was going on around her to be sure.

At the house she spent her time researching Sergei Pashko, with special attention to the Irish years of exile when he had painted *Blue Field*. Like a method actor, Liz had decided the best way to play her role—Jane Falconer, art-history student and Pashko enthusiast—was to embrace it. After the discomfiting interrogation by Greta Darnshof at the restaurant in the Hilton Hotel, Liz wanted to make sure she could perform credibly if the Danish woman put her though her art-history paces again.

But her real objective was to unearth as much information as she discreetly could, and pass it back to Peggy Kinsolving in Thames House. She was looking for anything that did not check out. The cook, Mrs. Grimby, was friendly enough, but busy and she didn't like to chat. On the other hand, Mrs. Warburton was a real gossip, almost a caricature of the traditional housekeeper who knows precisely what's going on upstairs and downstairs. Only Tamara, the secretary, was unwelcoming, offering the curtest of nods when she emerged occasionally from her office. But there was nothing in that to cause Liz to suspect that she—or Mrs. Warburton or Mrs. Grimby—was anything other than what she seemed. Though as Liz reminded herself, the same might once have been thought of the chauffeur, Jerry Simmons.

Liz had chosen her position next to the front hall, to give her a good vantage point for seeing who came and went, particularly visitors to Brunovsky's office, which opened off Tamara's at the back. But the previous day she had realised that she controlled only one of the entrances to Brunovsky's lair and that people came and went whom she never saw. In mid-afternoon, just after Mrs. Grimby had brought her a tray of tea and biscuits, she heard raised voices speaking in Russian coming from the office. One was Brunovsky and the other was female but not Tamara, whose voice Liz by now could easily recognise. The voices calmed to a dull hum only to be raised again and finally she heard the slam of a door and the sound of footsteps on the garden path. She realised that someone had come in through the French windows that led from Brunovsky's office into the garden and had then left, presumably through the gate into the mews at the back of the house. Why use that route she wondered, if it was not to avoid being seen by Liz? And if that was the reason, it must be someone who knew exactly where she would be.

She saw a lot of Brunovsky. The oligarch seemed to have the attention span of a gnat, and welcomed any excuse to distract himself from work. Though exactly what work do you do, thought Liz, when you are worth £6 billion? Try and make it seven? It wasn't clear, and the Russian was constantly emerging from his small office, popping into the dining room, apologising for interrupting Liz's "work," then starting a conversation about whatever had caught his perpetually wandering attention. Whenever he spoke to her, Brunovsky appeared relaxed, charming, like a little boy in his enthusiasms about everything from his pictures and his gardens to the spring weather. Increasingly, Liz was finding it difficult to equate this man with the ruthless exploiter of others that he must have been to acquire his present wealth. Billions don't just fall into your lap, she reflected. When empires fall it's the most ruthless who survive and prosper. Why are you putting on a performance? she wanted to ask the oligarch. Why do I feel like a character in a play you are directing? And who is the audience?

Now he was watching the gardener tie back a rose bush by the front step of the house, while Tutti dramatically extolled the merits of a Rodin statuette he'd found on a recent jaunt to Paris. You're on to a good thing, thought Liz as the Italian went on, so I wouldn't overdo it. It seemed that Tutti was not only in charge of decorating the interiors of Brunovsky's residences, but was involved in his art buying as well.

Brunovsky and Tutti strolled out of the room, now debating the merits of a painting Tutti had spied in a Lyons gallery. Liz turned her attention back to Google. It had as usual provided too much information—16,000 hits on "Sergei Pashko + Ireland

+ Blue Field," though most prominent were the press reports of the purchase of *Blue Field* by an anonymous telephone bidder.

Not that Brunovsky seemed to be trying to keep his acquisition a secret—if even his housekeeper knew he had spent millions on "some picture," it didn't seem possible that an inquisitive rival like Morozov would not sooner or later find out the identity of the buyer. Probably sooner, Liz thought, remembering the banker Harry Forbes's account of the other Russian's envy of Brunovsky. Even though both men were vocal critics of the Putin regime, Morozov and Brunovsky evidently disliked each other wholeheartedly.

She kept her eyes on her screen, while her mind mulled over this weird world with its strange alliances and hatreds, until a movement caught her eye and she looked up to find Monica Hetherington standing across the table from her. Just back from her trip, she was dressed in a sleeveless lilac dress that showed off both her athletic figure and deep tan; her ash-blonde hair was carefully tousled, and streaked as if by the sun.

"What the hell do you think you're playing at?" Monica demanded angrily, leaning across the table with both hands gripping its edge. There was no sign of her usual mild affability.

"Sorry?" said Liz, taken aback.

Monica pointed at the tall front windows. "Nicky says you think he should keep those bloody curtains."

"Steady on," said Liz. "I'm not here to decorate the house. He asked me if I liked the curtains. I said yes. That was the extent of it. Okay?"

Monica stared at Liz, her face hard. Liz hoped there wasn't going to be a second outburst—she had no wish to make an enemy of Brunovsky's girlfriend, especially over something as inconsequential as the oligarch's choice of curtains. And gradually Monica's expression softened. "Sorry," she said, "it's just that it's taken me three months to persuade Nicky, and now I come back and find he's changed his mind again. It's hard work trying to do anything round here, you know. Nicky is a great guy and I love him to bits, but he can get quite nasty if you go against him. He's Russian and I suppose they've got a different attitude to women," she said with a touch of wistfulness. "So I try to get my way by working on him slowly."

"Men," said Liz, sounding sympathetic.

"You're telling me," said Monica, and she laughed.

Liz motioned towards the curtains. "What do you want to put in their place?"

"Would you like to see?" asked Monica, and when Liz nodded, she went into the hall and came back with a small pile of sample swatches. She rifled through them until she suddenly stopped at a swatch with a lime green background. On this were stamped enormous pink and white cabbage roses. It was hideous.

Liz managed to say, "How lovely."

Monica nodded. "I've always loved roses," she said. "Even as a little girl."

"Where did you grow up?"

"Oh, here and there. My father was in shipping." She smiled vaguely. "We were always moving around. Portugal, Italy, the Caribbean, Singapore. Name a port, I've lived there. How about you?"

Liz gave a wry shrug. "The West Country. London's as far as I've got. But where did you meet Nikita?"

"Nicky? Oh, here in London. At a party." She detached the sample from its holder and went and stood by the window, holding it up against the cream-coloured curtains. "What do you think?" she asked.

"It's good. Really great," said Liz, trying not to grit her

teeth. I should get some of Tutti's commission for this, she thought.

"Tell Nicky that, would you? He's bound to ask."

"Of course."

She put the samples down on the table, then pointed at Liz's computer on the table. "How's it going then?"

Liz shrugged. "Okay," she said.

"Is everyone being nice to you?" The tone was big-sisterly. Liz sensed that for all her sudden aggression, Monica was a girl's girl.

"Absolutely."

"I bet Tamara's not." Monica laughed again. "Don't let that witch put you off. When she's rude to me once too often, I just tell her where to get off. It works a treat—for a while, that is. You try it if she gives you any gyp."

Liz's position in the household was hardly comparable to that of the oligarch's paramour, so she just nodded equably as Monica went on. "The rest are all right. Mrs. W. acts like she knows everybody's business, and she probably does. But she's a harmless old thing. Cook's a sweetie. One of the gardeners was a bit of a perv, but he's been sacked."

Liz noticed that as she grew more confiding, Monica's accent was slipping a social rung or two. Was it South London lurking behind South Africa, or pure Essex? Hard to tell, though if her father was a bigwig in shipping, thought Liz, mine was Lord Mayor of London.

27

Geoffrey Fane stretched out his long legs and leant back luxuriously against the well-padded banquette. For a brief moment he allowed himself to close his eyes. He had spent the last two hours in a particularly frustrating meeting in the Ministry of Defence, arguing over levels of MI6 representation in Afghanistan, and now he was waiting for Elizabeth Carlyle to join him. Liz, he said to himself, Liz. I must remember to call her Liz. She had seemed irrationally annoyed when they last met that he'd called her Elizabeth. I expect she thought I was patronising her, he mused. Though how it can be patronising *not* to use an abbreviation, I don't understand. These young women in MI5 nowadays are very defensive. Thank goodness in our neck of the woods we're still masculine. Well, nearly. It makes life so much easier.

He waved for another glass of Chablis. The service in the Savoy was still excellent and there was something sophisticated and faintly decadent about the American Bar, which suited him. That was why he went on using it, even though in the early evening it got excessively crowded. He rarely turned up there before eight.

His second drink had just arrived when Liz walked in. Fane stood up and waited until she was settled opposite him. As soon as she was supplied with a drink, he went straight to the business of the evening. He had grasped that she didn't like irrelevant conversation and he knew she would be wondering why he had arranged to meet here and not at Vauxhall Cross.

"Thank you for coming, Liz," he began. "I suggested here because I knew my meeting in the MoD would go on quite late. I wanted to find out how things were going in the Brunovsky household and to fill you in on a few things we've learnt from Moscow."

Liz looked at him over the rim of her glass. My God, her eyes are wary, he thought to himself. She doesn't trust me an inch.

"I told Brian I was meeting you," she said. So that's it, thought Fane. She thinks I'm trying to cut out her boss.

"That's fine. I told him too," he replied airily.

"Well, I quite like being an art expert," Liz confessed. "But to tell you the truth, I don't think I'm getting very far. I've seen nothing to make me suspicious. But whether that's because there isn't anything to discover or because I'm not well placed to discover it, I don't know. Quite a lot goes on in Russian. What I do understand seems all pretty normal—if you can call the life of an oligarch normal. He's just bought a painting for £13 million by someone called Pashko and now I've become an instant Pashko expert. Did you see it in the newspaper?"

"Was that Brunovsky? The reports I read said the buyer was anonymous," said Fane.

"That's how he wanted to play it," Liz replied, warming to her subject. "He's got some competitive thing going with another Russian called Morozov. He was bidding for the picture too. I can't say I fully understand it, but it's a sort of boy's game of one-upmanship as far as I can tell."

"Morozov. Never heard of him."

"Apparently he made his money in industrial diamonds. I suppose you could call him a second-class oligarch," she said with a smile. "Millions, not billions. I think Nicky just sees him as a nuisance. It's Morozov who's doing most of the competing."

So, she's thinking of him as Nicky, Fane noticed, with a slight feeling of alarm. "Eliz . . . Liz," he interrupted. "There's something we've picked up in Moscow that you should know. Stakhov has been arrested. If you remember, he was the origin of Victor's story that there was a plot being prepared in Moscow against an oligarch in London. Of course, it may have nothing to do with it. Victor said Stakhov was disillusioned and critical of Putin, so he may just have said the wrong thing at the wrong time. But there may have been a leak. It's possible the Russians have found out that he's talked and suspect we know something about what they're planning. In which case, you need to be careful. We are keeping our ears very close to the ground in Moscow and we can take decisions as and when we learn more."

Liz said, "Oh, I don't think I'm in any danger. The only one who knows who I am is Brunovsky and he's got his own safety to think about. He won't say anything. But I wonder, could your people do some research into Morozov? I'd dearly like to know what this feud is all about and how serious it is. What happened between him and Brunovsky and why did Morozov leave Russia? Did he have to, or was it simply because he wanted a life of luxury in London?"

"Probably a bit of both, don't you think?"

"Yes," Liz agreed, "but I'd like to know for sure. I don't understand why Morozov doesn't like Brunovsky. I know neither has any time for Putin."

Fane looked at Liz in surprise and thought to himself how typical of a female. One minute she thinks she's wasting her time, but as soon as I suggest that she might need to quit, she digs her heels in and gets all interested. She has the instincts of a bloodhound. Not for the first time he thought what a useful addition she would be to MI6.

Noticing Liz look surreptitiously at her watch, Fane changed the subject. He hadn't asked her here just to talk about Brunovsky, though this next part he hadn't shared with anyone. Recently he had been thinking more and more about his son, Michael. It was strange that when Michael was a boy at school, he had hardly given him a moment's thought. But since the Fane marriage had broken up, and particularly since Michael had joined MI5, Geoffrey Fane had found his thoughts turning towards his son.

He wanted him to do well—not just to reflect lustre on him, he reassured himself. Geoffrey Fane knew that Michael was not mature or even particularly stable, and he knew too that it was partly his fault. He had not provided his son with the role model he had needed. Unsurprisingly the boy's personality had not developed as his father would have liked. This woman sitting in front of him—Elizabeth, Liz, whatever she liked to call herself— she was all the things he would have liked Michael to be. She was calm, reliable, independent. She had inner reserves of strength, that was obvious. She was also extremely attractive, he acknowledged to himself. Michael was younger, inexperienced, and Geoffrey Fane knew that his upbringing had disturbed his development. The truth was that he had not played his part as a father and his son, Michael, had suffered accordingly.

"Before you go," he said to Liz. Immediately he saw the wariness come back. He knew she was thinking, What now? Is this where he produces some unwelcome rabbit out of the hat?

"My son, Michael," he said.

"Yes," she said levelly.

Fane kept his eyes on his drink. He felt damnably awkward, but he had to ask. "I just wondered if he was getting on all right."

"Wouldn't it be better to speak to him yourself? I'm sure he's got an accurate sense of how he's doing."

Fane flinched at her brusque reply and felt himself colouring, but having started, he was not going to stop now. "I shouldn't have brought it up, I know, but . . . how can I put it?" He felt immensely embarrassed. "There's a certain *froideur* between us. We're not in any kind of communication."

"I didn't know that," Liz replied, her voice warming slightly.

Fane shrugged. "It's just one of those things," he said. He added with a grim smile, "I know civilised divorce is all the rage these days, but Michael's mother and I didn't quite manage the trick. Not blood on the walls exactly, but not nice. I'm afraid Michael got caught in the middle. I never wanted him to feel he had to choose sides."

That's not quite true, he thought. I cut him out long before the divorce.

Liz looked at him thoughtfully. At last she said, "Michael's doing fine."

Fane picked up the momentary hesitation in her voice. She was letting him down gently. Michael wasn't really doing fine, but she didn't want to tell him. "Of course he's got a lot to learn." She paused. "But he is learning it."

"Thank you," he said, giving a small sigh. "You are very kind."

They both understood what had really been said.

Liz stood up. "Thanks for the drink," she said.

"A pleasure," said Fane. He stood up too to shake her hand. "Thank you for coming."

As he sat down and summoned the waiter again, he saw Liz casting a quick look back as she left the bar. Unusually for him, Geoffrey Fane felt foolish. He was also extremely annoyed with himself. He already knew the truth about Michael, and Liz, whatever she had actually said, had merely confirmed it. For no purpose at all he had exposed his vulnerability, his weakness. In the harsh world he moved in, a weakness was there to be exploited. He fully expected Liz to exploit his.

As Liz walked along the Strand to catch her bus, her mind was on Geoffrey Fane. She had not been entirely open with him about her emerging doubts about the Brunovsky household, but she preferred to wait until she had something more substantial than just a vague sense that all was not as it seemed. Perhaps something more tangible would come from Moscow.

Absorbed as she was, she had not noticed that as she walked through the foyer to leave the Savoy, a woman in a long dark coat, who had been packing away a laptop into her leather shoulder bag as Liz passed, got up and followed her out.

Liz was thinking how quickly one's attitude to someone could change. Fane was known to those in Thames House who had worked with him as the Prince of Darkness, for his dark aquiline looks and the air of sinister menace he exuded. He was generally thought to be ruthless in pursuit of his objectives and not at all careful about whose toes he trod on in achieving them. In the last hour he had shown her a very different side—was it real concern about his son or was it just guilt? Whatever it was, Liz was intrigued to find his guard had slipped, and she wondered how this letting down of his guard would affect their future relationship.

As Liz sat down on the bus, the woman from the Savoy was several rows behind her. Liz was reflecting on how complicated her life was becoming, living and working undercover not a mile away from her office in Thames House. She didn't think she could sustain it for much longer. She had decided to go back to Battersea tonight, though pure tradecraft would have dictated that, having just had a meeting with Geoffrey Fane as Liz Carlyle, she should go back to her own flat in Kentish Town. However, she had agreed to be at Brunovsky's house in Belgravia early the following morning, and she did not want to have to leave Kentish Town at the crack of dawn so that she could dry-clean herself before arriving at Brunovsky's house. Her mind moved on to the forthcoming weekend and further complications.

Dimitri had phoned that afternoon, suggesting dinner. He was coming down from Cambridge two days from now, on Saturday afternoon. It occurred to her that the only garment she had with her in Battersea suitable for an evening out was the dress she had worn to the post-auction dinner at the Windows on the World restaurant. It would probably be well over the top for whatever eating place Dimitri had in mind. When she'd last been at her own flat in Kentish Town, she had meant to bring more of her wardrobe over to Battersea, but she'd been distracted by—what was it? Oh yes, her mother had rung just as she was collecting more clothes. Hearing more about Edward had put Liz in such a foul mood that she had just scooped up a few things and left.

Now she was briefly tempted to change buses and go north instead of south, pick up something suitable from her flat and then go on to Battersea. But she didn't have the energy or the patience for all the kerfuffle that would involve. It would take the rest of the evening just to collect a few clothes. I'll make do with what I've got, she decided. She could dress up a work skirt with a silk blouse and wear her grandmother's garnet earrings or the glass bead necklace her mother had given her on her birthday. That would surely do for whatever Dimitri came up with.

Traffic was light and as she was wrapped up in her own thoughts, the bus was moving quickly down towards the river, then along the Embankment and across Albert Bridge. She was one of just three people who got off at the stop in the quiet street one away from the mansion block. As the other two turned left and began walking off, Liz suddenly felt how eerie it was on this street at this time of night, when most people were already at home and dusk threatened to turn to dark. The tall branching plane trees cut off much of the remaining light in the sky and the widely spaced street lights created pools of darkness. She walked quickly to the street door of her block, checking behind her as she put her key in the lock. The only people in the street were a man, walking quickly away from her, and another woman in the distance. She couldn't see her very well.

Once in the flat, she turned on Radio 3, then, unattracted by the atonal music it was playing, moved the dial to Classic FM. She had had nothing to eat since the morning and the Savoy's delicious Chablis on an empty stomach was beginning to make her feel quite weak. Her inspection of the small food cupboard revealed tins of soup but not much else you could actually eat.

The thought of one of the gastropubs in this gentrified neighbourhood didn't appeal. They were noisy and she needed some peace to collect her thoughts and reposition herself mentally after her rather confusing day. Then she remembered the sedate old-fashioned pub a couple of streets away, where a single woman could sit alone, unmolested, and read a book over a simple plate of cold roast beef and salad. As she left the building, she wondered if Dimitri would fit in there.

28

A4 was very stretched. An urgent counter-terrorism operation had absorbed all their free resources. Brian Ackers had been putting as much pressure as he could on the head of A4 to make at least one team available for the Rykov link with Jerry Simmons, but even he had had to concede that the possible kidnapping of a soldier home on leave by a gang of Al Qaeda–influenced militants took precedence. But at the last minute, one of the extremists had been arrested by the local uniformed police for shoplifting, and was in custody, so the team that had been allocated to him was free. Luckily, this was Wally Wood's team and they knew Rykov well.

This evening had seemed easy enough, just like others on

which they had watched Rykov. He had been in the embassy for most of the afternoon, then had drinks with an unidentified blonde in the penthouse bar of the Kensington Gardens Hotel. He'd left at six-thirty and taken a taxi into the West End, where he'd had early supper with another woman—identified as Mrs. Rykov—at Chez Gérard on Dover Street. When they'd come out at eight-thirty, Wally Woods, sitting in his car at the corner of Piccadilly, watched as the Russian walked past him and held his arm out to hail a cab. It was still light, and the lowering sun turned the clouds into pink puffballs over Green Park.

It seemed straightforward: the Russian couple would head north to Highgate and their flat at the Trade Delegation. But when a taxi pulled over, to Wally's surprise Rykov bundled his wife into it, slammed the door, crossed the road and walked off west on Piccadilly towards Hyde Park Corner. By the time Wally had negotiated the small Mayfair streets and re-emerged on the correct side of Piccadilly, his colleague Maureen was calling in over the radio that Rykov was flagging down another taxi. Wally was in time to join his colleagues, now intently following this second taxi.

Fifteen minutes later the taxi turned off Cheyne Walk and crossed Albert Bridge. On the south bank it turned into Parkgate Road, then stopped in a smaller tree-shaded side street of brick mansion blocks. Wally pulled over just around the corner. Bernie Rudge had turned off Albert Bridge Road further south and was now circling back. "Target coming your way," said Wally. He named the street Rykov's cab had gone down, then pulled out and drove around in a slow circle to the other end of it.

"I have eyeball," Bernie announced. "Chelsea 1 is getting out. Going into a building. I'll take him."

Wally wondered what the hell was going on. He knew there was an operational flat in a block on this road. He'd dry-cleaned a contact attending a meeting here for the Counter-Terrorist Branch a few months ago. Surely they'd have been briefed if Chelsea 1 was one of theirs and was going to a meeting. But it beggared belief that he had picked this obscure street in Battersea coincidentally.

"Target's on the move," said Bernie. "Walking fast. He's seen something. Heading back to you, Maureen. Can you take him?"

"Affirmative," came back from Maureen. "I have eyeball."

"There's a female coming from the opposite direction. She's crossed the street. She's gone into the same block of flats the target went up to. She must have been what spooked him."

Odd, thought Wally. If Chelsea 1 was meeting someone in the safe flat, why had he turned tail and run away? What was going on?

"Confirming. A female has entered the same building. She's one of ours. There's an unknown female approaching. Passing the block now and coming your way."

From A4 control in Thames House came the instruction for one car to stay on the street long enough to confirm the address Rykov had approached and for the others to keep with Rykov and ignore the unknown female. Control confirmed that there had been no briefing about any meeting with Rykov.

Wally sat in his car in the pool of darkness between two street lamps, watching the door of the mansion block. After a minute or two the door opened and Liz Carlyle emerged, crossed the road and walked off down a side street. Wally was dumbfounded. Possibilities spread like wildfire in his mind, some of them ones he didn't want to contemplate. He could hear from the radio traffic of his colleagues that Chelsea 1 seemed to be making his way back to Highgate by cab. The second woman had disappeared, so having checked the address, he radioed in that he was standing down.

Battersea Mansions. Yes, that was certainly where he'd helped dry-clean that meeting three months before. Well, there'd be an interesting wash-up tomorrow about all this. Either they hadn't been properly briefed or something very strange was going on. He just hoped Liz Carlyle knew what she was doing.

29

The last message from Moscow had not come as a total surprise. It warned her that the operation might have been compromised. The British authorities could have information to endanger the plan. It was not known at this stage precisely what the British knew. A suspect was in custody in Moscow and was being questioned. More information would be forthcoming.

She needed to find out where this Jane Falconer woman lived. Asking the chauffeur was out of the question, though she had overheard him telling Brunovsky that she lived in Battersea. There was nothing under her name in directory enquiries; nothing on the electoral roll. But it had proved easy enough to follow her this evening to the Savoy. She'd met some man for drinks, then down here to Battersea, within a long stone's throw of Albert Bridge Road.

She was sure she hadn't been spotted on the bus and she had turned the opposite way when she got off at the same stop. She had made it back to the corner before her target had disappeared from sight into a large block of flats further down this narrow street. Though she had looked back before she went in, Jane couldn't possibly have recognised her as the same person who'd got off the bus with her. Night was drawing in now, and she walked slowly down the pavement, ready at any moment to cross over to avoid suspicion. Outside the Victorian block, built like an armoury out of orange brick with black ironwork, she cast a casual look and registered the name—Battersea Mansions.

As she continued down the road, she wondered how to find out which was the right flat. There were probably at least two dozen in the building. She could ask another resident, but would the flat be in the name of Jane Falconer? Almost certainly not. And getting in would be risky. It would be more dangerous outside, but there seemed to be no real choice.

She was about to turn and head back when she saw a man with a blue overcoat on the far side of the street. He was standing in the shadow; he seemed nervy, peering around, turning his head from side to side, walking a few steps forward then back into the shadow, manifestly ill at ease. She kept her own head down to avoid attracting his attention and as she passed him on her side of the road, he seemed to make up his mind and he walked off quickly towards the lights of Parkgate Road.

She waited until he had reached the corner of the larger road before turning around herself. Then she noticed the beat-up Ford parked across the road. Its lights and engine were both off, but there was a man sitting behind the steering wheel. He looked as if he were dozing.

Odd. Normally, you'd sit with the lights on if you weren't going to be there very long and were waiting to pick someone up. So why were his lights off?

She reached the end of the road and walked around the corner. She passed another parked car with its lights off. This time two people were in the car, a man and a woman behind the wheel. She wondered if they were watching the same house she was. Hard to tell—they might just be minicabs waiting for fares, or a glum couple waiting for tempers to subside after a row. But two cars? No, this was a surveillance team. But who were they watching?

She turned again and went back round the corner, torn between leaving and her curiosity about these other watchers. Then out of Battersea Mansions she saw a woman emerge, in a raincoat. It was Jane Falconer.

Time to leave the area, the woman decided, and as she walked on, the car from round the corner came past her, briefly flashing its lights as it passed the parked Ford. Her suspicions were correct, then—they had been waiting for Jane. And the man on foot, was he with them too? Then why had he gone away?

She struggled to make sense of the Chinese boxes of watchers watching watchers. If Jane was just a low-level agent, placed in Brunovsky's household to help protect him, then what were all these other men doing here tonight? Why would they be watching Jane? It didn't make sense, unless for some reason they thought she needed protecting.

They were right.

The message she sent later that night was unambiguous, as was the reply she received six hours later:

Permission granted.

30

Hello, Liz. Long time no see. I hear you're in the arms of the Prince of Darkness. Why do you get all the best jobs?"

Dave Armstrong, Liz's old friend from Counter-Terrorism, got into the lift as it opened on the fifth floor.

"Whatever you've heard, it's disinformation," said Liz with a grin. "And as for best jobs, you know you'd run a mile rather than work with Dracula. Believe me, you're in the best place, Dave, and I'd stick your feet firmly under the desk, if I were you. By the way, is there any news of Charles coming back?" she enquired with a casual air that did not fool Dave for a moment.

"Sorry. Nothing firm on that front yet." He grinned. "Are you coming to drink out old Slater?"

"I'd forgotten all about it," replied Liz, "but I'll come along if you're going. I've always had rather a soft spot for the old boy."

Colin Slater had spent almost thirty years in MI5, rising to assistant director. Most of his time had been spent in Protective Security, and until the last few years he must have thought he was on the last leg of a peaceful voyage towards his pension. His work, though not without its challenges, had never been especially stressful.

Then, like virtually everyone else in the room tonight, he had been drawn into the post-9/11 maelstrom. Shifted, with the whole Protective Security Branch, into Counter-Terrorism, he had spent the last two years doing what so many of Liz's colleagues spent all their waking hours doing—working to stop the unthinkable from happening. Now, at his retirement party, there was an enervated air to the man as he stood, in the bright central atrium of Thames House, wine glass in hand, accepting the congratulations and goodbyes of his colleagues. He looks more like seventy-five than sixty, thought Liz. Is that how we'll all end up?

There were rules in Thames House about retirement parties, as about everything else. When a director retired, DG made the speech. When it was an assistant director retiring, the speech was made by the director. So it was Michael Binding, acting director of Counter-Terrorism in Charles's absence, who called for silence and began the ritual trawl through Colin's career. Liz found herself joined at the back of the semicircle of listeners by Geoffrey Fane. He'd already spoken to her that evening, showing no embarrassment over their awkward conversation at the Savoy. If anything, he seemed to feel it had broken through some barrier and his manner was noticeably warm.

Slater's reply to Michael Binding's remarks was mercifully

short and Liz was just preparing to slip quietly away when she heard someone say, "Good evening, Liz."

The voice was so low that at first she didn't recognise it. Turning, she found Charles Wetherby just behind her. He was dressed in a tweed jacket and flannels, and looked quite different from his usual formal self. Impulsively, she kissed him on the cheek, then stood back as he smiled at her.

"You look very well," she announced. Which was only partly true—he looked fit, with a ruddy bloom to his cheeks that must have come from lots of long walks, but his face was drawn, his eyes colourless and tired.

"So do you, Liz. New job suiting you?" he said.

She shrugged. "It's not what I expected." He raised an eyebrow, and she seized the unexpected opportunity to unburden herself. Once she had started, she found she couldn't stop, even though she knew she was going on too long. She described her odd status in the Brunovsky household and the machinations of Henry Pennington of the FCO that had put her there. She couldn't altogether disguise her frustration, though she tried to sound light-hearted—"I never thought when I was hunting the mole last year, that I'd end up as a mole myself."

But Charles didn't smile at this. "I hope you're being very careful," he said grimly.

She was a little taken aback. "Of course," she said. "Though I don't feel in any danger."

He was staring at her intently, with the fixed gaze she had come to recognise. It was the "X-ray stare," as Dave Armstrong had labelled it. When she first worked for Charles she had found this look unnerving but over the years she had grown to understand that it was a sign of concentration, a sign that he was taking something very seriously and thinking about it.

"You're at risk, Liz. You're there for a reason. Brunovsky

knows what you really are; for all you know others in the house-hold know too. If this plot exists, you are very exposed if anyone suspects you."

"It's a big 'if,' Charles, but I understand." He seemed so seri-ous that she wanted to change the subject. But the one thing she most wanted to ask—when he would be back at work—was the one topic she didn't feel she could bring up. Dave Armstrong had told her that Joanne Wetherby was no better.

"Good," he said. He smiled, as if aware of his own gravity. "You said you'd keep in touch. I'm holding you to that."

"All right, Charles," she said.

"Feel free to ring me at home until I'm back," he said.

As she stood in line to shake Colin Slater's hand before leav-ing, she saw Charles in earnest conversation with DG, who was frowning and looking worried.

31

How on earth does he afford this place? thought Liz, watching Dimitri taking a long swig from his glass of wine. They were in the library of the boutique hotel in Covent Garden where Dimitri was staying, an intimate Georgian town house where guests poured their own drinks.

Observing him, Liz thought how much he reminded her of Brunovsky. He had the same gusto, a sort of boyish quality, an innocent enjoyment of everything, though Dimitri had none of the oligarch's manic edge. Instead, there was something sensual and appreciative about his approach to life, as if he wanted to spread his large, long arms and embrace the world.

"I was reading about our prime minister's trip to Russia

next month," said Liz. "It said that after he's been in Moscow he's going to visit St. Petersburg. Apparently, his wife is keen to see the Hermitage. Did you know that?"

"Of course," he said. "I will be escorting her myself through the Fabergé exhibits in the Winter Palace."

"Will the prime minister be with her?"

"No, he will not," said Dimitri.

"Too bad."

"Not really." He shrugged. "Have you met many politicians?"

"No," said Liz truthfully. Bureaucrats were a different matter.

"They are all the same," he declared. "How lovely to meet you," he said in a mincing voice, turning and making a little bow. "I am most impressed," he went on, giving a fatuous smile. Liz laughed, and he said in his normal voice, "They believe in nothing, those people."

"And what do you believe in, Dimitri?" asked Liz.

"I believe in Russia," he said, lifting his glass in a toast.

"And art?" she asked. He seemed startled momentarily, then his face broke into a broad grin. "Art, of course. But what I mean is I belong to no political party; I have no religion. I am not a democrat or a Communist. I am Russian."

Liz smiled back, thinking about the glorious simplicity of this. What an escape it was from difficult issues. But what did it mean? Surely no one could seriously take that line in this day and age. Certainly no one with half a brain, and certainly not an art historian.

Could she imagine herself saying "I believe in England"? Well, of course she might, in certain circumstances, but would it mean any more than a sort of nostalgic attachment to places she knew—the River Nadder in summer, when the meadows were full of wild flowers in the high grass; or St. James's Park late in autumn, when the ducks huddled together against the November cold, and men started wearing overcoats on their way to work? Or would it mean a set of values—the civility that still hung on, somehow, in a distinctly uncivil age, even here in the bustle of London; the enthusiasm and loyalty that made Dave Armstrong work all hours on counter-terrorist operations even though he might earn five times as much in the City? Was that the sort of thing Dimitri was talking about? She suspected not. In fact she was beginning to suspect that he wasn't actually talking about anything.

"Where are you, Jane?" She looked up startled, to find Dimitri stirring from his chair. "You seem to me very far away. Let us go to supper."

Outside it was still light, and in Covent Garden a busker stood in the piazza, strumming a guitar. A teenage boy with a painted face juggled oranges in the air, and they stopped and watched before moving towards the Strand.

"I thought since you are English and I am Russian, we could compromise," said Dimitri as he opened the door to Joe Allen's, a restaurant Liz knew as a theatre haunt that served American food—immense hamburgers and barbecued ribs, corn bread and Boston bean soup. Just the sort of thing she would normally avoid like the plague.

They stepped down into a noisy, brick-lined cellar. At a long mahogany bar people stood drinking, waiting for their tables, and the restaurant itself was packed. But Dimitri spoke to the greeter, and they were shown at once to a table in a far corner. It was slightly quieter here, and Liz could just about make out what Dimitri said.

"I recommend the barbecue," he said when the waitress came to take their order.

"Very American."

"Of course. Three days in California was like—how would you say it? A crash course."

"That's right," said Liz, thinking of her own week of intensive tuition with Sonia Warschawsky. She asked Dimitri if he had seen her.

"I have," he said. "She is very excited about the Pashko."

"You mean the *Blue Field*?"

"Yes. She wanted to know who had bought it, because in the papers all it said was an anonymous buyer. I asked among some friends, and found that naturally enough, it had been bought by an oligarch."

"Someone you know?" Liz asked casually.

Dimitri said, "I have met the man, but I do not know him well. He is more cultured than one might expect, so perhaps he will let people like Sonia come and see the picture."

Liz nodded blankly, slightly disconcerted that he knew Brunovsky. The last thing she wanted was for Dimitri to find out she was spending time in the Brunovsky household.

"What about *Blue Mountain*?" she asked, moving the subject away from Brunovsky. "Could that turn up too, do you think?"

Dimitri shrugged as their waitress put down a large platter of spare ribs. He grinned wolfishly at Liz, whose grilled tuna looked positively sedate by comparison.

As he cut one of the ribs from the rack, Dimitri said, "I used to think talk of *Blue Mountain* was just another crazy conspiracy theory. But they found *Blue Field*, so who knows? It may turn up. I am told the country houses of Ireland are very beautiful, but many are decayed relics full of the webs of spiders, dusty corners with snakes and possibly lost pictures."

"There aren't any snakes in Ireland," Liz interjected. "St. Patrick charmed them all away."

Dimitri nodded appreciatively. "Ah. The power of religion. I like that story."

Dimitri recounted a story about his friend who bought art for the oligarchs and had almost paid $10 million for what turned out to be a phoney Rothko. "I told him to take advice, and fortunately for him he did. When he buys in my own period, I help him sometimes. For the purposes of authentication. He pays me," he added. "A little."

Liz nodded. Perhaps this explained Dimitri's lifestyle—the restaurants and expensive hotels.

Suddenly she heard a chirping noise like a twittering bird. It was only when Dimitri reached for his jacket pocket that she realised it was his mobile phone. "Excuse me please," he said, and answered it. As he listened his features tautened, the happy smile of the evening gradually replaced by a frown. He spoke tersely, in Russian, and when the call had ended and he put away his phone, he looked concerned.

"Is everything all right?" asked Liz.

"No," he said bluntly. He gestured with annoyance. "It is that friend I spoke about. He is in London and requires my help."

"What? Now?" she said in surprise. She hadn't been quite sure where the evening was heading, but she had not anticipated it ending like this.

"I am terribly sorry. I would ask you to come along. But my friend, he has managed to get himself into a . . . ." He paused, searching for the word.

"A fix?"

"Yes. A fix. It would upset him if I brought someone along

he does not know. Damn!" he cursed, putting one hand to his forehead.

"Don't worry," Liz said. "I understand." She had done much the same thing herself on occasion, called away from dinner, even once from a concert, but never by a friend, only by her work.

Outside on Exeter Street, Dimitri offered to walk Liz to her car. "Don't worry," she said. "Let's find you a taxi. Your friend needs you."

As he opened the cab door, the Russian looked at her earnestly. "I hope I have not spoiled the evening for you. I have enjoyed it immensely."

"Likewise," she said.

"When will I see you again?"

"That's up to you, Dimitri," she said lightly. "Let me know when you're coming to London."

His features momentarily lost their anxious cast and he smiled broadly again. "I will make it a priority," he said and, leaning over, kissed Liz squarely on the mouth.

What on earth was all that about? Liz thought as she walked to her car. Though she had enjoyed Dimitri's company in Cambridge, somehow he didn't translate to London. His little-boy enthusiasm did not quite ring true. It was almost as though he was acting, though she didn't know why he should. Perhaps he just felt uneasy now he was on her home territory. Perhaps she was imagining it. But with her mind back in Cambridge, she remembered the odd incident in her hotel room. She had never satisfactorily explained that to herself. She suddenly thought of Charles and what he had said about risk. For the first time she felt uneasy.

32

After a day of clear sky, cloud had moved in, obscuring the moon and darkening the street. Just in from the corner of the mansion block, steps led down to a basement door where the building's rubbish bins sat on a dank square of concrete, handy for their weekly collection on the kerbside.

She had watched the street for several nights but there had been no sign of a surveillance team. Now she stood halfway down the steps, able to see either way along the narrow street, lit dimly by old-fashioned street lamps. When anyone came past, she moved silently down the steps and crouched, hidden, behind the bins until they'd passed, then emerged to resume her vigil.

She wore a black hooded jacket, trainers and trousers with

large pockets. From a distance, she could pass for a teenage boy, and she was being careful to ensure that no one saw her up close. What she'd planned with clinical calculation was intended to look random.

She heard the brisk sound of footsteps as someone turned the corner a hundred yards up the street. Venturing a quick look, she saw the woman approaching, walking quickly. There was no one else in sight. This time she didn't withdraw and hide, but crouched motionless against the iron railings of the stairs, certain her dark clothes would allow her to stay undiscovered until it was too late to matter.

The footsteps grew closer, then closer still, their sound now vying with the *thump thump* of her own heartbeat as her adrenaline surged and her pulse quickened. She reached into her pocket as a faint elongated shadow appeared on the pavement, not three feet from where she crouched. The shadow passed and suddenly the woman was above her on the pavement, moving quickly, a handbag hanging from her left shoulder.

She sprang out of her crouch and took two quick steps until she was right behind her. With one large sweeping movement, she threw an arm around the woman's neck, jerking her so suddenly to a halt that her heels momentarily lifted right off the ground. A classic choke hold. The woman started to cry out, but then the pressure from the encircling arm had her fighting for air instead.

In her left hand now she had the Stanley knife, its blade extended full out. "Don't move," she hissed in a low voice, pressing the point of the blade against the woman's arm. "I won't hurt you if you don't move."

She kept her right arm taut around the woman's throat, and with her left reached for the handbag. In one quick movement she cut through its strap, and the bag fell with a thud to the ground. "Relax," she said. "I've got what I wanted."

But the woman stiffened in her grasp, twisting and hooking her left leg round her attacker's ankle, throwing the threatening left arm momentarily against the railings. She just managed to regain her balance, surprised by the defensive move. The woman was a more difficult target than she'd expected. She must finish the job quickly. As she raised the Stanley knife to slit the woman's throat, a voice shouted, "Hey! What are you doing? Stop! Stop!"

Distracted, she looked over her shoulder and saw a group of people coming down the street. Pub leavers or partygoers, there were at least six of them, and they must have seen the struggle. The shouts grew louder, and she could hear running feet coming towards her.

She must not get caught—that was the highest priority, higher than finishing this job. She twisted her hold on the woman's throat and through sheer strength forced her to turn towards the steps going down to the rubbish bins. Suddenly releasing her grip, she shoved the woman hard and briefly watched as she stumbled, then fell facedown on the steps, landing with a crash against a metal dustbin.

She reached down, grabbed the handbag and ran, sprinting in her trainers, away from the voices coming nearer, running all the way down the street and around the corner, then along two more streets to the safety of her parked car. She opened the car door and stood for a moment, listening intently. Nothing. If anyone had given chase, they had given up. She quickly took off her jacket, threw it and the handbag on to the back seat, then got in, started the car and drove carefully but at speed until she reached Albert Bridge Road. As she crossed the bridge a police car came past her from the opposite direction, its lights flashing.

She would have more chances to take care of this woman, but she would only get caught once. She realised what a close call it had been.

33

girl, you think. Are you sure of that, Miss?"

Liz looked up from the cheap plastic chair, relieved that she was no longer seeing two of everything, though her head still throbbed and she felt very sick. "I said it was a female. I don't know how old she was."

Liz had already been three hours in St. Thomas's, which she supposed wasn't actually too bad for Accident & Emergency this late at night. In the waiting room overhead fluorescent strips cast a bright, unforgiving light over the crowded room of waiting casualties. A couple sat right across from Liz—the man holding one arm and moaning in pain, while his girlfriend fiddled with her nails. In the corner a smelly old drunk in a dirty raincoat stretched over three chairs, snoring. A teenage boy, equally the worse for wear, had been sick on the floor and no one had come to clear it up.

There had been nothing to do but wait patiently, skimming through the battered copies of *Hello!* magazine, willing her eyes to focus, until at last they'd called her name. The nurse had cleaned the long, painful scrape on her forehead, then taken her to Radiology for her shoulder, which was bruised and incredibly sore from hitting the concrete. When she came back, the two policemen had been waiting for her.

"Did you get a look at her? Could you describe her?" asked the younger of the two. He was tall, with an earnest expression on his face and searching eyes.

"Not really. I saw something move out of the corner of my eye and the next thing I knew she'd grabbed me from behind. I think she was wearing something on her head."

"A balaclava probably. To hide her face," said the older policeman. He had a puffy, beat-up face that looked as if he had seen it all.

"Did she say anything?" asked the young policeman.

"Not much. She said something like, 'Don't move and you won't get hurt.' Then once she'd got my bag she said, 'I've got what I wanted.' " She thought those had been the words, but Liz remembered even more vividly the Stanley knife and her instinctive sense at the time that it wasn't the bag the woman wanted. Not that Liz was going to tell these policemen that.

Fortunately, the older cop seemed content to treat it as a simple mugging; he was keen to get out of there. His younger sidekick was less sure. "It seems odd," he was saying now, "a mugging by a single female. They usually work in packs."

Liz said nothing, and the older cop spoke up. "Happens more and more these days. I arrested a girl last week in Tulse

Hill who'd robbed an old man at knifepoint—believe me, you wouldn't have wanted to meet her in a dark alley."

He laughed but the young cop frowned. Leave it alone, Liz pleaded silently. The last thing she wanted was any kind of investigation. It wouldn't take them very long to find out that there wasn't much to "Jane Falconer"—she dreaded having to ask Brian Ackers to ring Special Branch and have them call off the dogs.

"Are you through with Miss Falconer, officers?" It was the nurse from the desk. "The doctor wants to see her now."

The young one hesitated, but the old pro nodded. "Yeah, we're done all right." He gave Liz a smile. "You look after yourself, young lady, and we'll be in touch when we have any news."

"Thank you," said Liz, more grateful than he knew.

The doctor had a thin moustache and looked harassed as Liz came into his small, stuffy consulting room. He motioned her impatiently to a chair sitting at right angles to his unadorned desk, and told her that the X-ray showed nothing broken. He argued only briefly when Liz declined to stay in overnight for observation.

"All right," he relented, "I'll get an ambulance to take you home. Have you got someone there to look after you?"

"Yes," she said, trying not to think of the cold, bare flat in Battersea she was going back to. "My mother," she added. Which at least was potentially true, since Liz knew if she needed her, her mother would come up right away.

"Stay in bed for a day or two," he said, "and just let yourself recover in your own good time. If you're sick, or your eyes go out of focus again, come back here straightaway. Don't be surprised if you find yourself getting a bit weepy—you've had one hell of a shock. It's just one of those things, I'm afraid. It could have been anyone they attacked—pure bad luck that you got picked."

As she waited for the ambulance Liz thought about this. Maybe it had been a random thing after all, she told herself. But no, she had an instinctive feeling that the attack had been professional—well planned and targeted specifically at her. But what did that mean? What would a professional attacker want from her? In her present half-concussed state, she wasn't able to work it out. Even thinking about it made her head throb more. So she parked the thought at the back of her mind to return to later.

As her transport arrived at last, Liz suddenly shivered; she saw again the knife two inches from her throat. That woman hadn't been after her handbag; she'd been after Liz. And as a nurse helped her up into the ambulance, she suddenly heard in her head the twittering sound of Dimitri's telephone.

34

I wish they'd just get on with it, thought Peggy Kinsolving, turning to her phone and willing it to ring. It didn't.

She was feeling stymied. She'd done her bit; now all she could do was wait until other people did theirs. She stared at the hydrangea in a pot on her desk. It was brown and wilted. I suppose it would help if I watered it, thought Peggy. Her father, who'd had a small greenhouse tacked on to the back of the house where she grew up, used to say that she had a black thumb.

Peggy was experienced enough to know that *everyone* had something to hide. After all, her own claustrophobia was something she kept to herself. What was troubling her as the days passed and she did her best to act on the snippets of information Liz produced, was that none of the members of Brunovsky's circle appeared to have a hidden past.

Yes, Mrs. Warburton's ex-husband had once done six months in prison for GBH, and the new maid, a Slovakian girl named Emilia, had lied to the immigration authorities at Heathrow about how long she planned to stay in the country. But it was inconceivable that these offences were part of a plot against Nikita Brunovsky. As for the others, Peggy simply didn't believe they had nothing to hide. It was just that she hadn't found it.

She looked idly at the first two issues of *Private Collection*, the new art magazine which Greta Darnshof had founded. It was produced on thick glossy paper, full of colour illustrations—and singularly free of ads. Unless its circulation was remarkably large, the publication must be subsidised. By whom? Peggy wondered. A philanthropic art-loving millionaire? Russian perhaps? Or was Greta wealthy enough to fund it with her own money? She had asked the Danish authorities to check out Greta Darnshof. So far there had been no reply.

Similarly, she had contacted the FBI in Washington about Harry Forbes. They had taken their time, but eventually, after she'd sent several chasers, they had come back with nothing recorded against him. Forbes was apparently just what he purported to be: a private banker, ex–Goldman Sachs, with a strong network of clients and contacts in the art world.

Then, in this extraordinary game of Cluedo, there was Marco Tutti, the decorator–cum–art dealer. Remembering young Signor Scusi from the conference in Paris, Peggy had called him in Rome. His English had not improved but he'd been charm itself over the phone, immediately agreeing to run a check on Tutti. When he'd rung back it was with some embarrassment—not only had he found nothing criminal in Tutti's past, he had been unable to locate Tutti at all. Could she please confirm the spelling of the man's names? She promptly did, but had heard nothing since—and that was ten days ago.

Peggy hated waiting for other people. She was at her happiest doing her own research—like a bloodhound pursuing the scent, going where her nose took her. Now her frustration was increasing by the hour. For the first time she was beginning to feel that her enquiries were urgent. Two days before when she'd seen Liz, walking with a slight limp with a large bruise on her forehead, Peggy felt the first chill of anxiety. She'd been mugged, Liz had explained. She'd said it was pretty common in those streets just south of the river. Then Peggy had heard the report that Rykov had been seen by A4 snooping round the safe flat in Battersea that Liz was using. Yet Liz had not said a word to suggest that all this could be connected. Surely there must be some link; could it be to Brunovsky? Peggy had a gut feeling there was; and wasn't it Liz who always urged her to follow her instincts?

A message came on to her desk. From Beckendorf, the veteran intelligence officer of the German BfV, it told her that Igor Ivanov, the economic attaché at the Russian Embassy in Berlin and suspected Illegal support officer, was planning to travel to London in the next few days with a trade delegation. Peggy grabbed the sheet of paper and walked quickly along the corridor to Liz's office, where she found Michael Fane in mid-flow. "Anything interesting?" he asked, as Peggy gave the paper to Liz.

Peggy ignored him as Liz read the message then pushed it across the desk to him to read.

"What's he really coming for?" asked Michael, frowning.

"If we knew that," said Peggy sharply, "we wouldn't be sitting here chatting, would we?"

"Michael," said Liz "find out where Ivanov's staying and

let's see if we can get a telephone intercept on his room. Also, let's try to get A4 to cover him while he's here. This might be our chance to get a sight of this Illegal, if there is one."

Later, after Michael left, Peggy looked at Liz. "You've had your hair cut. I like the fringe, but I can still see the bruise."

"Thank you, Peggy," said Liz sardonically.

"I'm worried about you. You could have been badly hurt." When Liz merely shrugged, Peggy said, "Did you tell Brian about it?"

"Of course. He says street muggings happen all the time, and they do, you know."

"I suppose so," said Peggy, but she was not convinced.

35

On Tuesday May arrived and for the first time the temperature climbed into the seventies. As Liz walked from Hyde Park Corner Underground station to the Brunovsky house, turning over in her mind all the recent events, she glanced wistfully at her alabaster arms, bare in her short-sleeved top, and wondered briefly whether this summer she might for once develop a decent tan.

Though she had made light of it with Peggy, she did, of course, continue to wonder whether the mugging and Rykov's appearance in Battersea were connected. It was the latter which puzzled her most. How had Rykov got the address of the safe house and why had he been hanging around there? Did he know about her and that she lived there or had the address been blown on some completely unconnected operation? He could have found out her address from Jerry Simmons, who had driven her home after the auction. But if Rykov had been asking Simmons about her, why hadn't Simmons mentioned it to Michael Fane, who was supposed to have recruited him? And did that have any connection with the attack on her? Had it really been a chance mugging, or something more sinister? Well, it was definitely a woman, so it couldn't have been Rykov. Anyway a Russian diplomat, even if he was an undercover intelligence officer, wasn't likely to mug anyone.

There was an alternative possibility. That someone else in Brunovsky's circle knew about her and had some reason to want to kill her. At present she had no answers, but whatever else she did, she was going to move out of that flat as soon as possible.

As the maid let her into the house she put it all out of her head and switched into her cover role. She sensed immediately an air of excitement in the house. Tamara was bustling along the corridor, not even offering her usual curt, acknowledging nod. In the study Liz could hear Brunovsky on the phone—his voice raised to a high pitch in excitement. Mrs. Warburton was busy checking the tables in the hall for dust.

Walking through to the dining room, Liz was about to put her laptop on the table when she noticed two figures sitting on the front window seat. They looked like a pair of garden gnomes, huddled together face-to-face. Seeing her, one of them stood up. It was Marco Tutti, dressed formally today in a charcoal suit with thick pinstripes. The other man rose more slowly. "Hi there," he said, and she saw it was Harry Forbes, looking very American in a striped shirt and red braces.

"Sorry to interrupt," she said, but Forbes shook his head. His grin was distinctly boyish.

"No problem," he said. "Just having a chat with Marco here."

Now she heard other voices in the hall. Looking through the door she saw Tamara and Greta Darnshof, standing waiting tensely.

"Come on," said Forbes, looking out of the front window towards the street. "The baby's arrived."

The front door was open. Brunovsky stood on the steps with Tamara and Greta, while Liz, Tutti and Harry Forbes peered out from the hall. Three Securicor vans had stopped in the street in front of the house, and half a dozen uniformed men in helmets converged around the back of the middle van. Its door was open, and two men emerged, wearing gloves and green aprons, and carrying between them a large flat package, wrapped in white sheeting. Joining them on the pavement was a thin, bespectacled figure in a three-piece suit. The man from the insurance company, thought Liz. He looked as white as a ghost, though she thought his pallor probably came from nerves about the cargo's arrival rather than a lack of sun.

As they came to the front steps, Brunovsky suddenly began clapping, short sharp smacks of his hands. Gradually all of them followed suit. Liz felt faintly ridiculous applauding a painting, but there was something touching about the oligarch's boyish excitement that *Blue Field* had reached its new home.

They followed the painting upstairs. It had been put down on the small dining room's table and the insurance executive was slowly unwrapping it, with an ostentatious delicacy that was belied by the slight trembling of his hands. At last the final covering was removed. He looked at Brunovsky. For a moment no one said anything. Then Brunovsky nodded and the two men in green aprons moved forward to secure it to the wall and wire it up to the alarm system. "Brilliant," said Marco Tutti, suddenly coming forward to stand next to Brunovsky in front of *Blue Field*. "But you know," he said, lowering his voice and sweeping an extended arm around the room and its other pictures, "you may need to find another space soon."

Brunovsky looked at him quizzically. "Space for what?"

"Another Pashko perhaps," said the Italian, with the tantalising air of a man who has a secret.

Brunovsky turned and faced Tutti. "What are you talking about?" he demanded.

Tutti lifted both hands. "Perhaps nothing," he admitted, "but perhaps not. A little bird tells me that there is a possibility that *Blue Mountain* was not destroyed after all. It seems the publicity surrounding *Blue Field*"—and he gestured to the picture on the wall—"has led to the most intensive search for its twin."

"It was destroyed," the oligarch said flatly.

"These are not just vague rumours," insisted Tutti. Liz had to admire his persistence, since Brunovsky seemed close to losing his temper. And she realised that for all his sharp clothes and swish manner, what Tutti really had was the consummate panache of the true hustler. He'd sell you back your own shoes, she thought, listening as the Italian explained. "I have a dealer friend who lives near Cork in Ireland," he declared. "He told me several senior people from Northam's visited the area last week. One was Archie Davenport-Howse."

"Their Russian expert," whispered Harry Forbes, who was standing next to Liz.

"Ach," said Brunovsky with disgust, "I don't believe it." He looked sharply at Tutti. "Has anyone seen this picture? What you say is pure fantasy."

"I would not be so sure," said a measured female voice. It was Greta Darnshof, standing near the door, looking, Liz had to admit, extremely attractive in a classic Chanel suit. If Monica's dress sense was It girl, Greta's was strictly haute couture. "Grigor Morozov believes it."

"Meaning?" asked Brunovsky, but he was not dismissive with her.

"I've heard Morozov sent two of his henchmen to Ireland to follow up this news."

"Is he crazy?" Brunovsky looked around the room, searching for moral support.

"No," said Greta patiently, "just determined to own *Blue Mountain.*"

Tutti laughed now. "Or determined to keep you from owning it."

Brunovsky nodded at this and looked down at the floor, thinking hard. "This must not happen," he said. He raised his face and looked at Tutti. His expression was calm now, but determined. "If *Blue Mountain* exists, I want you to find it for me," he said. "I don't care what it costs."

Later that morning Liz was in the downstairs dining room when Brunovsky came in, looking contemplative. He shut the door to the foyer behind him. "I have been thinking, Jane. We both know why you are here. I take it you have not uncovered anything suspicious."

"No," she said carefully, "I haven't." The only person who'd been in danger was Liz herself, but there was no reason to tell the Russian that. Perhaps he was wondering if there was any point to her presence, and she was momentarily cheered by the prospect of leaving this bizarre household and getting on with her proper job.

"I am not surprised," he said. "Still, it is very nice to have you here, even though that is not what I am worried about."

The invitation to probe seemed undisguised. So Liz did not hesitate to ask, "What *is* worrying you?"

He hesitated, walking halfway around the dining-room table before he replied. "Have you ever been followed?"

"No," said Liz, lying as smoothly as she could.

"I was once, for three months by the KGB. In the old days." He gave a weak smile. "I am older than I look. When that happens, you feel like you have gone out on a hot day but for some reason are wearing an overcoat. Try as you may, you cannot take the coat off. If eventually you manage to, then *presto*, suddenly it is back over your shoulders."

"How unpleasant," said Liz, struck by the accuracy of his description.

"No, it is not nice. But that is how I feel with Morozov. Not that he follows me physically—as far as I know—but he casts a shadow wherever I go."

"When did that start?"

"Over ten years ago. In Russia. He came to me to ask my help protecting one of his associates, a man called Levintov, a Jew from Kiev, who had offended one of the big criminals. I spoke with some people I knew in the security services. Also, a policeman I had once bribed." He said this quite unself-consciously, and Liz remembered that in the cowboy ethics of the Russian state, bribing a policeman was perfectly normal.

"I found Levintov a bodyguard. Morozov was pleased," continued Brunovsky. "In fact, he could not be grateful enough. He showered me with presents, asked me to his dacha. But then one night, when this man Levintov was returning home from the ballet in Moscow, two cars followed him, men got out carrying

Kalashnikovs and fired over fifty bullets into his car. Levintov was killed immediately—with his bodyguard and his driver."

"The mafia caught up with him then?"

Brunovsky was shaking his head. "It turned out not to be the mafia at all. I was told on the highest authority that it was a renegade group of ex-KGB men. Levintov had crossed them in a deal and they took their revenge."

He stood by the window now, looking out at the front garden's roses. He spoke softly. "When I told Morozov this, he didn't believe me. He said I had betrayed his friend and he would make me pay. I took very little notice at the time, and then I moved to England. But then he came to live here too. I can't help feeling I was the reason for that."

36

Michael Fane was excited. This was his first real involvement in operational work and he could hardly sit still. Igor Ivanov had arrived the night before and was staying at a small hotel in Bloomsbury. Four teams of A4 were in place to follow him wherever he went. "Any news?" he asked, sticking his head round the door of the Ops Room for the third time that morning.

"No," said Reggie Purvis crossly. "And there's not going to be. Your operation's off. Counter-Terrorism has taken all the teams."

"What?" said Michael angrily. "I'm going to complain."

"Do what you like, sonny," replied Reggie, as his radio

sprang into life with a burst of static, "but push off, will you? I'm busy."

Back in the open-plan office, Michael asked Peggy, "Why have they pulled A4 off Ivanov?"

"There's been an alert. A suspected Al Qaeda operative has flown in from Turkey; they think he may be meeting with a cell in North London."

"So no one's watching Ivanov while he's here?"

"Nope. And he's flying back to Germany tomorrow."

"But he could go anywhere in the meantime," Michael protested.

"You'll see, if you look at the transcript of his calls, he's having lunch with Rykov. Rykov phoned him to confirm this morning. They're being very English—Wiltons on Jermyn Street."

"Where else is he going?"

"I've no idea. And without A4 we're not going to know."

"That's outrageous," Michael said. "What about the Illegal? How are we going to identify him if we don't follow Ivanov? I'm going to complain to Liz."

"I wouldn't," said Peggy, but Michael was already out the door.

"No," said Liz firmly when Michael made his complaint. "It's unfortunate, but not outrageous. It's a matter of matching resources to priorities. That's always the problem."

She was not willing to argue the point. When Michael tried, she cut him off, making it clear he shouldn't raise it again.

He went away dissatisfied, certain that a mistake was being made. He supposed he shouldn't care—after all, he was just an underling, new to the game. But there was an opportunity here being carelessly thrown away. He was surprised Liz didn't seem to realise this.

Show some initiative. Wasn't that what his father used to say when Michael was at a loose end, bored, with nothing to do? Especially that last fateful summer before his parents' divorce, when post-A levels, pre-gap year, Michael had nothing to occupy himself. His father had said it repeatedly then, to Michael's intense annoyance.

But maybe his father had a point. All right, Michael decided, initiative here we come. And he went back to his desk with an idea starting to take root. When Peggy Kinsolving came into sight he hailed her like a taxi. "What are you doing for lunch?" he asked.

"I'm going to the Public Records Office," she said firmly and kept walking.

Be like that, thought Michael. Who else might better appreciate his offer? He thought suddenly of Anna, his ex-girlfriend—she couldn't very well call him immature now. He picked up the phone, and five minutes later found himself explaining, "No, not sandwiches. Quite the contrary, I assure you," he added as suavely as he could.

He listened for a moment. "Oh come on," he said finally. "Do it as a favour. Weren't you the one who said you wanted to stay friends?"

Roland Phipps was bored. Really, he thought, he shouldn't have been surprised. Tony Caldecott had warned him that though the lunch would be top-notch, the conversation might not be scintillating. Too true, but this one really was the pits. You had to hand it to Russian officials—only they could bore you until lobster and Puligny-Montrachet tasted like cardboard and cold pee—and this at Wiltons.

He and Tony went way back together—to the second rowing eight at Winchester to be precise, which was enough to keep them twice-a-year friends. He'd gone into Lloyd's after Winchester and Tony into the military. They'd never quite lost touch and then Tony had resurfaced in the City, with an investment bank, channelling venture capital into Russian gas exploration.

"It won't be too bad, old man. Strictly social," Tony had said. "My friend Vladimir at the Trade Delegation's got some bigwig in tow that he needs to impress. I need you for local colour."

Well, Tony was a pal, but my God, Roland had earned this expensive blowout. He didn't mind Russia in principle, even though his partnership had taken a bit of a bath after Chernobyl. He didn't even mind bores—there were plenty at Lloyd's. But Tony hadn't prepared him for just how boring these two chaps were going to be.

One—Rakov? Rykov? Who knew? Who cared?—spoke English well, so well in fact that he never seemed to shut up. But the other fellow was a nasty piece of work—a sinister-looking Slavic bastard, straight out of a James Bond film, barely said a word. It didn't make for a lively exchange of views.

Another thirty minutes maybe, thought Roland, sneaking a look at his watch. Would Tony's hospitality stretch to a largish brandy with the coffee? Now, there was a pretty girl at the table just behind the Russians—pity she's not with us, thought Roland. He wondered if it would be rude to go for a pee, then thought the hell with it and offering his excuses made his way rearward to the gents.

It was on his way back to the table—he'd taken his time—that he noticed the young fellow sitting with the really splendid girl. There was something familiar about him, and then it clicked.

"Excuse me," he'd said, leaning over the table, emboldened by several glasses of Wilton's best and a strong desire to delay his return to his deadly luncheon companions. "Aren't you Geoffrey Fane's boy?"

The boy blushed and the girl looked surprised at the figure leaning over their table.

"I'm Michael Fane," said the boy quietly. He seems shy, thought Roland, not at all like his father. Geoffrey had always been smoothly self-assured, polished, even at school.

"Roland Phipps," he said amiably. "Sorry to interrupt. All well with your father?" The boy just nodded. "Well, give him my best then," said Roland, and nodding benignly at the pretty girl, clapped the boy on his shoulder and went back to his table.

"Remember Geoffrey Fane?" he asked, as Tony came to the end of some lengthy remark about bond issues. "That's his boy over there. I met him at Lord's with his papa, years ago." He nodded. "Pretty girl he's got there. Chip off the old block."

He turned to the voluble Russian. "Sorry, it's just I've seen the son of an old acquaintance." He paused, wondering if he was about to be indiscreet. No, not these days. "We've always thought his father was a spook."

When Rykov looked at him blankly, Roland explained. "You know, the Secret Service." He gave the stolid Ivanov a glance. "James Bond. That sort of thing."

And for the first time Ivanov's eyes lit up. Yes, he understood. How amusing, his smile seemed to suggest.

Jesus, thought Roland, another half hour to go.

37

From Rome, Scusi replied at last to Peggy: he was very sorry not to have answered earlier but he had got married ten days before and been in Umbria on his *luna di miele*. Unfortunately his colleagues had been unable to locate Marco Tutti. As a courtesy, he attached a list of people in the Italian art world who had been convicted of offences in the last ten years.

Peggy sighed, wondering just how she could provide enough information about Tutti to have Scusi run background checks. She was confident a request for A4 surveillance would get turned down, and in any case there was no reason to think it would uncover anything criminal about the Italian.

She looked idly through the list of names Scusi had sent.

Nothing there even remotely resembling "Marco Tutti." Near the bottom was another list, of people deported from Italy, presumably for more than average bad behaviour—smuggling antiquities out of Italy, she knew, was almost commonplace. She looked at a virtual smorgasbord of international surnames: Erickson, Goldfarb, Deschamps, Forbes . . . she stopped and looked again. Harry Forbes, expelled from Italy.

She picked up the phone and dialled Rome. *Pronto*, a voice declared and by the time she was put through, after a succession of non-English-speaking secretaries, Peggy was almost regretting the call.

"Signor Scusi, I am sorry to bother you again, but I know one of the names of the deportees on the list you sent me. Harry Forbes—it says he was expelled from Italy for involvement in an antiquities smuggling ring. What I'd like to know is if anyone else was involved."

"*Uno momento*." She could hear him ruffling through pages. "*Si*. Two other men were caught. But they were not deported." He gave a small derisory snort. "They went to jail because they were Italian citizens. Their names are Camurati and Marcone."

Peggy could not have explained her next request—she was operating solely on instinct now. "Could you send me the details on these two men?"

Four hours later she was examining Scusi's latest message. She walked into Liz's office and put one of the attachments on her desk.

"Why are you showing me a picture of Marco Tutti?" asked Liz.

"Because his real name is Luigi Marcone. He was convicted of art fraud in Italy and spent three years behind bars in Sicily. The authorities also arrested Harry Forbes, but he was only expelled from the country. Both were accused of helping *tombaroli*—tomb raiders—smuggle gold coins out of Sicily for American collectors.

"When he got out of prison, Marcone changed his name to Tutti and moved to England. Though from what you've said his interest in art is as strong as ever."

Liz nodded, then mused for a moment. "I can't see how this makes him a threat to Brunovsky. Except to his pocket of course. He's obviously cheating Brunovsky in some way or another but there's no reason to think he has any Russian connections."

"I know."

"Still, he's worth keeping an eye on. Along with Harry Forbes."

"What I can't understand," said Peggy, "is why the FBI didn't turn up Harry Forbes. They must have a record if he was expelled from Italy."

"Two departments not speaking to each other, I expect," replied Liz. "Anyway, I don't think they're interested in anything except terrorism nowadays." She fixed Peggy with a look. "I'm impressed you've found this," she said.

"The Italians are very good," said Peggy modestly.

"Actually," said Liz, "so are you." And Peggy felt her face turn bright red.

There was a tap on the open door, and Michael Fane loomed in the doorway. "Could I have a word, Liz?" he asked. He glanced at Peggy. "In private please."

Peggy got up. "Speak to you later," she said to Liz. As she left she noticed that Michael did not seem his usual confident self. He looked worried. Oh good, thought Peggy uncharitably, maybe he's screwed up.

．　．　．

He had. His account of following Rykov to lunch in Wiltons emerged haltingly, but when he had finished Liz could not conceal her astonishment. "You total idiot," she exclaimed.

He hung his head like a runaway dog come home.

"What on earth possessed you?" she demanded.

"I couldn't believe A4 was pulled off." He lifted his head now, and scratched his cheek while he tried to marshal his defence. "I thought somebody should watch Ivanov. And I wanted to show some initiative."

"That wasn't initiative, Michael, that was stupidity." She cupped her chin firmly in her hand, and he could see she was trying to control her anger. "Look," she said sharply, "why didn't you ask me before you did it?"

"I thought you'd say no."

"You were right—I would have. And saved you from the mess you've got yourself into. Michael, what you've got to understand is that we do things here for a reason. A4 are the surveillance professionals, not you or me. They know how to avoid being seen. You don't, as you've proved. You always have to remember, Michael, that in an investigation you only know a part of what's going on. Has it occurred to you that you may well be looking at the Rykov-Ivanov connection from the wrong angle? There may be something going on completely different from what you think, and by acting so stupidly you've given away information. They know now that we're interested. Just think about that," and shaking her head with exasperation, she reached for the phone.

"Does that mean I'm in trouble?" he asked.

But Liz was already speaking. "Brian, I need to see you

urgently. Yes, I'll be right down." When she hung up she got to her feet without looking at Michael.

"If you'd kept your eye on the intelligence, instead of trying to be James Bond, you'd see that Rykov's suddenly being sent home," she said as she left the room. "Why don't you go back to your desk and try to work out what that might mean?"

38

Brian Ackers's office, like Charles Wetherby's, faced the Thames, but unlike Charles, or anyone else with an office on that side of the building, Brian had positioned his desk so he had his back to the view. What sort of a person would do that? thought Liz, as she walked into his office. Sitting in the chair in front of his desk she could see over his shoulder that the bright sun had turned the river lapis blue. A speedboat slowly puttered through the light chop, towing a wetsuited man on a surfboard with a charity banner floating out behind him. *Look, Brian*, she almost said, but seeing his expression, she changed her mind.

His desk was preternaturally tidy, with a clean pad of A4

centred on the blotter and a neat stack of files to one side. The only adornment was a green marble pen holder he never used; it had been given to him, he'd explained with ironic appreciation, by the KGB on their first visit to Thames House at the end of the Cold War. On the wall he'd pinned an enormous map of the former Soviet Union, so vast it must have come from a military operations room; facing him against the far wall were floor-to-ceiling shelves, crammed with a lifetime's collection of Sovietology.

Liz gave a brief account of Michael Fane's home-made surveillance operation. From Brian's pursed lips as she talked, she could tell that he was not inclined to go easy on the young man. Her own initial anger had subsided—Michael had been foolish and impulsive, his mistake was serious rather than fatal. She wanted to keep Brian from overreacting.

"What Fane's done is grounds for dismissal," he said when she'd finished.

"I know," she agreed. "But I do think there are mitigating circumstances."

"Really? What could conceivably excuse his running off half-cocked this way?"

"Nothing could excuse it," she agreed, "but he thought he was doing the right thing." She added quickly, "Obviously he wasn't. Believe me, he knows that now. I'm confident he won't do anything so foolish again. Frankly, I think the problem is he's just so young and inexperienced, and he takes too much responsibility on himself."

"Well, we can soon change that," said Brian, returning to disgruntled mode. "A transfer back to a support role in Protective Security where he came from might just do the trick for our Mr. Fane."

"Of course," Liz said placatingly. "But there's no guarantee he'd be replaced, is there? Not with the current situation."

Brian nodded grudgingly. "That's true. And I suppose even Fane is better than no one. Do we think he's done any real damage?"

"I hope not," said Liz, whose concern had been just that—that the Englishman in the restaurant might have mentioned Geoffrey Fane's MI6 connection to Rykov and Ivanov; that the Russians would immediately fear that whatever they were up to had been blown. "What's really bothering me," she went on, "is that Rykov has suddenly been sent home. We've had a report from one of his contacts that he's rung him up to say goodbye. He sounded almost hysterical. Apparently he's going back under a cloud. I can't help wondering whether all this is connected."

Brian sat forward in his chair, an owlish look on his face, his hands clasped primly on the desk. "I don't suppose so. But even the fact that you're having to wonder about it, shows how stupid young Fane has been. What are we going to do about him?"

"I'd leave it to be honest, Brian. It will come up at his next review, and I'll certainly let him know that he's on thin ice. Hopefully he'll learn from this."

Brian considered, and for a moment Liz feared he would overrule her. Finally he said, "He'd better," and reached for the stack of files on his desk to show the meeting was over.

As she left Brian's office, somewhat relieved, Liz was turning over in her mind what this chain of events could possibly mean. Brian was prepared to accept the proximity of Rykov's departure and Michael's impetuous mistake as coincidence, but Liz wasn't so sure.

39

You on for a drink?" It was Monica, suddenly appearing behind Liz as she peered at her laptop.

"Sure," Liz said slowly, masking her surprise.

"I'm going upstairs to change. Why don't I collect you in half an hour?"

Liz nodded and watched Monica as she moved towards the stairs. She wore designer jeans and a silk shirt that showed half an inch of navel. Casual but trendy. Liz felt positively frumpy, in her M&S skirt and a favourite lilac blouse that she wouldn't claim was on the cutting edge of fashion.

Suddenly a shout came from Brunovsky's study. "Tamara!" Liz heard scurrying footsteps and the secretary appeared, dressed in a black sweater and skirt, heading breathlessly towards the back of the house while Brunovsky yelled again— "Tamara! *Idite siuda!*"

Tamara's arrival in his office did not appease the oligarch, for he continued to shout, in an uninterrupted torrent of Russian. Eventually Tamara came back along the corridor, her usually cold, passionless face crumpled in unhappiness. Tracks of mascara-stained tears ran down one cheek.

Liz was tempted to console the woman, but seconds later Brunovsky himself came through and began to yell at her again. Monica reappeared, still wearing the same clothes. She gestured towards Tamara's office. "Maybe we should go now."

"Okay," said Liz with relief.

"When he gets like this," Monica said wearily, "it can take hours for him to calm down."

It was called the White Palace, though the large Georgian town house in Knightsbridge was of burnt-orange brick. As they entered the softly carpeted foyer with its massive overhanging chandelier, a dark-haired man in a dinner jacket came forward to greet them. "How nice to see you again, Miss Hetherington. And how is Mr. Brunovsky?"

"In fighting form," said Monica, winking at Liz. "We're just here for a quick drink, Milo."

She led Liz down a cast-iron spiral staircase into a vast cellar with a brick vaulted ceiling and a sunken floor of bleached oak. Tables were positioned in alcoves against the walls, lit by recessed spots. Monica picked a corner alcove, and they sat down on a cushioned banquette. "Whew!" Monica exclaimed. "I'm glad to get out of there."

Liz looked around the half-empty room, and noticed that

almost all its occupants were female. Well-dressed stylish women, but noticeably different from the Sloane Rangers recuperating after an exhausting afternoon shopping in Harvey Nichols, who could be found in the coffee shops of this part of London. Most of these women had a slight but discernible foreignness: a Roman nose, high Slavic cheeks, gaudy jewellery that was more Budapest than SW1. "Is this a private club?" she asked Monica.

"Not really—you just have to be introduced to Milo. This early in the evening it's mainly wives of the Russians who come here. You won't see any men."

"I noticed—it's like an upmarket Women's Institute."

Monica laughed. "Later on, the singles come in, searching for Mr. Right. Or should I say Mr. Russian? It's a bit of a pickup joint for the oligarchs. That's why I don't let Nicky near the place. No point putting temptation in his way, is there?"

"No," agreed Liz, wondering if this had been where Monica had met Brunovsky.

A waiter came and Monica ordered a bottle of Cristal—over Liz's protests that she only wanted a glass of wine. "Go for it, girl," said Monica, and gave her diamond bracelet a shake, like a high roller at a craps table. With Brunovsky absent, Liz realised, Monica was a different girl—outspoken, high-spirited, even wild.

"This is my shout," Monica announced. "Well, let's be honest—it's Nicky's." She gave a satisfied smirk, then pointed across the floor at two women entering the room. They were both tall, slim and blonde—looking rather louche, in dresses a size too tight and sharp stiletto heels. "See those two? They're looking. But it's too early. There won't be many Russian men in until later."

"So they've miscalculated?" said Liz a little dryly.

Monica misunderstood her. "They're dressed a bit tarty, I know, but it's what Russian men like." She thrust her chest out and wiggled seductively, in a parody of a bathing-suit contest entrant, and Liz laughed, but a more doleful look spread over Monica's face. "At first that's all they're looking for, but then it changes. 'I want you to be an English laa-dy,' " she said in an uncanny imitation of Brunovsky's voice. She looked at Liz. "You're lucky: you don't have to try."

I suppose that's a compliment, thought Liz, pushing her hair back self-consciously. Monica stared at her. "Ah," she said, still looking at Liz. "I thought it was a shadow, but it's not. You've got a wicked bruise on your forehead. How did you get that?"

"I walked into a door at my flat."

"It's always a door, isn't it?" said Monica knowingly. She laughed sarcastically. "I've met lots of doors. There was a Philip door, and one called Ronnie—that was the worst door of all. And then, of course, there's the Nicky door."

Liz didn't see any point protesting that she hadn't been hit by a boyfriend. Did Monica get knocked around by Brunovsky? It sounded like it, though looking at Monica's tall trim figure, honed by daily visits to the gym, Liz wondered whether she could hold her own with the oligarch. Probably not—he was short, but wiry and very fit. And then she found herself wondering if Monica was strong enough to have shoved her down the mansion-block stairs. *Don't move*, the voice had said. Could that have been Monica? "Tamara seemed upset," she said.

"Yeah, well don't go feeling sorry for her. The witch."

"I've never seen Nicky lose his temper before."

"Stick around, Jane, and you'll see him lose it again." Monica was already on her second glass of champagne, and she drained it, then reached for the ice bucket.

As Monica kept talking, now describing her recent trip to

Paris, a few men came into the room. And Liz noticed a raven-haired woman, with a strong face and a revealing dress, who was sitting by herself at the bar. There was no pretence; with each new male arrival she gave a frank inviting stare. One man went and joined her, but after a brief conversation shook his head and moved along the bar.

"I must say," Monica declared, with a hint of a slur to her speech as she finished her third glass of champagne, "I think the Plaza Athénée is overrated. Give me the George V any day. Do you travel much, Jane, in your line of work? What exactly do you do, by the way?"

"I'm a researcher at the moment. Working on a thesis."

"Can't bring in much bread," said Monica. "You want to get yourself a Russian."

Liz grinned but didn't comment. And suddenly she had had enough. This is not my scene, she decided, looking around the room, which seemed nothing more than a marketplace for spending power and lust. She reached for her bag. "Monica, thank you very much. This has been fun, but I've got to be going."

Monica looked at her watch. "Christ!" she exclaimed. "Me too. Nicky will be fuming—we're meant to be going out to dinner."

On their way out, the black-haired woman at the bar, still alone, still looking, caught sight of Monica. With a wry smile, the woman blew a kiss.

Upstairs, Liz asked, "Who was that?"

"Some trollop I knew years ago," said Monica breezily, and Liz sensed the champagne speaking. Then Monica seemed to catch herself. "Just joking," she said, putting a friendly hand on Liz's arm. "I've never seen her before in my life."

40

Unusually, Geoffrey Fane had offered to come across the river to call on her and now he was twenty minutes over-due. His imminent arrival was preventing Liz settling to anything and she was just about to ring his secretary at Vauxhall Cross to find out whether he was coming or not when he strolled into her room.

"I'm so sorry to be late," he said, throwing his raincoat on to a spare chair against the wall. He sat down across from Liz and leisurely crossed an ankle over the other knee, casting his eye round her office as he did so. Liz found herself wishing she had done a little more to personalise the room. The only addi-tion she had made to the bland government furnishings was a print of the Nadder Valley which she'd bought at an antiques shop near her mother's house. "That's very fine," said Fane, getting up to admire it. "Do you know that area well?"

"It's where I was brought up," replied Liz, feeling unaccountably pleased at his approval.

"Wonderful part of the country. I fish there." He paused reflectively, then said briskly, getting down to business, "I've heard back from Moscow Station about Morozov. They've sent us quite a detailed report. The most interesting thing in it from our point of view is that Morozov is ex-KGB, first chief directorate, postings in New York and East Germany, where he had a heart attack in 1989. He was posted back to Moscow and left the KGB in 1990. His two eldest children both live in the United States. He's got a younger one here."

"That's remarkable," said Liz. Then, pausing for a moment's thought, she went on, "But it doesn't seem to square at all with what Brunovsky told me about him." And she related Brunovsky's story of what lay behind Morozov's enmity.

Fane listened intently, frowning from time to time. When she'd finished he said, "That doesn't fit. What Moscow Station says is that after Yeltsin's rise, Morozov made his move into the private sector. With a bunch of investors he managed to procure one of the concessions granted to private individuals under the sell-off of state assets. He and his co-investors paid a relatively small sum for a sector of industrial diamonds that was underexploited and that's how he made his money. Not that much by oligarch standards perhaps"—and he looked whimsically at Liz—"but certainly by ours.

"Once he'd made a small fortune, Morozov wanted to make a bigger one by cornering part of the diamonds market. But cornering a market doesn't come cheap. Morozov and his associates weren't sufficiently well heeled to fund their caper on their own, so they brought in someone who was. To cut a long story short, as the price started to rise this new partner sold out, the price spiralled downwards, and suddenly all the diamonds they were holding were worth less than they'd paid for them. Morozov in particular got shafted, since he had the most money invested, probably half his fortune. Guess who the partner was."

"Don't tell me. Brunovsky."

"That's the rumour."

"So Brunovsky's story was a total fabrication."

"It appears so. Though remember, this is the story from Morozov's friends."

"It rings true, though. And it could be the first indication we've had there genuinely is a plot against Brunovsky. If Morozov is ex-KGB, and is harbouring a serious grudge, he'd have the means to take a very nasty form of revenge."

"Yes." Fane reached for his coat. "Let me see about this Levintov fellow," he said, standing up. "I have a feeling if he did die, it was from old age rather than a bullet, but you never know."

"Right," replied Liz. "And I'll get Peggy to find out if the Americans or the Germans have anything to offer about Morozov's time with them. Thanks for coming back to me so quickly about all this."

"Not at all," said Fane. "I regard this as a joint operation." He paused, and his eyes looked searchingly at Liz. "Brian tells me that you want out. I can understand that. But I would be grateful if you would hang on in there for a little longer. We may just be getting somewhere."

He stood there, holding his raincoat, making no move for the door. Suddenly he seemed hesitant, unassured. "By the way," he said at last, "I gather that my son, Michael, has stepped out of line."

God, thought Liz, trust Brian. I thought we'd agreed to take it no further. She shrugged. "No great harm done."

Fane shook his head. "We must hope not."

"We all make mistakes," said Liz, latching on to the first platitude that entered her head. "At least Michael had the sense to own up to his."

Fane nodded, but did not look reassured. "Brian tells me that you recommended that no action be taken. Thank you for that," he said awkwardly. And as he left her office Liz wondered if Geoffrey Fane thought she had intervened for his sake, rather than Michael's. What bothered her was that he might be right.

That was not the end of it. Leaving work, Liz retrieved her Audi, ageing but reliable, from the Thames House basement garage and pulled out on to the street at the back of the building. Ahead of her, she saw a tall figure on the corner of Marsham Street and realised it was Fane, looking for a taxi. With parliament in session, the chances of a cab this side of the House and at this time of the evening were slim. Liz hesitated, then slowed down and pulled over.

"Can I give you a lift, Geoffrey?" she called out through the side window.

"Gracious, it's you again," he said brightly. "That would be very kind. I don't want to take you out of your way," he said, but his hand was already on the passenger-door handle.

"Kensington?" she ventured.

"More Fulham, actually," he said, getting in. "She may live in Paris now, but Adele's still the owner of Phillimore Gardens," he added, with a touch of resentment.

Liz turned down Horseferry Road towards the Embankment. At this time it would be the quickest route, and she always liked the view of Albert Bridge, lit up in its pink and white paint like a decorated cake.

They drove in silence for a few minutes, while Fane looked out his window towards the river. "Astonishing how much they're building over there," he said, pointing towards the south bank, where new blocks of flats loomed like Lego towers. "When I was a boy all of that was wasteland."

"Did you grow up in London?"

"Sussex," he said. "Though my grandmother had a house in Pelham Crescent. I hate to think what it's worth today," he said with a touch of acidity that sounded more to do with reduced circumstances than nostalgia for the house itself.

"Did you see her much?"

"I'd come up on school holidays and stay for a few days. She was a game old thing—took me all over the place. Pantos at Christmas, the Tate, concerts—the whole cultural *shebang*." He seemed to delight in the sound of the word. "And you?"

"Once a year with my mother. We'd come up from Wiltshire for the sales after Christmas."

"So we're both from the country," said Fane. "That explains it."

"Explains what?" she asked, a little sharply.

"Why we get on," he said smoothly. But Liz felt sure that was not what he meant.

They passed Cheyne Walk, and Fane began to give instructions. She turned right and drove towards Fulham Road, before turning on to a quiet residential side street. A man stood patiently, holding the lead while his terrier sniffed at the base of a lamp post; a gate slammed shut further down the road; otherwise it was deserted. At Fane's direction Liz slowed about halfway down the street, in front of a large stuccoed house that had been divided into flats.

"Would you like a drink?" Fane asked. He pointed at the kerb. "You could park here. This time of night you're fine."

"Thanks," she said. "Perhaps another time."

"Sure?" he asked sharply. He seemed surprised by her refusal.

"Early start," she said, and he nodded reluctantly. Thanking her for the lift, he got out of the car.

As she drove off, she saw him in her rear-view mirror walk up his front steps. Was he cross she hadn't come in? she wondered. Probably. He didn't seem the type who was used to rejection. Was his offer of a drink innocent? Probably not.

Unlike many of her colleagues, Liz had never gone out with someone from work. She'd come close—at one time her friendship with her colleague and fellow agent runner Dave Armstrong might have blossomed into something more. And deep in her heart, though he was unavailable, there was always Charles. So it wasn't due to principle so much as simple circumstance.

In his flat Geoffrey Fane poured himself a whisky and sat down to contemplate the evening ahead. It was a pity Liz wouldn't come in, she was an attractive girl and an evening or even a few hours in her company would have been pleasant. Thinking about her, as he gazed into his glass, he had the vaguest feeling that he had seen her before, a long time ago. A memory came back to him. It was the year he had been in the Winchester XI— the Eton match. He had been sitting with his pads on, waiting to bat, when he had noticed a girl on a deckchair a few yards away—the daughter of an Eton master or somebody's sister, he didn't know. She was deeply attractive in a way he couldn't define. He had wanted to catch her attention, but she was intently watching the cricket, and then a wicket fell. As he got up to go in, she had unexpectedly called "Good luck" and smiled at him—a wonderful smile. That day he had scored seventy, and as he came back to the pavilion, holding up his bat to the applause, he had looked for her. But she had gone, and though he had searched all around for her, he had never seen her again. Life was like that: dreams, vanished opportunities. And now—Liz couldn't have been born the day he got seventy against Eton, but she was that same girl, or her double.

41

T ell Jane," said Brunovsky.

She looked up warily as he came into the sunlit dining room, with Marco Tutti by his side. The Italian was exuberantly dressed this afternoon, in a suit the colour of milk chocolate and a pink shirt. He hesitated, but Brunovsky poked him in the ribs. "Go on, tell her." He sounded very excited.

"We believe we have located *Blue Mountain*," Tutti said stiffly.

"Really?" Liz tried not to show her scepticism. "Where?"

"In Ireland. Where else?" said Brunovsky. He was just back from his weekly tennis match with another oligarch and was still wearing white shorts and a lime green Lacoste shirt. Liz noticed that his pale legs, matted with swirls of curly black hair, were heavily muscled—like those of a professional cyclist.

"Of course," said Liz evenly.

Brunovsky looked at Tutti, and taking his cue the Italian started talking again. "An old lady called Cottingham is the owner. She lives about forty miles west of Cork."

"Why is she coming forward now?"

"It seems the sale of *Blue Field* was in the local newspaper. There was a photograph of the painting which was almost identical to one Miss Cottingham has owned for years."

"And no one else had ever noticed the likeness? Or was the picture in the attic?" asked Liz, a trace sardonically, wondering why on earth Brunovsky couldn't see through this nonsense.

Marco shrugged. "Perhaps it was. But also, she is a—what is the word for someone who sees no one?"

"Recluse," said Brunovsky, whose English vocabulary never failed to impress Liz. She tried not to groan—Tutti's story was dismayingly predictable.

"Thank you," said Marco. "Miss Cottingham got in touch with a nephew in Dublin and asked him to try and find a buyer."

"And he approached you?" asked Liz.

"Actually, he spoke to Northam's and they rang Harry."

Brunovsky interjected. "Harry was the front man for the auction. Tamara did the phone bidding. I didn't want it traced back to me." He was tossing a glass paperweight back and forth between his hands, clearly impatient with these details. "None of this is so important, Jane," he said sharply, though he smiled to take the sting out of his words. "Do you not see? *Blue Mountain* has been found and I want it!"

"Has anyone seen it yet?"

"No," said Brunovsky, "but we know what it looks like. I have photographs in my study. Come."

The three of them went down the hall towards the back of the house. In the oligarch's office a smart leather file case lay on the partner's desk, on top of a mound of newspaper cuttings and handwritten notes. Brunovsky picked it up and handed it to Liz, motioning her to the two-seater sofa. He stood facing her, his back to the desk, while Marco settled in the chair underneath the large portrait of the Cossack. Glancing up at the painting, Liz noted the horseman's bellicose eyes.

Opening the folder, Liz saw several 10x8 colour stills, taken front-on but from various distances—the closest near enough to show the artist's signature in a lower corner of the canvas. The painting was barely distinguishable from *Blue Field*. The same blue-black waves filled the canvas, the same thick texture to the paint. The only difference Liz could make out was an absence of the yellow slash she had taken for a tree, and a sense in this second painting of a looming, vertiginous height—presumably the "mountain" of the picture's title. Otherwise the pictures were uncannily alike. Or cannily, thought Liz, who was now convinced this was a scam.

"What's this?" she asked suddenly, pointing to a rust-coloured streak that ran across the upper right corner of the painting in the photo.

"Ah," said Marco, lightly touching his goatee with a finger. "That we believe to be water damage."

"Don't tell me," said Liz. "The burst pipe."

"Exactly," said Brunovsky, clapping his hands as if to praise Liz's astuteness.

"But how did the picture get lost for so long?"

Brunovsky looked at Tutti, who started fiddling with his watch strap. "That remains a great mystery," Tutti said. "No details have been forthcoming. But Miss Cottingham will explain everything when we meet her."

"Meet her?"

"Yes, if we can come to terms," said Tutti.

Tutti looked enigmatic now, but Brunovsky said impatiently, "I have no secrets from Jane, Marco. Not about my collection anyway," he added with a sly grin.

"The picture will be rather expensive, I suppose," said Liz dryly.

"More than *Blue Field*," said Brunovsky, as if he liked the idea. "Twenty million pounds will be enough, so Marco says." A bagatelle, his attitude suggested, but then for Brunovsky it was.

"Marco says they want some money before they'll meet us," Brunovsky went on. "I believe the expression is earnest money."

"What are they asking for?" enquired Liz sceptically.

"One million pounds," Marco said, and shrugged to show it was out of his control. Liz noticed that this time when he stroked his goatee his hand was shaking. "If the sale falls through they will retain £100,000 for their trouble."

Brunovsky clucked a caustic tongue. "Tell them that *half* a million is sufficient earnest money. To be returned in full if the sale falls through."

Marco Tutti clasped his hands together, pursing his lips in a show of prim obedience. "Of course, if you say so. But I do not think Miss Cottingham will be flexible. She seems confident someone else will be happy to pay for the right of first refusal, if we don't."

Brunovsky stared at him. "Someone else?" he said. "Who do you mean? I thought she had come to us first. There's someone else, is there?" He looked at Marco wide-eyed. "You don't mean to tell me . . . Is it who I think it is?" He smacked a hand against his forehead and turned to Liz in almost comic consternation. "*Morozov!*" he hissed.

There was a silence. Brunovsky turned back to Tutti. "Forget what I just said. I'll pay a million."

For once Marco didn't overplay his hand. "Do not concern yourself," he said submissively. "I will tell the nephew that we accept their terms."

Liz stared in amazement. She could not but admire Tutti's tactical acumen. So this was the way oligarchs did business? A million for just an option to buy? With a sizeable non-returnable chunk. Suppose there was no painting, or just a fake? Surely Brunovsky must see how crazy this was? But maybe he was crazy—about Pashko at least, or perhaps about Morozov. She told herself she couldn't hope to understand the rivalry between these two men.

42

'll have to take this," said Brian Ackers, picking up his purring phone. Liz had just finished relating the news of Marco Tutti's background and his "discovery" that a second Pashko painting was available. Brian had seemed preoccupied, and listening to his end of the conversation now Liz realised there was an operation going on that she didn't know anything about. The time she was spending at the Brunovsky house was putting her out of touch with developments in Counter-Espionage.

And for what? For all the anxiety about Victor Adler's so-called plot, Brian didn't seem particularly interested in what she had to tell him. She seemed to have been sent off down a sidetrack. Maybe it was a sidetrack leading to something important, but so far she'd seen no sign of it. Rykov's recruitment of Jerry Simmons didn't seem to disguise anything more than a clumsy attempt to keep tabs on an oligarch—if there'd been more to it, surely Simmons would have had more to tell Michael Fane. There was no indication that Rykov's lunch with Ivanov, or indeed Ivanov's visit to London, had anything to do with Brunovsky. It was true that Rykov's sudden recall to Moscow, apparently under a cloud, was an unusual overreaction to Michael Fane's clumsy surveillance operation. But maybe there was something else behind it.

Certainly the people surrounding Brunovsky were what her father would have called a "rum bunch," but they were probably no rummer than any other billionaire's entourage. There seemed nothing particularly threatening about them. All kings had their courts; all magnates had their sycophants and freeloaders. The only remarkable thing about the Belgravia household and its hangers-on was that Brunovsky himself couldn't see that he was being exploited. Or maybe he could and didn't care, thought Liz. After all, he had to have a life.

"Sorry about that," said Brian, putting down the phone. "There's been another approach to a government scientist by the Russians."

"Someone from the embassy?"

He shook his head, and she noticed his eyes were bloodshot from a lack of sleep. "No. This time it's a Russian scientist over here on an exchange. Always something new from our Moscow friends. Anyway, is there anything else you wanted to tell me? I need to get on to the Home Office."

"Well," she said, "what Tutti's up to, as far as I can tell, is just a good old-fashioned scam. Why Brunovsky's falling for it is beyond me—I'd have thought he'd spot it a mile away."

"Yes, yes," said Brian impatiently. "We all have our weaknesses. But your point is?"

"My point is, this is one for the police—don't they have an Art and Antiquities Squad? It's certainly not for us. Frankly, the only danger I can detect for Brunovsky is losing his shirt buying this fake picture."

"Right then, let's contact the Met and have them investigate this Tutti chap. Can I leave that to you?" He looked down with obvious impatience at some notes he'd made during his call.

"Of course," she said, suppressing growing irritation. "I also think we should seriously consider pulling me out of there now. My job's done. The only plot I've discovered is to bilk Brunovsky of his money, not that he can't afford it. But there's nothing I can see along the lines of Victor Adler's story."

"Yes, well let's talk about this when I have a bit more time. I know Geoffrey Fane is keen for you to stay on there for the time being. If we do pull you out, I'll need to discuss it with him and Pennington first."

Really? Liz was aching to ask why. Since when did the FCO or Geoffrey Fane's views determine what an MI5 officer should do? Yet from Brian's peremptory manner it was clear he wasn't going to spare the time for questions—in fact, he stood up, to show he didn't want to talk about anything with Liz right now. She got the message.

43

The bells of Westminster Cathedral were ringing for even-song as the woman packed away her laptop and its small black companion in their bags. Moscow had agreed that Jane Falconer, or whatever her real name was, now presented a serious threat to the operation. She had made it obvious that she disbelieved the Italian's discovery of a second painting. So far her scepticism did not seem to have affected anyone else. But it well might. The operation was on a knife-edge. Curse Brunovsky for inviting her into his household.

The woman knew she would be blamed for letting Falconer escape that night in Battersea. Those who had sent her here did

not take failure lightly. They had no understanding of the difficulty of direct action against such a target in a London street,
while being certain to escape unseen. But they had agreed that
another attempt of that kind might well jeopardise the whole
operation. Her task now was to remove the risk from Falconer
and it had been left to her to do it in whatever way she thought
best.

She was trained to work alone but now, aware of their criticism, she was feeling isolated. It was not her fault that Rykov
had drawn attention to himself by unauthorised interference in
areas he did not understand. As a result the messenger Ivanov
had failed to make the meeting.

Her phone rang as she mused. The voice was fraught. "I
need to see you right away. It's urgent."

"Keep calm," she said coolly. "Tell me what's happened."

"Not on the phone."

She sighed. Another stupid man. Italians were completely
unreliable. If it rained when it was meant to be fair, if a train was
twenty minutes late, if the sandwich bar ran out of prosciutto—
hysteria ensued. Orderly people, the Germans or the Swiss,
stayed calm over small mishaps. Citizens of chaotic nations
(how many post-war Italian governments had there been?) were
outraged that anyone else should replicate their own complete
lack of organisation. "When can you meet?" she asked.

"Tonight. Come to my flat."

She thought for a moment, assessing the risk. "Give me the
address," she said, and as he told her she memorised it instantly.

"Come at eight," he ordered, seeming to forget in his near-
hysteria that she held the whip hand.

"No," she said bluntly. "I will be there at ten." It would be
best to arrive under cover of darkness.

· · ·

He lived in a converted loft a few streets north of Oxford Street, in what was still known as the home of London's rag trade, though many of the buildings now housed the offices of solicitors and estate agents. A few were being converted into flats, but on a weekday night at this hour, the neighbourhood was quiet, half-deserted.

She had taken a taxi to Tottenham Court Road, then walked the rest of the way, half a mile or so, knowing that she was far more likely to be remembercd at the address by a cab driver who dropped her there than by anyone who simply passed her in the street. She was dressed in trainers, dark waterproof trousers with deep pockets and a jacket with the hood up, covering her hair and obscuring her face.

The entrance to his building was off a main thoroughfare, in a cobblestone alley empty of cars. She pressed the bell and looked around her. There was no one. The door buzzed; in the small bare hall there was nothing but a metal lift. Pressing the button for the top floor, she rose smoothly and silently up through the building. The door opened and he was standing there, holding a large, well-filled brandy balloon.

"Come in, come in," he said and walked ahead of her into the vast converted loft. Large, colourful squares of stencilled fabric hung on the walls; the floorboards were waxed and buffed to a burnt-orange shine. In the middle of the floor square brick pillars, spaced at intervals, harked back to the days when the floor had been divided into small offices. Now the space was uncluttered—a large, sleek television screen hung flat against the wall. Two black leather chairs and a long sofa were grouped like modernist icons around a glass coffee table. Further back sat a dining area, with a grey slate table and steel chairs, and behind it a restaurant-sized cooking range, shining black wall-to-ceiling cupboards, and a fridge-freezer built deeply into the wall.

She took all this in, while mentally assessing the flat for vantage points, visibility, means of access and egress. One side of the room overlooked the alley from which she'd entered, the other fronted a building undergoing restoration, pitch-black inside. Facing her, she could see a short corridor, which must lead to a bedroom and bathroom. She doubted there was a second entrance to the flat.

He didn't offer her a drink but sat down immediately in one of the chairs, motioning her to take the sofa, where at one end a skinny black-and-white cat was curled up asleep. Ugh, she thought, sitting at the other end. She disliked all animals, especially house pets.

"Have you come from the gym?" he asked, gesturing irritably towards her clothes. His agitation was obvious.

"Yes. I've not been home. Now tell me, what is the matter?"

"Everything," he said brusquely. Beside her the cat stood up and stretched. "I had a telephone call this morning from the police. A detective at the Art Squad. He said he wanted to talk to me as soon as possible. I tried to delay him, but he wasn't having it. I am due to see him tomorrow."

"Is he coming here?" she asked quietly. The answer would be crucial.

"No. I said I'd go to him."

"Do you know what he wants to see you about?"

"He wouldn't tell me, but it's obvious, isn't it? He must know about *Blue Mountain*."

"I don't see why."

"What else could it be?" When she looked at him with

raised eyebrows, he shouted, "That was in the past. No one here knows about it except you. Besides, I served my sentence—what more could they want from me? No, it must be *Blue Mountain*."

"All right," she said quietly. "Let's suppose they have heard something—possibly from Morozov's people. Why should that alarm you? You can say that Forbes got in touch with you about the find and you simply relayed the news to Brunovsky. That's not hard to remember, is it? And it has the merit of being perfectly true."

"That's easy for you to say." He groaned and put his head in his hands. "I should never have listened to you. You said it was foolproof, if I did what you said I would have no worries. *Che incubo*." He raised his head and stared at her, his eyes red and strained.

"I'll put the kettle on," she said soothingly, and got up and went to the large range at the back of the room. He was getting hysterical, she realised. She would have to calm him down. And this time there was no one to disturb her.

44

As Peggy dialled the sixth cruise company on her list the rain was streaming down the glass of her office window. Caribbean Leisure Works ("Your Leisure, Our Pleasure") had its headquarters in Bridgetown, Barbados. Their website showed the city's sun-soaked harbour, a flotilla of berthed cruisers and sailboats forming a white armada on an azure sea. If only, thought Peggy.

The friendly Barbadian voice at the other end stopped in its tracks when she explained what she wanted, and went off to consult, leaving her on hold, listening to the thump, thump of reggae. Eventually a cut-glass English voice came on the line.

"This is Marjorie Allingworth. I'm the personnel director. You wanted to know about Monica Hetherington?"

"That's right. I'm ringing from the North Middlesex Hospital in London. I'm trying to find her because her mother's not well," said Peggy smoothly. "The last information I have, she was with your company—I believe she worked on one of the cruise boats."

"That was a long time ago." From the curtness of her voice it was clear that Marjorie remembered Monica, and not fondly. Peggy could hear the tap of computer keys. "Let me see—1996. She was only here for two seasons."

"Would you have any record of where she went next?"

There was an audible sniff. "No idea. She didn't keep in touch."

"Would anyone there be able to help? It's really important," Peggy pleaded.

There was a long pause. "Let me see."

Peggy waited, listening as she heard the cut-glass voice making brisk enquiries in the background. Eventually she returned to the phone. "One of the girls here says Monica was great friends with Sally Dubbing. She still works for us during the season. The rest of the time she lives in London. Hold on and I'll give you her address."

Wow, thought Peggy. I don't think much of her security. I could be anybody.

Tulse Hill was alien territory to Peggy. She had walked from the bus stop, past a betting shop that belched cigarette smoke through its open door, a newsagent with steel protective bars on the windows, and a unisex hair salon that specialised in straightening hair. Some boys wolf-whistled at her from a hoopless basketball court, and a pregnant woman wheeling a buggy had sent her the wrong way. Now she was sitting in a living room four storeys up a decaying sixties block, while Sally Dubbing made coffee in the kitchen.

Peggy looked around at the shabby furniture and stained walls hung with photographs of faraway exotic places—Tahiti, an aerial photograph of a string of small Caribbean islands, the harbour of Key West. They were meant to bring some sunshine into the flat but to Peggy's eye they just brought home the cramped grimness of the place. It seemed a long way from Belgravia.

"Here you go. No sugar, right?" Sally set the mug down on the stained table next to Peggy's chair, where it sloshed gently as it cooled. Peggy looked closely at Sally sitting opposite her on the small sofa. She was a sweetly pretty baby-faced blonde—except for the inch-wide band of blotchy pink that stretched like watery jam from one ear to her nose. No one could call it a beauty mark; it was far too big even to say it had "character."

"So you want to talk to me about Monica?" The accent was South London mixed with aspiration.

"Yes," said Peggy, getting her notebook out of her bag, "it's for an article about the wives and girlfriends of these Russian oligarchs."

Sally nodded. "I saw her in *Hello!* magazine a few weeks ago. Is that who you work for?"

"No. It's a new magazine, not out yet." She smiled and pushed her spectacles up her nose. "Tell me, do you ever hear from Monica these days?"

"Are you taking the piss?" she said curtly, reaching for a pack of cigarettes. She lit up and, blowing out some smoke, said, "I haven't heard from Monica for over two years."

"But you used to know her, didn't you?"

"Oh yes," she said easily. "I knew her. She was my best friend. She was a different Monica then." She stared at Peggy for a moment, with a glazed look that suggested her thoughts were elsewhere. She seemed to make up her mind about something, for she got up and went into the kitchen, returning with a half-bottle of Bell's whisky. Peggy shook her head when she proffered the bottle, then watched as Sally poured a neat two inches into her own coffee. Sitting back, she sipped the mixture carefully, and then she started to talk.

That winter when they met they were just two teenage girls fresh out of school without a GCSE between them. Monica was selling kitchenware in Debenhams' basement and Sally was learning more about Hoover bags than anyone should ever know. They'd become friends at once, joined by a simple detestation of their jobs, and a common passion for clubbing.

"Monica was always the leader," said Sally reflectively, pausing to sip her coffee. It was Monica who had come up with the idea. A friend of a friend of a friend worked on a cruise ship in the Caribbean—and was having the time of her life. Monica made it sound like one big party in the sun. Six weeks later both she and Monica were crew members of SS *Prince Albert*, sailing from Tobago to Miami.

Sally always knew there was no such thing as a free lunch, and she'd had to work hard as a waitress in the on-deck bar and in the industrial-sized dining room. But they let her sing sometimes at night, between the professionals. And the weather was wonderful, food was free and drinks were cheap.

"How about Monica?" asked Peggy lightly, wanting to get back to the subject.

"Oh, she was a waitress too. At least at the beginning. Then they made her hostess for the restaurant," she said, with a hint of pride.

The first season had passed without a hitch, and the girls had got back to London with money in their pockets. The second year was almost as good—for Sally at any rate. Monica had got in trouble just before Christmas, for fraternising with one of the paying guests, a retired policeman from Miami.

Sally looked at Peggy knowingly. "Of course we were paid to be friendly, but the company had strict limits and Monica was a bit *too* friendly."

They gave her a formal warning, but it didn't seem to worry her much. "Who cares?" she'd said to Sally, showing her a gold choker that the former cop had bought her in St. Lucia.

Then at Easter it happened again, and this time the company gave Monica her cards. Sally had expected her to be very upset, but she just said, "Good riddance."

It turned out that the offending passenger was offering her five grand to go with him on a cruise through the Greek islands.

After that, Sally had watched with a mixture of admiration and concern as her friend started a new, altogether different career. She was still working on cruise ships, but not for any company—Monica had gone into business on her own.

"Didn't the cruise companies object?" asked Peggy, doubting they'd be eager to have a reputation as a floating brothel.

"She was very careful. She'd buy a ticket like anybody else, then mix with the other passengers during the cruise. She'd single out one bloke—usually a widower, they seem to have a thing about cruises once the wife's dead. And what could the company say about that?" She raised an eyebrow. "You can't forbid 'love' can you? The cruises are meant to be romantic."

A tabby cat came out of the kitchen, slinking towards the window. Ignoring him, Sally went on, "After that, I didn't see Monica so much." Occasionally they would coincide in a harbour; and back in England during the summer they always got together. Interestingly Monica never plied her new trade in her home country: "I think she was still hoping she might meet Mr. Right, and she didn't want a reputation—not here anyway." By then, of course, Monica was in a different league financially from Sally, but she was always generous with her old mate. Once she even paid for Sally to join her on a cruise as a passenger.

"Did she expect you to join her"—Peggy hesitated, unsure of how to phrase this—"professionally?"

"No," said Sally, and gave a sad smile. Then she put her fingers against the ragged ribbon of pink on her face. "This kind of disqualifies me, don't you think?" She didn't seem to expect an answer. "Actually, Monica didn't work on that trip. It was just two girlfriends on a treat together. We had a lovely time."

But then why aren't they still friends? wondered Peggy, watching as the cat hopped up on to a pine table, littered with toast crumbs and a folded copy of the *Mirror*. "When did Monica stop working the cruises?" she asked.

"Three years ago. I came home in the summer and rang her up, like I always did. She was nice, but she said she was very busy—she was living in Beirut or somewhere like that. She'd got some Middle Eastern guy in tow, very well heeled, she said, only she didn't think he'd be crazy about what she used to do for a living. Then I saw her picture a couple of months ago in *Hello!* with a Russian guy. It said he had more money than the queen."

"And you haven't heard from her since?"

"No. I gave up trying. I know when I'm not wanted," she said fiercely. Behind this show of pride, Peggy sensed, was a festering hurt. About the disloyalty of her old friend; perhaps about the way things had turned out for her; possibly about the shocking blazoned stripe nature had deposited across her face like paint. "You know," she said, "Monica was wonderful to be with when things were going her way. I worshipped her, I did really—but underneath she was as hard as nails. I thought—yes—I thought she'd kill you to get what she wanted."

Suddenly a tear formed in the corner of her eye. She dabbed at it with a tissue. It was time to go. "Thank you very much for talking to me," said Peggy as she rose from her chair.

"Don't you want to take my picture then?" Sally was almost defiant.

Peggy looked at the dismal room: the cat was cleaning himself on the floor now, beside a grease stain that ran up to the kitchen door. "I'll ask my editor," she said.

"Whoever he is, he can't be very nice," said Sally, making no effort to get up. She sloshed another inch of whisky into her empty mug.

"Who?" asked Peggy, puzzled.

"This Russian bloke."

"Why do you say that?"

"Before she started picking them for their money, Monica never liked nice men. She always went for the rough ones—you know, the kind who'd rather belt you than talk things over. I know she's very grand now, but I bet that hasn't changed."

"Do you still work on the cruise ships?" asked Peggy, turning at the door, wanting to be polite.

Sally nodded, but there was nothing happy in her face. "I'll be back there in autumn." She paused, and a summary bleakness settled in her eyes. "But they don't let me sing any more."

45

This was the third time Detective Constable Denniston had tried the flat without finding anyone in. Only three months into his posting to the Art Squad, he did things strictly by the book, but he was starting to think that continuing to ring the bell of Mr. Marco Tutti was a major waste of time. On this occasion, however, he tried the neighbours as well and was surprised to find himself rewarded right away.

"Who is it?" demanded a woman's voice over the intercom, and when he explained she buzzed him in.

Getting out of the lift on the third floor, he found himself face-to-face with an exotic figure. The thin, pale young woman wore a purple minidress over black leggings. Her bright red hair was tied back in a ponytail and in her arms she held a meowing Siamese cat with a rhinestone-studded collar.

"You looking for Marco?"

"Yes, madam. Have you seen him?"

She shook her head and scratched the cat's ears. "Not for a couple of days."

"Do you know anything about his movements? Could he be away?"

"No, I don't think so. He does travel a bit, but I always know about it because then I look after Gobbolino."

"Who's that?"

"His cat, of course."

As if I should know, thought DC Denniston. Just what I need—a dodgy neighbour. He sighed. This Marco bloke was going to stay on his list until he'd either found him or discovered where he'd gone. He was about to go back down the stairs when the woman said, "Come to think of it, Officer, now that you mention it, it's a bit odd."

He looked at her enquiringly and she explained. "When Marco goes away he always tells me so I can feed his cat. But I haven't heard him around since the day before yesterday. And I've been at home a lot because I'm between jobs. I'm a dancer with Cupid's Children but we haven't got any bookings till June. Do you think something's wrong with Marco?"

"I don't know, madam," said Denniston, though for the first time he wondered if something was. This could be a real nuisance, he thought, wondering how much trouble this enquiry was going to cause him. I'll have to get into the flat first, he supposed, just to confirm the man had done a runner. The guvnor isn't going to like that one bit; they'd need a warrant, which meant paperwork and time and no guarantee of getting one at the end of it all.

"Couldn't you just check on him?" she asked.

"I've rung his bell. He didn't answer." He shrugged. "There's nothing else I can do right now."

"Why don't we go and have a look?"

"Pardon?" he said, startled. "Do you have a key to his flat?"

"Of course. How else do you think I feed Gobbolino?"

DC Denniston took out his notebook. He knew the rules. This had to be done properly. "May I have your name and address, madam?" he asked.

"I'm Amanda Millbrook. My stage name's Mandy Mills. I live here. Number 8."

Upstairs, she opened the door and led the way into Marco Tutti's flat. A small black-and-white cat immediately shot out from somewhere and ran for cover under the sofa, skidding slightly on the polished floor. "Here puss, puss, here Gobbolino," said Mandy, bending down with her hand out. The cat didn't budge until, as Mandy moved towards it, cooing, it suddenly broke cover and streaked for the back of the flat.

Mandy followed it while DC Denniston looked around. The flat was spic and span and he supposed that if you liked modern furnishings, it was very nice. Tasteful—a bit too tasteful for the policeman's liking. Wasn't there something a bit prissy about keeping your home like a trendy restaurant? Mandy stuck her head out of the rear hall. "He's not in the bedroom," she said, then disappeared again.

Did she mean the cat or Tutti? Denniston shook his head wearily when, like a squad car's siren, a scream filled the air. He ran through the doorway to the back and found Mandy leaning against the wall in the bathroom, the light on, an expression of horror on her face.

Reaching her he saw why. A man, obviously dead, lay naked in a bath of what had once been water, but was now a murky, sable-coloured soup. The body was fully extended, its feet splayed out like gruesome chicken wings, its arms draped over the sides, each wrist with deep gashes that were partly obscured by congealed gumdrops of blood. At the end of the bath, the man's face lay half-submerged under the sepia slime of blood and water, a trim goatee just visible below the surface. His eyes were wide open and staring—staring horribly at his pale white toes.

Mandy stifled a sob and said, "It's Marco."

You mean it *was* Marco, thought DC Denniston, reaching for his radio.

46

This time Liz didn't care what operation Brian had on, he was damn well going to listen to her. He was reading the *Evening Standard* article she had clipped for him; she'd first seen it the previous evening as she took the Underground back to Kentish Town. It had given her such a shock that she had missed her stop.

The body of Marco Tutti, an Italian fine-art specialist based in London, was found naked in the bath in his luxury W1 penthouse yesterday morning. According to police he had filled the bath, climbed in and then cut his wrists with a Stanley knife found nearby. A police spokesman said there was no suspicion of foul play, but would not confirm reports that prescription drugs and a note were found in the flat.

Tutti, 44, was well known in the gay clubbing scene. Clients of his exclusive interior design business include prominent Russians based in London, among them Prince Rupert von Demski and Nikita Brunovsky, the oligarch and art collector. Neither were available for comment

Dancer Mandy Mills, 23, of Cupid's Children, a neighbour, who was with police when the body was found, said that Mr. Tutti had shown no signs of depression. "He was a gentle man, who was particularly fond of animals," said Mandy. "I used to look after his cat Gobbolino when he was away. We are all shocked by this, and Gobbolino is devastated."

A friend, Alvo Bertorelli, commented, "He had no reason to be depressed. I don't know why he should do this. But he did tell me he did not want to grow old."

The accompanying picture showed an exotic-looking young woman clutching a small cat.

"So," said Brian, finishing the article, "Marco Tutti killed himself. Was he that frightened of the Art Squad?"

"Possibly. Perhaps he was afraid of his fake identity being uncovered. But he's survived brushes with the law before and he was a con man through and through."

"So why do himself in?"

"I'm not sure he did." She handed him the report she'd had from the police, and with her eyes dared him not to examine it carefully. As he read, she looked out the window, where a brisk shower was spotting the placid surface of the Thames.

Finished, he looked up at her doubtfully. "Have I missed something? This also seems to say he committed suicide."

Liz said, "I know it does, but look at the facts. The blood tests indicate he'd drunk over ten ounces of cognac and taken at least twelve Valium."

"Presumably he wanted to sedate himself first. It must be rather painful cutting one's wrists." Brian sniffed to indicate his distaste.

"Sure. But three Valium would do that. Why take twelve? Why not take seventy and kill yourself that way? It would have been much less messy, and painless."

"Who knows?" said Brian bluntly. He put the report on his desktop and slid a hand back through his thinning hair. "In his state of mind he might have done anything. Suicide isn't exactly rational behaviour, so why expect him to behave rationally?" He pointed to the police report. "This looks straightforward to me. I know there will be a coroner's inquest, but I can't see how he'll have any option but to call it suicide. Especially as there was a note."

"A pretty enigmatic one."

"Because it was in Italian?" There was a cutting note to his voice. He read from the report, "*La mia vita é diventata un incubo*. What does that mean?"

" 'My life has become a nightmare.' "

"There you go then. It couldn't be much clearer than that." He tossed the file across the desk at Liz, but threw it too hard, and it slid off the front of the desktop. Liz didn't reach down to pick it up.

Brian looked at her appraisingly. "Is something else the matter? Are you all right?"

"I'm fine," she said swiftly, then realised she sounded touchy, just like Brian often did. "There was another thing."

"Yes?" he said, sighing.

"Tutti's wrists were slit with a Stanley knife. It was left behind the taps on the bath."

"Tidy to the end," said Brian blithely.

"When I was attacked in Battersea, the mugger had a Stanley knife. I know because she waved it in my face." And she was going to do more than wave it around, thought Liz. But saying so would probably only fortify Brian's feeling that she was being paranoid.

He gave her a sharp look that suggested his patience was running out. "What are you trying to say, Liz?"

"I think I should be pulled out of Brunovsky's house. Contrary to what I said before, I think Brunovsky may need protection after all. The kind of protection I'm not qualified to give. We should explain this to him and get him to up his protection level or get Special Branch to take my place if it's considered a matter of national importance."

Brian made a show of thinking hard about this, but from the way his eyes hardened Liz knew his mind was made up. "I can't agree with you. It's exactly your presence that is needed. And Brunovsky's already got his own bodyguard."

She wanted to argue but Brian held up a warning hand. "That's my decision, and it's final." He suddenly leant forward, his features softening in a way that immediately struck Liz as false. "However, if you're concerned about your own safety that's another matter. If you're frightened just say so, and I'll pull you out of there right away."

Liz could not believe her ears. Of course she was frightened—what sane person wouldn't be? When she'd read about Tutti's death in the bath, she'd remembered something else— that unpleasant pool of red in her bath at the hotel in Cambridge—but she wasn't going to mention that to Brian. She was damned if she'd give him the satisfaction of thinking she couldn't cope. She felt so outraged that she could hardly trust herself to speak.

"No, Brian. If that's your decision, I'm not going to argue with you," she said at last. She looked down at the floor and the strewn pages of the police report. When she left the room a moment later they were still on the floor.

Walking into Liz's office, Peggy could see immediately that she was upset. She hesitated, wondering if she should come back later but Liz waved her in and pointed to a chair. Liz herself was standing up, looking with even greater distaste at the government-issue prints on her wall. I really can't put up with these much longer, she thought. There were some pleasant watercolours in her old bedroom at South Lodge. Her mother couldn't object if she reclaimed them. "Edward" might even be happy to get rid of what little presence Liz still had there. The last time she'd been at Kentish Town she'd had a long phone conversation with her mother. Most of it was about Edward and the things they were doing together. Even though she hadn't met him, Liz had created a mental picture of the man. He had grey hair and wore tweed suits and brogues—some days, when she was feeling down, she gave him a moustache and a pipe. In her mind, he spoke in a military voice and she didn't like him. Thoughts of Edward snapped her out of her reverie, as did Peggy's question, "What did Brian think about Tutti?"

"He thought it was suicide. An obvious suicide," said Liz, raising an eyebrow.

"You must be joking." Peggy had seen the police report and shared Liz's doubts. They'd both agreed that it seemed far more likely that Tutti had been drugged, stripped, put in the bath, then had his wrists slit.

"Afraid not," said Liz, frowning. She seemed to pull herself together. "What's your news?"

"I've found out a lot more about Monica's background. Seems she's been an upmarket tart for years, living on whoever would support her in the style she enjoyed. The only slightly odd thing is that immediately before she shacked up with Brunovsky she was living with some man in Beirut. I did wonder whether she could have been recruited and then targeted against Brunovsky, but it seems rather unlikely."

"I'm beginning to think anything's possible."

"Yes. Well, I've also been talking to our friends at PET in Denmark. I'd asked them to check out Greta Darnshof and I only heard back from them this morning." Peggy glanced at her notes. "Greta Darnshof was born on the island of Samso in 1964. She has no criminal record of any kind, owns a small flat in Copenhagen, and has a healthy balance in a savings account with the Jyske Bank."

"But?" asked Liz.

"Someone at PET was pretty diligent and took a second look. They discovered that there was no record of any Greta Darnshof attending a Danish *gymnasiet*, taking the baccalaureate exam, or attending university."

"She probably grew up abroad."

"That's what they think at PET. But I still haven't been able to discover who's backing her magazine. One company leads on to another. I'd have said it was money laundering but I wouldn't have thought an art magazine was ideal for that."

"Don't say she's another crook," said Liz with a sigh. "Poor Nicky's surrounded by them."

"Absolutely," agreed Peggy. "Every one of them is dodgy—Tutti, Monica, Harry Forbes and now Greta. At least the secretary Tamara seems to be what she claims to be. She's been with Brunovsky for fifteen years."

"What about your other operation?" asked Liz, only too pleased to change the subject. "What does Herr Beckendorf make of the fact that Ivanov was out publicly lunching with Rykov?"

"He's sure it was meant to be cover for something else. He was pretty annoyed when I told him we'd had to withdraw surveillance at the last minute. Catching an Illegal before he retires turns out to be his ambition and he thought Ivanov was going to lead him to one."

"The question," said Liz, reverting to the subject that most interested her, "is whether this bunch of crooks round Brunovsky are part of some Victor Adler–type of plot or whether they're just hovering like wasps round a jam pot."

"And whether Tutti's death has anything to do with it," added Peggy.

They both sat silent, thinking. Then Liz said, "Peggy, do you think I'm being paranoid? Marco Tutti's wrists were slashed with a Stanley knife and when I was mugged, my attacker threatened me with a Stanley knife. If we hadn't been interrupted by some people down the street, I think she was going to cut my throat."

"Why didn't you say so?"

"I wasn't sure. It could have been just a street robbery. The police thought so. Brian agreed with the police," she added with a shrug. "He thinks I'm another hysterical female, gone wobbly at the first hint of violence."

Peggy's alarm was now too great to disguise. "Liz, if you think that the attack on you is connected with Tutti's death, I don't think you should stay a moment longer in the Brunovsky house."

Liz stared at Peggy, wondering how best to hide the fact that she agreed with her one hundred percent. "Whatever's going on, I can't believe they would try anything in the house," she said finally, using a smile to disarm her younger colleague. "And I'm sure I won't be there much longer."

After Peggy had gone back to her office Liz sat on at her desk, gazing out at the unprepossessing view. Her intuition was telling her loudly now that something about the Brunovsky household did not add up—or it added up in some way she could not yet fathom. She'd be wise to get out, though she had to confess that sheer curiosity had her in its grip. And there was no way she would let Brian or Geoffrey Fane think that she couldn't cope. She would not reinforce whatever their female stereotype was—"Okay for desk work but can't really deal with the sharp end."

What are you trying to demonstrate? a small voice in her head was saying. That she was just as tough as a man in dealing with personal risk? Probably. But it could be a liability, that kind of macho posturing. Women had different skills, intuition and empathy—the "feminine skills" so many men lacked. She knew what hers were telling her. But this time she wasn't going to listen.

Down the corridor, Peggy was worried. Her mind raced. She knew she'd never change Liz's mind, but that didn't mean she was prepared to sit and do nothing. Who could she turn to? She knew better than to tackle Brian Ackers. He was the problem. Could Liz's old friends in Counter-Terrorism help? They'd tell her to go through the correct channels, which brought her back to . . . Brian again. Geoffrey Fane? No. Liz would never forgive her and anyway he'd be no help.

Unless . . . and the more Peggy thought about it, the more her heart thumped like an out-of-control drum. There *was* a way to help Liz, provided that Peggy was eloquent and forceful enough not to get sent off with a flea in her ear, or worse, an official reprimand. She wasn't that worried about being blamed for doing the wrong thing—she had enough pride to ignore any qualms about that—but she was worried she might make a hash of it, and end up with Liz in the same dangerous situation.

She waited until she got home that evening and then, pushing her spectacles firmly up her nose, she sat down, picked up her phone and rang the duty officer at Thames House. "It's Peggy Kinsolving here from Counter-Espionage. I need to speak to Charles Wetherby urgently. Could you give me his home number please?"

"You know he's on extended leave, don't you?" came the reply.

"Yes. But I still need to contact him."

"Are you at home? I'll ask him to ring you."

A few minutes later her phone rang. "Charles Wetherby," said a quiet voice. "I gather you want a word."

"Charles. Thank you so much for ringing. It's about Liz Carlyle."

47

I t was an eventful morning. Arriving at the house in Eaton Square, Liz had not expected to find a residence in mourning, but still thought there would be a subdued atmosphere in the Brunovsky household. Yet there had been no sign at all that Marco Tutti's death was affecting business as usual: as Liz arrived, Brunovsky was shouting for Tamara, Mrs. Grimby had brought up a pain au chocolat, still warm from the oven, and Mrs. Warburton was supervising Emilia the maid's dusting with an eagle eye.

Only Monica had made reference to the recent mortality, stopping in the doorway to the dining room. "Poor Marco," she said, before asking Liz if she had ever been in the Royal

Enclosure at Ascot. It was not so much callous, thought Liz, as Monica's usual way of dealing with the past—sticking her head in the sand.

Then Brunovsky had shouted again, this time calling for Liz. Has he started to think I'm working for him? she'd wondered as she rose from her chair.

"Yes," she had said coolly when she got to the door of his study.

He was standing by his desk, holding a passport. "Do you have one of these?" he'd asked. It sounded urgent.

"Of course," she'd said, for she had long before taken the precaution of having one in the name of Jane Falconer.

"With you?"

She nodded. The mugger had got some of her cover documents when she stole her handbag, so for the time being, until they were replaced, she was carrying her passport with her as proof of identity. He breathed a huge sigh of relief. "Thank goodness," he'd said. "You can come along then."

"Where to?"

Brunovsky looked at her with surprise. "Why, Ireland, of course. With Marco dead, I got in touch with this Miss Cottingham right away. She is not keen to visit London, so I thought why not let the mountain visit Muhammad, no? My plane is at Northolt and it will take only an hour to fly there. Harry will meet us and we can drive to this lady's mansion in thirty minutes. We'll be back in time for supper. Well, late supper anyway."

Liz stared at him incredulously. He was obviously determined to go, indeed he seemed to have instigated the plan. Liz was certain he'd be walking straight into a fraud, if not something worse. She was convinced that *Blue Mountain* was no more authentic than *The Protocols of the Elders of Zion*. But now that Tutti was dead, who was running the scam? It must be Forbes, the American—he'd been tied up with Tutti in the past. Both of them had been after Brunovsky's wallet since the beginning.

She hesitated. Brunovsky returned to the charge. "Jane, you must come. I need you," he said in his little-boy voice. "Not perhaps for your Pashko expertise," he winked at her, a rare acknowledgement that she was working undercover. "It's just that I respect your judgement. These are complicated matters—you will look after me." He smiled at her winningly.

"Are you taking Jerry Simmons?"

He seemed surprised by the question. "Of course. I will need him to drive me when we land."

Thank God. If Brian wasn't going to move Special Branch in to protect the Russian, at least his bodyguard should be around.

Liz glanced around. There was no one in the room or in Tamara's office outside but she walked with deliberate slowness to the door and closed it. As if surprised, Brunovsky sat down at the table, and Liz came to a stop in front of him.

"Nikita," she said—it was the first time she had ventured his Christian name but suddenly it seemed appropriate—"it's not my job to protect you. But you did ask for me to be here to keep an eye out and give you advice about your security and I'm doing that now. You know that you are under a threat. *Blue Mountain* could be a fake or a fraud as you are well aware, but it could possibly be some kind of a set-up to catch you and your protection on the wrong foot in the wrong place. What I'm saying is that I don't think it's wise for you to go to Ireland."

She stopped, wondering what on earth his reaction would be.

For a moment he gazed at her with simple unfeigned astonishment, his mouth opening and then closing. "Thank you for the warning," he said, "but it is very important to me to go. There will be no danger."

Then suddenly he grinned expansively. "You'll come then? That's my girl! Is that the right thing to say to a member of the British Security Service?"

And ninety minutes later she was walking with Brunovsky out on to the tarmac towards an Embraer Legacy jet, its steps down and the pilot, casual in a windcheater, standing on the top step. She'd tried to ring Peggy but she was not at her desk. The message she left must have sounded inane to the young woman— flitting off across the Irish Sea spontaneously, in search of a painting that didn't exist. It was all getting out of hand. When I'm back, Liz decided, I'll tell Brian to get me out of here or I'll go and talk to DG.

48

He had never, ever, had an interview like that in all his time in the Service. DG had spoken, not emotionally, not even overtly angrily—either would have been preferable to the icy coldness of the dressing-down he had just received. When Brian had been eight years old, he had been caught cheating on an exam at his boarding school and sent to the headmaster. That was how he felt now.

Barely noticing the river view, he stood resting his forehead on the window of his office, until it clouded up from the exhalation of his breath. Absentmindedly he drew a grid for noughts and crosses, etched a large O and a smaller adjacent x, then forgot about the next move as he played back in his head DG's accusatory tones.

You have placed an officer's life in danger. And for what purpose? I want you to act at once to retrieve the situation. And the final terse warning: *I must warn you that I shall be taking disciplinary action.*

Was that how his career was going to end? Thirty years' service abruptly terminated because someone got nervy. He didn't doubt for a minute that Adler's original story had been correct. The Russians were up to something—they were *always* up to something, that's what people didn't understand. But it was Brunovsky they wanted, not Liz Carlyle. Silly, panicky woman. It was his misfortune to have got stuck with her on this operation.

He sat down at his desk and stared at the green marble slab and its unused pen. He wondered where DG had got his information. Who had spoken to him? Who had gone around his— Brian's—back? He'd find out in the end who'd undermined him. But that would have to wait—he had to act immediately, if only out of self-preservation, and do what DG had ordered.

He sighed, then dialled the mobile number, only to get a voicemail's recorded announcement. Damn. It was bad enough having to eat humble pie, but worse having to postpone the meal. He put down the phone, then picked it up again, and dialled an internal number. "Could I see you please, right away?"

Peggy Kinsolving came in within sixty seconds. She seemed an efficient sort of lass, if a bit too close to that Carlyle woman for his liking. Very young, but a competent investigator. He did not ask her to sit down; this wouldn't take long.

"I'm trying to reach Liz Carlyle but her mobile's on voice-mail."

"I've been trying to reach her too. You know that we've been in touch with the Danes and the Germans to try to identify the Illegal that they thought might have come here. I've just had a message."

Peggy took a piece of paper from the folder she was carrying and put it on the desk under Brian Ackers's nose. He gazed abstractedly at its few terse sentences and at the name.

"Has this woman surfaced here in any way? Do we know anything about her whereabouts?"

"She is close to Brunovsky."

"My God!" said Brian excitedly. "This could be our first sight of Victor Adler's plot."

Then suddenly the implications of Peggy's statement struck him like a thunderbolt. Liz Carlyle could be in real danger after all. Trying not to look as shaken as he felt, he began issuing rapid-fire orders. "I want you to go to the Brunovsky house and find Liz. Pretend you're an old friend, or her sister—I don't care, just make sure you find her. Tell her I want her to get out of there at once—she can think up any excuse she likes but she must leave immediately. Is that understood?"

"I can't, Brian," Peggy said, looking at her feet.

Jesus, he thought angrily. What's wrong with these women? "Nonsense," he said harshly. "Do as you're told." If DG could talk to him like that, then he could act the same way with his subordinates. "This is your immediate priority. Is that clear?"

"I'm sorry, Brian," said Peggy, but she was not apologising. "Liz isn't there. She's gone to Ireland with Brunovsky. She left a message for me about an hour ago from Northolt. They're taking his private jet."

"Oh God," Brian groaned. "What is she doing there?"

"She said they've gone to try and buy this picture from some old lady west of Cork."

"Will this . . . woman . . . be with them?"

"I don't know."

"All right," said Brian. He knew now how wrong he had been, but he found himself almost eerily calm. There was no point in self-recrimination. "Get me Michael Fane," he said to Peggy. "I'm going to send him over there as quick as we can manage. I want you to get on to the Garda right away. Tell them we're urgently trying to find a colleague. Get them to meet Michael when he lands at Cork."

"All right," said Peggy. "Shall I tell them the whole story?"

"No, for goodness' sake," said Brian. "Just tell them what they need to know." He waved a bony hand to indicate she'd better get a move on. So why wasn't this girl going? She was looking at him in a way he found unsettling. It was a look he'd never seen before in one of his staff—contemptuous but pitying at the same time.

"Don't you think, Brian, you'd better speak to Geoffrey Fane and the Foreign Office? We don't know how this is going to turn out. And I think I'd better try and find out who's gone to Ireland with Brunovsky and Liz."

49

The view of the lake had not changed for a hundred years (when the last of the woodland had been felled), and Letitia Cottingham had been alive for eighty-six of them. This morning as she took her small constitutional around the box hedge of the terrace, she wondered vaguely who all these people were flitting in and out of her house.

Perhaps they would have a party. That would be nice, like her childhood again, those days before the war when Thomas, her brother, would bring friends all the way from Cambridge to stay. The house was filled with laughing voices then, and they played lawn tennis and swam just down there, next to the boathouse. In the evenings there was dancing, and she was allowed to stay up and watch from the stairs.

But it had all ended with the war. The locals had been unhappy when Thomas had enlisted in the British Army—some of their mutterings had been positively pro-German. But even they had shown sympathy after that bleak morning when the postman had cycled up the drive, carrying the telegram announcing Thomas's death at El Alamein.

Her parents had never recovered; both were dead within five years. And so the place had come down to her—plain Letitia Cottingham, whom nobody had wanted to marry until she had inherited the estate. She'd had her revenge, saying no to half a dozen suitors after that, and though she had never made a success of the place—selling off parcels of land every few years—she was still here. The roof leaked so badly there were buckets in the attic; the sash windows were rotten to the core; woodworm and rot in the floorboards meant that half the bedrooms were uninhabitable; but the fact was, the house was still Letitia's. They would have to carry her out with her boots on.

The new carer was nice. Better than the last one who'd come from Dublin and seemed to hate the countryside. What was this girl's name? Svetlana? Something like that. From one of those countries in Eastern Europe everyone used to complain about. She was such a gentle girl, even if her English wasn't very good. Her friends were nice as well, though those foreign men who'd been the week before were rather brusque. And that unpleasant woman. Still, it was good to have life in the old place again.

50

Brunovsky was in love with his aeroplane. He sat in one of the vanilla leather-padded chairs, wearing a fawn cashmere blazer and Gucci loafers that looked as soft as slippers, talking to Liz in loving and monotonous detail about the attributes of the Embraer Legacy 600: its range of 3,400 nautical miles, wingspan of 68 feet, approach capability of 5.5 degrees (whatever that meant), and last but not least, its $23.6 million price tag.

The engines revved and the jet accelerated down the short Northolt runway until they were pushed back against their seats. It cleared the outer perimeter fence with what looked to Liz no more than twenty feet to spare; for a moment she wondered if the pilot was planning to join the cars heading west on the M40.

A friend of her father's had once flown in the Concorde back from New York, and said that its interior was like a padded cigar tube, but Brunovsky's jet was remarkably spacious. It could seat fourteen passengers, but on board now were only Liz, the oligarch and Jerry Simmons, sitting by himself on a two-seater sofa near the galley in the rear. As soon as they were airborne a slim young blonde stewardess in a smart navy blue suit with the shortest skirt Liz had ever seen on a uniform offered them smoked salmon and cold Sancerre. This is the life, thought Liz, settling back in her chair, realising without any feeling of guilt that she was the only one to accept the wine.

Sitting up front, alone with Brunovsky, she was wondering how much if anything she should tell him about Peggy's recent discoveries. But she hesitated. She didn't see it as any part of her job to tell Brunovsky that all his pals were crooks. He might well be aware of it already and he wouldn't thank her for pointing it out. Tutti, for example. It was remarkable that Brunovsky had not even mentioned his supposed suicide. He might well know more about Harry Forbes than she did, and if that club was where he had met Monica, he must have a pretty good idea already of what sort of a girl she was.

As for Greta Darnshof, Liz determined to find out how much Brunovsky knew about her mysteriously funded magazine. She was about to raise the topic when Brunovsky finished his lunch, unbuckled his seat belt and stood up. He pointed towards the cockpit. "Excuse me, Jane, I must leave you for a little while. Monica hates flying, and when we travel together I have to sit and hold her hand. Now I have the rare opportunity to keep my pilot skills sharp. Hopefully, you won't know if it's me or the regular pilot who lands the plane." He laughed and moved towards the nose of the plane.

Looking through the small window, Liz watched the Severn grow larger, then after a short time begin to shrink in the distance behind them. She thought about Brunovsky, trying yet again to get a fix on the man—difficult, since he was so volatile: one minute charm itself, the next volcanically bad-tempered. The deference he'd shown her at first had slowly diminished as she had become a familiar in his household. He obviously had some kind of confidence in her and had listened to her warning like a little boy being told what was good for him, but increasingly he was treating her as his property, in the same peremptory, demanding fashion he treated Monica or, God help us, the hapless Tamara. Another three weeks in Belgravia, thought Liz, and he'd have me taking dictation.

She undid her seat belt and walked back to the galley in search of some water, passing Jerry Simmons in his blue chauffeur's suit. There would have been something imposing about his gorilla shoulders and big, bland face, had he not been sound asleep, snoring softly with his mouth open.

As they reached the eastern tip of Ireland the cloud thickened and the view disappeared. The plane descended slowly and bumpily until suddenly, only a few hundred feet above land, a gentle, rolling landscape of silky green appeared like a watercolour below. Liz could make out small farms, a hamlet of six or seven cottages, a stream no bigger than a large ditch, and then the wheels gently touched the runway with a delicate kiss.

A jubilant roar came from the cockpit, and as the plane rolled slowly towards the tiny terminal in the distance, Brunovsky emerged with a grin on his face. "I have not lost my touch," he declared happily as he rejoined Liz, who was taking her mobile out of her bag. As she turned it on, Brunovsky reached out a large hand. "Could I borrow that for a moment?" he asked. "I left mine behind, and Monica likes to know when I have landed."

Liz was extremely reluctant to surrender her phone, since it held a battery of Thames House numbers, but with Brunovsky's hand held out, it was difficult to refuse to lend it to him. He took the phone and went back to the cockpit as the plane continued to traverse the long cross-axis of runway.

At last the plane came to a stop outside the terminal, and the pilot pushed open the cabin door, then unfolded the steel stairway. As Liz and Brunovsky came down the steps, with Simmons behind them, a chill westerly wind that had not yet reached London swept across the tarmac, catching them as they walked quickly to the tiny new terminal building of tinted glass and charcoal steel. There was a Boeing 737 parked outside the far end of the building, and a line of Cessna propeller planes on the grass fringe by the airport fence, but otherwise no sign of traffic.

Inside the terminal, landing formalities were cursory. A cheerful young man in a uniform gave a quick look at their passports and waved them through. Baggageless, they moved past an unattended customs desk into a small outer hall, where a solitary girl sat doing nothing behind a desk. Liz thought she had better let Peggy know where she was. "Can I have my phone please?" she asked Brunovsky.

"Of course," he said, and felt in his jacket pocket. He tried another pocket, then patted all of them with an anxious look on his face. "Oh no," he said, "I've left it in the cockpit."

"I'm sure I can go back and get it," said Liz. She couldn't believe the man at passport control would object.

Brunovsky shook his head. "I am so sorry, Jane, but the

plane won't be there. The pilot's taken it for refuelling." He looked at her apologetically.

"There must be a pay phone here."

Brunovsky looked irritated. "Jane, we are late already. Please wait. We will be at the house in half an hour—you can ring from there."

51

Your call is being forwarded to the voicemail service . . .

Peggy had already sent a text message—RETURN TO LONDON URGENTLY. RING ASAP—and had phoned half a dozen times to no avail. What had Liz said in her message? *I'm going to Ireland with Brunovsky in his private jet to see this new picture that's turned up. We'll be back this evening but I'll ring again when we get there to let you know where we are.* But no call had come, so where were they?

Normally, this was just the sort of problem Peggy enjoyed solving but she wasn't enjoying herself now. The possibility that Liz was in danger was making her heart thump uncomfortably as she worked. She began by checking back through all Liz's reports to see if there was any mention of the location of this supposed new picture, but all Liz had said was that it was owned by a Miss Cottingham who lived near Cork. Peggy had great faith in the Internet as a starting point for puzzles and she was pretty sure that she would be able to find Liz within a few minutes. Googling "Cottingham + Ireland" produced only the useless information that Lewis Cottingham was the architect of Armagh Cathedral. Liz had said the old lady owned a large country house, but a trawl through landowners and tourist sites turned up nothing useful. The Irish telephone directory listed only four Cottinghams in the entire country—three in Dublin and one in Belfast, none of them obvious owners of large country houses, none of them likely candidates for the perpetration of an art fraud.

Airports next, thought Peggy, trying to keep calm. Where would a small plane land? They were heading for somewhere near Cork, so probably Cork airport. But it could be Kerry. Or even Shannon—if they had a helicopter standing by they could reach almost any point in southwest Ireland within half an hour. There were thirty-six airports in Ireland and even when she had discounted the twenty-one with unpaved runways, that still left fifteen possibilities.

At this point Peggy telephoned the office of the Garda Siochana in Cork and found herself speaking to a soft-spoken man named O'Farrell, head of Special Branch. She told him that she needed urgently to contact a colleague who was on her way to visit a country house somewhere in the county, owned by an old lady. "I don't know the name of the place, and was hoping you could help."

O'Farrell gave a gentle laugh. "Ireland's full of old country houses inhabited by almost equally old ladies."

"I've got the owner's name," she said eagerly. "It's Cottingham—a Miss Cottingham. But I can't find her in any directory."

"The name doesn't ring a bell, but then, I'm not a student of the Irish gentry. Let me ask around. I'll get back to you."

What next? thought Peggy, drawing what felt like her first breath for half an hour. "When in doubt," her Anglo-Saxon tutor at Oxford had once told her, finding her half in tears when stuck with a particularly tricky passage in *Beowulf*, "the answer is to move on." So now Peggy did.

The news in the message from the Danes that she had shown to Brian, that Greta Darnshof was not who she claimed to be, would in other circumstances have thrilled Peggy. Now it frightened her. The Danes had run Greta Darnshof's name against a programme intended to help expose identity theft and they'd hit the jackpot. At first the search had come up negative—the Danes had focused on 1964 when Greta claimed to have been born, and 1965. But when they widened the search they found Greta Darnshof, a five-year-old girl, died with her mother and father in a car crash in 1969, thirty kilometres from the town of Horsens. About six years ago someone else had assumed her identity and three years later, the new Darnshof had moved to Norway. Herr Beckendorf was convinced this was his Illegal and now she was living in London, dead thirty-eight years yet miraculously reborn as the editor of *Private Collection*. Neither the Danes, the Germans nor Peggy knew what her mission was, but it was looking increasingly likely that it had something to do with Brunovsky.

Peggy rang the office of *Private Collection* in Hanover Square. "Miss Darnshof is unavailable," said a tired, Sloaney voice over the phone.

"Will she be available later on?"

"I'm afraid I don't know," said the voice, this time audibly suppressing a yawn.

"Well, is she in town? I'm an old friend from Denmark,"

added Peggy, wishing she'd thought of this in time to add a slight accent. "I'll ring her flat—unless you think she's gone to Ireland."

"I don't know if it's Ireland, but she was flying somewhere." The Sloane seemed to wake up at last, and regret her indiscretion. "What did you say your name was?"

"Thanks very much," said Peggy, and after this non sequitur put down the phone, suddenly feeling sick at the thought of Greta Darnshof in Ireland. If anything happens to Liz, she thought with sudden helpless anger, I hope they hang Brian Ackers up from a lamp post on Millbank.

Why didn't Liz ring? She must have landed by now. Perhaps she couldn't find a private place to make a call, but Liz would always find some way to keep in touch. She tried to still the racing thoughts in her head, stretched both arms out and took a few deep breaths to keep her circulation flowing. Pushing her glasses firmly up her nose, she reminded herself that sometimes the answer was so obvious you ignored it. What obvious thing had she missed?

Suddenly, for no apparent reason at all, she remembered that even a private plane had to file a flight plan. A few phone calls got her to Northolt, then a brief argument, another call to the airport police, and eighteen minutes later Peggy was staring at the faxed copy of Brunovsky's itinerary. Then she rang O'Farrell of the Garda again.

"You say Shillington airport?" he said when she'd explained. "That would make sense. It's new, about thirty miles west of Cork. Small but with a long enough runway to take private jets. It gets a lot of use from the money that's been coming into Cork by the coast. Do you want me to send someone there to pick her up?"

And then Peggy looked at her watch and with a sinking

feeling realised it was too late. Liz would have landed by now. Brian Ackers had told her to play it low-key with the Garda. "We don't want to cause an unnecessary international incident," he'd said. She decided to disobey him.

By the time she had given an astonished O'Farrell a version of what she thought was going on, he had agreed to send two officers to meet Michael Fane, now en route to Heathrow, when he landed at Cork airport. Then they would take him to . . . where? Peggy hoped that by then she would have been able to make contact and would know where Liz had gone.

She thanked O'Farrell, agreed to keep in close touch, hung up, then picked the phone up again.

Your call has been forwarded to the voicemail service.

52

We will be landing at Cork in twenty minutes." Michael Fane did up his tie and ran a comb through his hair. It wasn't that he was expecting the Garda officers meeting him to be particularly spruce, but they'd be looking to him to lead and he was determined to be authoritative.

He wondered if they would be armed. I hope so, he thought a little nervously, recalling Brian Ackers's warning. Brian had kept stressing the possible danger Liz might be in, yet seemed perfectly happy to be chucking Michael into the middle of it.

Not that Michael could complain. When Brian had summoned him, he had assumed, despite Liz's assurances, that he was going to be reprimanded for his surveillance of Ivanov.

Brian had looked furious—red in the face, his eyes darting about unnervingly. But Michael quickly discovered that Brian's agitation had nothing to do with him, and he was so relieved that at first he didn't take in what he was being told to do.

"You're to go to Ireland right away," Brian said at once. "Liz went there early this morning—we don't know exactly where she's gone yet. Take the first flight you can get to Cork. Peggy Kinsolving has talked to the Garda. Keep in touch with her and she'll arrange for them to meet you. If there's any trouble, you're to defer to them, but otherwise they'll look to you for direction."

"What do I do when I get there?"

Brian looked at him as if he should have known. "Find Liz," he said shortly. "Wherever she is, locate her and bring her back. I don't care who she's with or what she's doing, you're to remove her at once and return with her to England. Is that clear?"

It couldn't be much clearer, thought Michael, though he could see an obvious problem. "What if she won't come? I mean, she usually gives the orders, not me."

"For the time being, you report directly to me. When you find her, tell her you are just a messenger, conveying my orders."

Thanks a lot, thought Michael, but he was excited by the challenge. As he left he almost missed the tall, slim figure standing in Brian's secretary's office, looking through the window down into the inner atrium. As the man turned, Michael saw that it was his father.

"Hello, Michael," said Geoffrey Fane.

His father was his usual elegant figure in pinstripe suit and silk tie and Michael, seeing him there in his boss's office, felt the familiar feeling of inferiority and anger swell up. I don't know what you're doing here, thought Michael, but trust you to show up just when I've got something real to do at last. Here you are to muscle in on it and spoil it.

But just as the fog of all the usual emotions started to settle, he stopped long enough to cast a sideways look at Geoffrey, who was just standing there looking at him. He suddenly seemed to Michael—there was no other way to describe it—forlorn. And then, for reasons Michael could not have described or explained or even halfway understood, he saw in this bogeyman figure of a father something he had not seen before, something that had nothing to do with the figure he had created in his mind, something that instead seemed entirely, unexpectedly *human*.

"Dad," he found himself saying, "I'm in a bit of a rush. I've got to go to Ireland." And he paused, wondering where these words were leading, until out of nowhere new words came to him and he said suddenly, "When I get back, maybe we could have lunch."

Geoffrey Fane looked so surprised that Michael started to regret his impetuous proposal. "Yes," his father finally said, "I would really like that." And he smiled, but uncertainly, awkwardly—something Michael had never seen in him before.

"I'll ring you when I'm back," said Michael confidently.

He basked in that feeling now, as the 737 dipped one wing and the Irish coast disappeared from view. The prospect of this trip no longer seemed so daunting. It would be an anticlimax to get sent out with such urgency, only to find there wasn't a problem at all; part of him secretly hoped to see some action. It would be nice to have something to tell his father.

53

Jerry Simmons was driving them in an enormous black car which had been waiting at the tiny little airport where they had landed. A Mercedes-Benz S600, the safest car in the world, Brunovsky had boyishly declared. He wasn't talking about road accidents. The way the back doors clunked as Jerry closed them suggested that the side panels were armour-plated. Why on earth hire an armoured car in rural Ireland? wondered Liz.

Now Brunovsky was studying some spreadsheets he had produced from his briefcase and was clearly not in conversational mode, so they travelled in silence. Liz was concentrating on the route, trying to memorise the names on the fingerposts at each crossroads. Simmons was driving fast but carefully through the thin Atlantic rain that spattered the windscreen, relying on his satellite navigation system to direct him.

At first Liz found it quite easy to keep track of where they were as they drove west through a succession of building sites and roadworks, but then, as they turned north, away from the coast and its influx of new money, she began to get confused. Gradually the villages became smaller, the roads narrower and more twisted and the cottages older. The few people they passed stared at the bulletproof limousine negotiating their narrow streets, and two pigs nonchalantly forced them to a halt on a mud-covered track on the outskirts of a town.

At last Simmons turned off a valley road and, carefully steering through a gap in an ancient iron boundary fence, drove on to a gravel drive. On either side was parkland, studded by huge oaks, with a dozen scraggy sheep grazing on the lush grass. Ahead, through gaps in the sentry lines of towering lime trees, Liz could see a vast grey stone Georgian house. Two enormous pilasters flanked the entrance, with wide stone steps leading up to the front door. Above the attic windows a balustrade ran the width of the house, and as they drew nearer, a side wing of Victorian brick came into view.

Simmons pulled the car to a halt on the gravel in front of the house, and got out to open the doors. As Liz stepped out she looked up into the chauffeur's eyes, and they held hers meaningfully for a moment before he looked away.

What was that about? she wondered as she followed Brunovsky up the steps. The door was answered by a tall, thin old man in a frayed black jacket covering a dingy jumper, his face mottled purple by weather or drink. "Will you come in?" he said in a voice full of Ireland, and they walked into the hall. Four impressive Corinthian pillars soared up to the roof and a staircase swept up to a landing in an arabesque of stone. But the paint on the pillars was peeling like loose onion skins, and most of the floor's tiles were cracked. It was cold, even colder than outside, and the strong smell of damp was as pungent as the salt air in a seaside town.

Liz walked behind Brunovsky into the drawing room, a long salon running across half the width of the house. She paused inside the door to take in the room—the ceiling decorated with plaster friezes of cherubim, family portraits on three of the walls and in the fourth long, vertical windows looking out over the terrace and overgrown formal gardens. Her attention distracted, she did not notice the young woman in a nurse's uniform standing in front of the fireplace until she spoke. "Welcome," she said. "I am Svetlana."

"*Zdravstvujte*," said Brunovsky, shaking her hand and they exchanged a few words in Russian.

Noticing Liz's surprise the woman spoke in English. "Miss Cottingham is slightly indisposed today, though I hope she will join us later."

"Is Harry Forbes here?" asked Liz. With Marco gone, he was the intermediary in this deal, if that's what it was going to be.

A woman's voice behind her said, "He is not well."

Liz turned to see Greta Darnshof standing in the doorway. Her leonine blonde hair was tied back in a tight bun, and she wore a severe grey suit. In the cold light her fine-featured face seemed hard, almost fierce. Greta advanced towards Brunovsky, ignoring Liz. She said, "I left Harry in the hotel. Everything has been prepared."

Prepared? thought Liz. I thought we were here to see a painting.

"Come into the library," said Greta.

She was speaking directly to Brunovsky, and Liz decided to use the opportunity to find a phone. In response to her question, Svetlana led her towards the back of the house, past a small sitting room, a cloakroom and finally the larder, until they came into an enormous kitchen. There among rows of copper pots hanging from hooks on the wall, opposite an enormous ancient Aga, its once white enamel stained caramel by years of cooking, hung a wall phone on a rickety bracket.

But when Liz picked up the phone there was no dial tone. Puzzled, she turned to the Russian girl and said, "It's not working."

Svetlana shrugged. "Sometimes it fails. We are quite remote here."

"I'm sure. Do you have a mobile I could use?"

"No," said Svetlana.

Since Greta's unexpected appearance, Liz had begun to grow suspicious. This seemingly straightforward day had developed disturbing possibilities. Now this. How could this woman look after an invalid, if that's what Miss Cottingham was, without a phone? Liz's mind was whirling with questions. Was she deliberately being kept incommunicado? Whatever was going on here, she wasn't going to show any disquiet to this woman. "Doesn't matter," she said cheerily. "Can you show me the library now?"

There was no sign of Brunovsky or Greta in the library, and Svetlana left Liz alone there. It was a windowless circular room in the centre of the house, lined with floor-to-ceiling shelves crammed with musty books. A wrought-iron staircase leading up to a walkway gave access to the higher shelves and a domed glass roof provided the only light. In one corner Liz saw the painting, mounted for viewing on a large easel, only half-illuminated by the weak light from the dome.

Liz was struck again by how closely it resembled the Pashko Brunovsky had bought. She looked at the thick strokes of its surface, then her eye was caught by the stain in its upper right corner. It was little more than a streak, which if she hadn't known about the burst pipe would have struck her as the accidental swipe of a paintbrush. The pipe must have been rusty, otherwise why should a water stain be coloured? Intrigued, she looked intently at the mark and realised she could make out small granules—of what? Paint! This wasn't water damage at all; this was paint. She listened for a moment, but heard no sound in the house; leaning forward she sniffed deeply, her nose almost touching the stain, and smelled the faintest aroma, a smell of lacquer, of glue, of aerosol spray.

Walking round the easel to the back, she saw that the canvas had been wrapped around a large wooden frame, its edges tacked down. In one corner a postage-stamp-sized piece of canvas flapping loosely gave Liz an idea. Rummaging in her bag, she found her nail scissors, and very delicately she snipped a sliver from the loose canvas and put it carefully into the inner pocket of her bag. No one here would notice, but back in London the Art Squad should easily be able to determine if the canvas was really a hundred years old.

"Usually people like to look at pictures from in front." She jumped at the sound of the familiar voice, and, stepping round the easel, saw that Dimitri had come quietly into the room.

"What on earth are you doing here?" she asked with genuine astonishment. Had he seen her snipping off the bit of canvas? Probably not. He was smiling at her, though there was no warmth in his face.

"How could I resist the news of another Pashko?" he said, advancing towards Liz and kissing her formally on both cheeks.

She noticed his leather jacket was spattered with rain. "And you are an extra bonus."

"Have you just arrived?"

Dimitri nodded. "I have driven from Dublin." He pointed to the painting behind her. "What do you think of it?"

Not bad, considering it was painted two weeks ago, Liz wanted to say, but wary now, not sure why Dimitri was there, she said only, "It's very like *Blue Field*."

"Unsurprising," said Dimitri. "They were painted within months of each other."

"Are you sure of that?"

Dimitri looked at her, slightly quizzically. "It is impossible to be precise about the dates. But certainly it was the same year."

Did he really believe this? She was not an expert, she couldn't know for sure, but the circumstances around the painting's redis- covery, the picture itself, all suggested it was a crude fake.

She said, "What I don't understand is who is negotiating for the owner. I thought she had a nephew."

Dimitri watched her appraisingly. "I don't know," he said at last. "But why all these questions, Jane?" He did not seem to expect an answer. "Let's go and join the others." Something in his tone had changed; when he walked to the door and held it open, pointedly waiting for Liz, she realised it was the same auto- cratic note she had heard recently in Brunovsky's voice. As if they were in charge, directing her. Or were they just being Russian?

In the drawing room Brunovsky and Greta were sitting on a long high-backed sofa at the far end of the room. Liz was sur- prised to see Jerry Simmons in the room too, sitting awkwardly on an Empire chair in the corner, leaning forward with his hands between his knees. "Come and sit down here, Jane," said Greta, and patted the cushion next to her.

"Are we waiting for Miss Cottingham?" asked Liz.

"You could say that," said Greta, and again she patted the cushion, this time more emphatically.

"I think I'll take a walk around," said Liz, pointing towards the terrace and gardens.

"In this rain? That's not a good idea." Greta's eyes were tense, focused on Liz, who in turn looked at Brunovsky. He seemed a million miles away, thoughtful and detached from the people around him. When Liz turned to Dimitri, he gave a slight smile and she noticed that he was now standing between her and the door.

Okay, she thought, perhaps I won't go for a walk after all. But she wondered, as she sat down on the sofa next to Greta, just what they were really waiting for.

54

Charles Wetherby was sitting in Brian Ackers's office. What an uncomfortable, soulless kind of room, he reflected, with its Cold War library, the war-room map and the desk with its back to the window. The situation was even worse than he'd feared, which made him feel less guilty about leaving Joanne and coming back to work. "They need you," she'd said firmly after DG's first phone call.

"So do you," he'd said.

"Not just at the moment, Charles," and he knew she was thinking of the doctor's candid assessment after the latest round of treatment. *I can't promise you more than a year but you should be stable now for at least a month or two.*

She looked him in the eye then. "A little time by myself is what I need. Don't worry—when I want you back with me, I'll tell you."

And so he'd returned, into this odd position—another man's desk, another man's job—trying to focus for the first time in many months on something other than his wife's slow dying.

Brian's secretary stuck her head round the door. She looked flustered, upset that her boss had gone off so suddenly. Charles wished she could explain why, having pressured Liz to remain in such a dangerous position, Brian had compounded his folly by sending Michael Fane to join her. From the little Charles knew of him, young Fane was inexperienced and headstrong—not the sort of officer to send into an unassessed situation on a rescue mission. Charles suspected it was this second misjudgement that had led DG to remove Brian Ackers from his post and send him on gardening leave.

"Geoffrey Fane's here," the secretary announced flatly.

"Ask him to come in please." He sighed inwardly at the prospect. He knew Geoffrey Fane; their paths had crossed over recent years in several counter-terrorist operations. Charles respected Fane for his intelligence and his skill at getting things done but he did not entirely trust him. The two men were products of the different cultures of their services. Fane came from a culture developed to train officers to be self-reliant, to work alone or in small groups, sometimes in hostile conditions, where the emphasis was on initiative and getting things done. Wetherby's style came from working on complex investigations, in interdependent teams, where everything that was done might ultimately face scrutiny by parliamentary committee, official inquiry, the courts or even the press. To Charles's mind Geoffrey Fane was devious and cut corners; to Fane's, Charles was over-cautious. Charles hoped Fane would be straightforward now;

the last thing he needed in this situation was a game of cat and mouse.

"Charles," said Fane coming into the room. He wore a dark pinstripe suit and a pale yellow shirt and spotted tie. They shook hands and sat down. "It's good to see you back. I hope all is well at home?" said Fane. "Pity about the situation here."

Charles ignored this; he wasn't going to discuss Brian Ackers's sudden departure with Fane, though he had no doubt it was all over Thames House and Vauxhall Cross by now. Instead he said, "I gather Liz Carlyle's gone to Ireland with this man Brunovsky. Apparently they're after some painting, but there seems good reason to believe something quite different is going on." He paused. "You should know that your son Michael's over there too."

"I did know that, actually. I was here to see Brian when Michael left."

"I gather you know the background to why Liz was involved with this Brunovsky character. To save time I've asked Peggy Kinsolving to come in and brief us both on what she thinks the situation is, and you can fill me in on the background as we go along. The priority seems to me to get Liz and Michael out of there unharmed."

Fane hesitated, then asked, "Is the situation dangerous?"

"It shouldn't be for Michael. He's with the Garda."

Fane nodded, but his relief was momentary. "How about Liz?"

Charles shrugged. "I very much hope not." He looked at Fane; it suddenly struck him that they were both equally worried about Liz. He's fond of her too, thought Charles with a twinge of jealousy.

While they waited for Peggy, Fane got up and went to the window while Wetherby sat slowly tapping the end of a pencil on the desktop. Fane said, "I could never understand why Brian put the desk there. You'd think that having earned a river view, he'd want to enjoy it."

The door opened and Peggy came in carrying a folder. She seemed surprised to find Fane there, and sat down carefully, looking apprehensive, as if she was walking into a trap. I sympathise, thought Wetherby.

Fane remained standing as Wetherby said, "Why don't you give us an overview of where things stand, Peggy? Geoffrey probably knows most of it, but I don't."

She nodded and opened the folder, though she didn't look at her notes. "Two months ago, we heard from MI6 that a trusted source had learnt about a possible plot against a dissident oligarch in London."

Wetherby asked, "What was this plot supposed to consist of?"

"It was thought an assassination might take place here in London."

"*Pour décourager les autres*," said Fane lightly, still looking out the window.

"Really?" Wetherby could not conceal his scepticism. Surely after Litvinenko, the last thing the Russian authorities would want was blame for another murder of a disaffected expatriate.

Peggy went on. "At roughly the same time, A4 saw a Russian intelligence officer, a man named Vladimir Rykov from the Trade Delegation, conducting a covert meeting on Hampstead Heath. When they followed his contact, they discovered he was an ex-SAS soldier now working as driver for Nikita Brunovsky. It was then decided to put Liz undercover into Brunovsky's household."

"I do not really understand that decision," interrupted Wetherby.

Peggy said nothing. Fane took a step back and shrugged. "One of Henry Pennington's dafter ideas, Charles," he said.

Charles looked at him sceptically. "Brian didn't have to agree, Geoffrey. It's not the FCO's call." But Fane just shrugged again.

Wetherby, knowing Fane, thought it likely that he had played more of a part in the decision than he was admitting. "What evidence was there to link this supposed plot with Brunovsky?"

"None," said Fane easily, glancing over before looking out the window again. "But the coincidence of hearing about a plot and Rykov's pass at the bodyguard seemed . . . too much of a coincidence. In any case, even if there wasn't a link, the fact that Rykov was suborning a Brunovsky retainer suggested Moscow had an interest in the man that couldn't be entirely healthy."

"That's precisely my point: surely it was a job for Special Branch, not us."

Fane kept his gaze firmly on the river, making it clear he wasn't prepared to argue. Wetherby shook his head, then gestured for Peggy to continue.

"Liz entered the Brunovsky household, posing as a history of art student—she spent a week in Cambridge being intensively tutored on Russian modernists, including a painter called Pashko whom Brunovsky was especially interested in. Brunovsky recently bought a Pashko that had long been thought lost." She looked studiedly at Wetherby. "It was rediscovered in Ireland, where Brunovsky is now, searching for another long-lost Pashko."

"This is starting to sound preposterous," said Wetherby acidly.

Fane laughed sharply enough for Peggy to look startled. Wetherby could see she too was worried about Liz. How differently we are each showing our concern, he thought: Peggy grows even more serious, Fane laughs and I get impatient with the mess I've inherited.

Peggy described what she and Liz had discovered about the people in Brunovsky's circle—his girlfriend had been an upmarket prostitute, his decorator and his personal banker had been in cahoots smuggling antiquities out of Italy. Pretty squalid, thought Wetherby, but hardly surprising, and almost certainly unconnected to Moscow. He said as much, and for once Fane turned around. "I agree," he said.

"Whatever you think," said Peggy fiercely, and both Wetherby and Fane looked at her with surprise, "Tutti was found dead in his flat. It looked like suicide, but Liz has her doubts."

"Well . . . ," said Fane, not without a note of condescension.

"And I agree with her," said Peggy quickly. Good for her, thought Wetherby. She's got nerve. "Tutti's wrists were slit with a Stanley knife. Liz was mugged, outside the safe flat, and her attacker threatened her with a Stanley knife as well."

"I didn't know that," said Fane sharply. He pulled over a chair and sat down next to Peggy, all languor gone.

"And then just to complicate things further, we were told that there might be an Illegal operating in the UK."

"Is that relevant to all this?" asked Wetherby.

"We didn't think so at first," said Peggy. "But I do now. There's a Danish woman who calls herself Greta Darnshof—she's editor of a new art magazine and she knows Brunovsky well. We've just learnt from PET in Copenhagen that the real Greta Darnshof died nearly forty years ago."

"Is this Darnshof in Ireland?" asked Fane.

"I don't know for sure, but she may well be. Her office said she was 'travelling.' "

"What's her role in all this?"

"I don't know exactly but I think she was the woman who tried to harm Liz. I can't prove it, but it certainly looks that way."

Fane broke the momentary silence: "I can't believe they'd want to harm Brunovsky: killing him in Ireland wouldn't be any better in PR terms than killing him here."

"So why *do* they want him in Ireland?" asked Wetherby.

"Because I think they'll abduct him and take him back to Russia. That's a lot easier to do in Kilkenny than Eaton Square."

"Killarney," said Peggy pedantically.

"But couldn't Brunovsky see the danger?" Wetherby broke in. "Why on earth did he agree to go to Ireland?"

Peggy spoke up. "Liz says he's desperate to get this other painting. Apparently another oligarch, a man called Morozov, also wants the picture. He and Brunovsky have got some sort of long-standing rivalry. Liz said that once Brunovsky learnt that Morozov was also on the trail, there was no stopping him."

"Morozov?" said Fane.

"Who is he?" asked Wetherby, almost resignedly. To him these people were like characters in a play. He wondered how many acts there were to be in this drama.

"He made his fortune in industrial diamonds," said Peggy. "Before that he was KGB, postings in New York and East Germany. We thought he might be planning something against Brunovsky on personal grounds—there's history between them. But we just don't know."

Wetherby turned to Fane, who was looking as if there was something he wanted to say but couldn't quite get out. I'll wait, thought Wetherby, and said nothing until the silence became strained. At last Fane broke it. "Liz asked us to find out about Morozov and I gave her a fairly detailed report from our station in Moscow. I told her he was posted in East Germany where he had a heart attack in 1989 and was sent home. But there was something else I didn't tell her. I didn't think it was relevant and the information wasn't mine to give. But I think I should tell you now."

He paused, weighing his words with care. "During his last few years in the KGB, Morozov was recruited by the West Germans. He was an agent-in-place for the BND all the time he was in East Germany. He was in the KGB station in Dresden. One of his KGB colleagues there was Vladimir Putin."

Wetherby lifted both arms in disbelief. "I would have said the plot thickens, if it weren't like treacle already. So where does that put Morozov in all this?"

"Not in Ireland, I hope," said Fane. "But it may be relevant that he's not altogether what he seems."

"I'm not sure Brunovsky is either," said Peggy quietly.

None of these people are, thought Wetherby. I just hope Liz realises that. It would have been nice if Fane had let us know this earlier. As if reading his thoughts Fane said quietly, "Sorry about that, Charles. Third-party information, you know, and it didn't seem relevant at the time."

Wetherby sighed. He was thinking that things had to be dire indeed when Geoffrey Fane apologised.

55

W e'd better be going," Brunovsky announced, looking at his watch anxiously. "Jerry, get the car round. We'll be with you in a moment."

But before Jerry could get up, the door opened. Liz found herself staring at what, at first sight, could have been an apparition. It was an old lady, with flowing hair the colour of snow. She wore a long embroidered cotton nightdress and slippers that scuffed the floor as she walked into the drawing room with slow regal steps. Her grey-blue eyes were blank, her lips set in a rigid smile. She's mad, thought Liz.

In a pure high voice, more English than Irish, the apparition spoke. "Welcome to Ballymurtagh. We do not often see visitors nowadays, but please make yourselves at home."

Liz noticed Brunovsky looking at Greta with astonishment. "Tonight," the old lady was saying, "we shall have music. There will be dancing for those who like . . ." A girlish coyness crept across her face.

Greta signalled to Dimitri, who went over to close the door, just as Svetlana ran in, her handsome Slavic face drawn and frightened. "I am sorry—she got away from me," she said, and started towards the old lady, reaching for her arm. But her target skipped forward out of reach. "Ha ha," she cried with delight, and Liz realised she was back in the nursery.

Greta moved quickly as if to grab the old lady, but it was Svetlana she was aiming for. The Danish woman approached the girl with her hands by her sides, then suddenly her right arm swung up and *crack,* with her open hand she struck Svetlana on the face. The noise was like a pistol shot. And Svetlana reeled back. In the utter silence that followed, the only movement came from the old lady, twirling her index finger into her hair.

Greta shouted something in Russian to Svetlana, pointing to Miss Cottingham. She was visibly struggling, but failing, to control her anger. "Go on, *move!*" she hissed. "Move." To Liz there was something oddly familiar about her intonation.

Svetlana was terrified, paralysed, crouching on the floor, and Greta moved again. She seized her roughly by the shoulder, trying to lift her to her feet. Dimitri came across the room to her side, and Miss Cottingham took the opportunity to scamper behind a chair, as if she were enjoying herself. For an old lady she was remarkably agile.

Dimitri and Greta approached her from opposite sides, trying to corner her, but the old lady had played this game before and she darted nimbly behind one of the sofas. Safe for an instant, she began to sing, in a high quavering voice, "You can't catch me, you can't catch me."

With everyone's eyes focused on Miss Cottingham, Liz saw her opportunity. She moved sideways to Jerry Simmons's chair. "Jerry," she whispered urgently, "give me your phone." Evidently mesmerised by the spectacle, he turned to her with an expression of disbelief, and she had to jab him hard with her finger to focus his attention. "I work with Magnusson," she said, relieved to have remembered Michael Fane's alias. "You know . . . MI5. I need your phone."

Meanwhile, Dimitri and Greta had with difficulty seized hold of Miss Cottingham. She was resisting with surprising strength, and singing at the top of her voice. Jerry's eyes, widening, were fixed on the old lady, but cautiously he reached into his jacket pocket, and the next thing Liz knew the phone was lying in the palm of her hand. As she closed her fingers on it, Dimitri picked Miss Cottingham up with both arms and carried her to the door and out of the room.

Svetlana was still sobbing. Greta, leaning down to the crouching girl, told her sharply to get out and see to her charge. Brunovsky, who had not moved a muscle since the beginning of the drama, rose to his feet and looked at his watch, for all the world like the chairman of a meeting declaring it closed. "Okay," he said. "Time to go. He won't be long now."

Greta hissed a word and it came sharply to Liz just where she'd heard that voice before. *Move!* Greta had shouted at Svetlana. *Don't move!* the mugger had ordered Liz on the darkened Battersea street. There was no mistaking that voice, with its menacing hiss. It was Greta who had attacked her, Greta who had wielded the Stanley knife. Greta, therefore, who had killed Marco Tutti.

And it was Greta who was in charge here, not Brunovsky.

Whatever she was, she was no Danish art expert. She was a Russian. No wonder the Danes had found oddities in her background, no wonder Peggy couldn't trace the ownership of her magazine. Greta must be the Illegal, a Russian intelligence officer. That was why Brunovsky was deferring to her. But what was she doing here? Who were they waiting for? And why did Brunovsky want to leave before the visitor appeared?

Liz looked at Brunovsky. "I need the ladies' room before we go. I'll be quick. I'll meet you out front."

Brunovsky nodded impatiently, reluctantly, and ignoring Greta, Liz left the room. From the rear of the house she heard snatches of song from the old lady, then Svetlana pleading with her to be quiet.

But she had no time to reflect on the bizarre aspects of the scene. Off the main hall she found an ancient bathroom and, going in, she carefully closed its tall door behind her. There was no lock. In the dim light she saw a cracked washbasin on a stand, a lavatory with a cistern high on the wall, its long chain ending in a porcelain handle. She turned on one of the taps and water gushed loudly. She must be quick. Brunovsky was impatient to be gone, and so was she. She needed to get out of the house quickly before Greta began to suspect that her cover had been cracked.

She looked down at the phone. Would she get a signal here? The display lit up, then showed SEARCHING for what seemed an eternity, until at last to her relief it registered. She dialled Peggy's Thames House extension, but almost immediately heard "The person at this extension is unavailable. Please leave a message after the tone." She hesitated, but this wasn't a time for messages. She needed urgent action. But who to call? Not Brian Ackers. Even if he were there, he'd tell her to calm down and report back later. Dave Armstrong, her friend and former colleague in Counter-Terrorism? He'd do something sensible but she might have no better luck reaching him.

She had no time at all, and her mind raced. Who could she count on to be there, to understand the urgency and to be able to act? Yes, there was someone.

The Kingston number rang twice and then a woman's voice answered. Liz spoke as loudly as she dared. "Hello, Mrs. Wetherby? It's Liz Carlyle. Is Charles there? It's urgent."

There was a pause. "Oh, Liz. He's at the office. I thought you'd know. He's gone back."

"I didn't know. I'm in Ireland." She thought of ringing off, then realised this was her one chance. "Please listen: I'm in trouble and I can't get through to the office. Please get hold of Charles and tell him Greta is here—G-R-E-T-A. Tell him she's Russian and I'm sure she's the Illegal. Brian Ackers can tell him what it all means."

"But it's Brian Charles is standing in for," said Joanne. "Didn't you know? Brian's gone on leave."

Thank God, thought Liz. But there was no time to rejoice— she had to go. "Okay. Tell him that I am at a house called Ballymurtagh, B-A-L . . . oh, you've got it? I'm leaving soon for Shillington airport. Yes, that's right—Shillington. We need the Garda here and at the airport, and they need to be armed. Can you tell him right away?" She tried to sound calm and decisive. "It's urgent."

"I'll call him now," Joanne said. "Take care." It was then that Liz remembered that Joanne had been a member of the Service herself. Twenty years ago; she'd been a secretary. That was how she and Charles had met.

But would she get through to her husband? Liz could hear nothing from the hall. It occurred to her that she might have time to text a message to Peggy and laboriously she began to compose one. She had entered BALLYM with her thumb when suddenly the bathroom door flew open and in the doorway stood Greta. She was holding a short-barrelled handgun, and it was pointing at Liz.

"Give me that," Greta demanded. Her voice was terse, emotionless. Liz held the phone out immediately.

Greta reached for it without taking her eyes off Liz or moving the gun from its focus just above her left eye. Keeping her foot in the door, she stepped back slightly and glanced at the mobile. "Have you sent this?"

"No," said Liz, "I'd just started. I need to let my boyfriend know where I am and that I'll probably be late for dinner," she added, trying to smile credibly.

Greta ignored her. She motioned to Liz to follow her into the corridor and with a grim "Move or I'll shoot," she backed off a couple of paces.

Liz had no choice. They walked back down the corridor, Liz leading. Once she tried to speak but "Shut up," was the terse response. In the drawing room they found only Brunovsky, standing impatiently. When he saw the gun in Greta's hand his face whitened with shock.

"What is going on?" he said. "We should have been gone ten minutes ago. Jerry is waiting with the car."

Greta moved away from Liz towards Brunovsky, keeping him out of her line of fire. "It's too late," she said. "I found her trying to text someone. She's already made a call."

Brunovsky was clearly agitated, looking to Greta for direction. Gone was the confident air of the tycoon used to having his own way, gone the boyish swagger.

Liz tried to stay calm, her mind racing to take in this new situation. So Brunovsky was part of the plot, not its intended victim. But their plan, whatever it was, had come off its hinges.

Greta spoke in Russian, gesturing towards Liz. Brunovsky replied in short staccato sentences. Clearly they were discussing what to do with her now the scheme for Liz to leave with him had gone awry. Brunovsky was asking questions and from the look on his face, he was not liking the answers he was getting. Liz noticed that he didn't look at her.

Would they kill her? She considered the possibility as dispassionately as she could, and rejected it. It would be impossible to cover it up, even if they put her corpse in a brick-filled trunk and dumped it in the lake.

Victor Adler had been right. There was a plot, but it had nothing to do with harming Nikita Brunovsky. There was some other target—presumably the person they were waiting for. But why on earth had Brunovsky wanted her with him in this remote part of Ireland, to see a painting that he surely already knew was a fake?

Then she understood. Brunovsky was a decoy to attract someone else. The plan was that he'd show up here, with Liz, reject the painting and then fly back to England. Whatever happened after that could not be blamed on him. Liz was to be his witness—who better than an MI5 officer, with him through the whole of his brief stay in Ireland?

Liz watched as the full scale of the disaster struck Brunovsky. Serves you right you bastard, she thought. It's goodbye London, goodbye the high life. Even goodbye Monica, though probably he wouldn't miss her much. You clever, clever bastard—only you don't look so clever now.

When first she heard the sound, it was so dim she wondered if she were imagining it. Then she thought it was just the pipes rumbling somewhere in the walls of this crumbling mansion. *Phut-phut-phut.* It was becoming more distinct, a noise from outside that was coming closer. *Phut-phut-phut.* Something up above, something in the air. Then the noise was so clear that of course it was a helicopter.

Greta said something abruptly to Brunovsky and without a word he left the room. Greta looked at Liz coolly. "We have a visitor."

"So I gather," said Liz, lifting an eyebrow skywards. "Somehow, I don't think it's Harry Forbes. Have you killed him as well as Tutti?"

"Tutti panicked," Greta said, then seemed to regret her words.

"Was it the same Stanley knife you held on me?" Greta did not reply, so Liz went on. "I couldn't understand how you got on to me. Only Simmons knew where I lived, but he didn't know anything else about me. Perhaps he told Rykov my address, but why did you suspect me?"

"Rykov is a fool," said Greta, spitting the words. "He got in the way. I already knew about you."

"Yes, you did," said Liz, starting to understand how early her identity had been betrayed. "It was you at the hotel in Cambridge, wasn't it? Trying to frighten me off. I suppose it wasn't hard to engineer a meeting between me and Dimitri."

Greta gave a small hard smile. "You didn't seem to mind," she sneered.

"So Brunovsky told you about me from the start."

"Brunovsky is a child," she said, and Liz realised the full arrogance of the woman. I suppose an Illegal needs that kind of self-confidence, thought Liz—how else could you put up with years of isolation, not even knowing for sure your long-term deception will get put to use? Hadn't Greta been tempted, after the fall of the Soviet Union, to pack it all in and get herself a life?

Liz was trying to keep Greta talking, anything to delay the moment when she and Simmons would be dealt with, in whatever way had been decided. She wanted desperately to know who they were waiting for and why. Clearly she had not been supposed to know anything about it—by this time she and Brunovsky were meant to be back at the airport.

"I can't hear the helicopter now," said Liz.

"It's landed," Greta said sharply as if Liz were another simpleton. "Keep quiet. Understand?"

Liz nodded. Greta's gun was still trained on her.

"Remember," said Greta. "Whatever happens, you say no word and you do not move. Afterwards we shall see."

She returned her pistol to her shoulder bag, keeping her hand on it.

56

As Michael emerged into the arrivals lounge at Cork airport he saw a tall, casually dressed figure with the obvious air of a police officer standing waiting. "Maloney," said the officer, offering his hand. "You'll be Mr. Fane." Michael felt like a visiting dignitary as he walked out of the airport behind Maloney, into the clear Irish light and climbed into an unmarked police car parked outside. In the driving seat was a much younger officer who introduced himself as Rodrigues. In spite of his Portuguese name, Garda Rodrigues had hair the colour of a satsuma and a face of freckles. Maloney was clearly in charge. Michael was relieved to see the message from London had got through and that, exceptionally, both Garda men were wearing side arms.

"Now, Mr. Fane. How can we help you?" Maloney asked and Michael realised with a sinking feeling that they had been given no background briefing, just the general instruction to take him where he wanted to go. He was in charge and he didn't feel ready for the responsibility.

"We need to go first to Shillington airport," said Michael in a voice more confident than he felt.

Maloney gave a mild groan and explained that he and Rodrigues had just come from near there. "Never mind," he said with a wry smile. "They also serve who only sit and drive."

Let's hope that's all we have to do, thought Michael.

As they drove along, the two Gardai sitting in the front of the car, Maloney pointed out local landmarks while Rodrigues drove in silence. The countryside they were travelling through had a wild, undomesticated aspect, made harsher by the bright light filtered through banks of high grey clouds. Crumbling stone walls ran along the edges of the fields, with the occasional rusting iron bedstead blocking up a gap. This was hinterland Ireland, Michael realised, a world away from the Cork coast one read so much about, the Republic's new Riviera.

Then Michael's phone rang. It was Peggy, speaking fast. "Where are you?"

He asked Maloney, then relayed their location to Peggy.

"Listen carefully," she said. "Liz has got a message through. She's at a country house called Ballymurtagh but she said they're leaving soon for Shillington airport. Try to get there before they go. Greta Darnshof is there. She's turned out to be a Russian— we think she's probably the Illegal we've been looking for. She's dangerous, and she's armed. The Garda are sending more officers to cover the airport and to the house. But you'll probably be there first. Try and get Liz out of it in any way you can. But be careful."

She rang off and Michael, his palms damp where he was holding the phone and his stomach churning painfully now, explained the change of destination.

"Ballymurtagh?" asked Maloney incredulously. "That old place?"

"That's what they said. And we've got to hurry. How far is it from here?"

Maloney shrugged. "About ten miles. It shouldn't take more than fifteen minutes."

Rodrigues spoke up. "Less than that if I use the siren." He looked questioningly in the rear-view mirror.

Michael shook his head. "Better not. There're other people there, and they may not be friendly."

Rodrigues gave a sideways look at Maloney and raised an eyebrow.

Michael explained. "I'm here to collect my colleague. She's called Liz Carlyle, but she's using the name of Jane Falconer. There's also a Danish woman there named Darnshof, who is really a Russian, and some other Russians. According to the call I just had, they may not want my colleague to leave. At least one of them is armed. There could be trouble."

Rodrigues blew through his teeth and looked at his partner again, this time with alarm. "No one said anything to us about Russians."

"It'll be fine," said Maloney to his younger partner, but when the older man turned towards Michael his face was sombre. "What exactly do you want us to do? Is the priority getting your colleague out of there, or dealing with these other people?" he asked.

"Getting my colleague," he said, remembering Brian Ackers's orders. But Michael, just fending off panic now, realised they might have to do both.

As they changed direction and turned on to another road, the radio crackled. Maloney answered and, listening to the transmissions, Michael realised that this was turning into a major incident and he was at the centre of it.

A pulsating sound overhead, a shadow, and then a helicopter passed over the car, barely 500 feet above the ground, and flew off into the distance. "Is that one of yours?" asked Michael, pointing through the windscreen.

Rodrigues shook his head. "No. But right now I wish it was."

57

In the drawing room the air crackled with tension. Greta stood in front of the fireplace now, very much in charge. Liz saw that someone, presumably Dimitri, had carried in the *Blue Mountain* canvas on its easel and stood it up in a corner where the light from the windows fell obliquely on it. Brunovsky had brought Jerry Simmons in from the front of the house and now they were standing beside the picture like some kind of uneasy reception committee. The whole scene resembled a stage prepared for "curtain up." Only the main character had not yet arrived.

Like Brunovsky, Dimitri was avoiding meeting Liz's eyes. She realised that he might genuinely be a gallery curator but he was no bystander here. From the assured way he was acting, he was obviously fully part of whatever was going on. That explained the small mysteries she'd found in the man: his excellent English (despite supposedly having been to the West only once before), his expensive lifestyle—the chic hotel, the expensive dinner. And, she remembered with a shiver, the sudden phone call that had sent her off home early to the waiting mugger.

Liz glanced at Simmons. How much did he understand about what was happening? He had been outside with the car while Greta was pointing her gun at Liz. She didn't know whether he was armed. Probably not. How would he act if events took an ugly turn or if she was threatened? His job was to look after Brunovsky. He'd interfere only if his principal was threatened—or in his own defence, and he was no quick thinker.

Her reflections ended abruptly when the French windows to the garden burst open and a tall, lean figure came into the room. Liz recognised the taut, scarred face of Grigor Morozov. Of course, this was the last piece of the jigsaw. The final act had begun.

Morozov wore a dark grey business suit and an open-necked shirt. Turning to face the room, he looked round, puzzled, his eyes moving from one figure to another, as he tried to understand the scene he had walked into. Then he saw Brunovsky standing by the sofa. "What are you doing here?" he said. "Where is the owner? Who are all these people?"

"Upstairs," said Brunovsky. He waved a hand airily. "But she has no objection to your looking at the picture."

"Forbes told me I would be alone," Morozov said tensely. "Have you bribed him too? If you have bought the painting, just say so and I will go back to London. But do not play games—I have had enough of your games, Brunovsky."

Brunovsky said something in Russian in a sharp, harsh voice. The explosive anger Liz had seen before seemed close to surfacing, but she noticed Greta give him a cautioning look. He contrived a small, phoney smile.

"The picture is there," he said in English, pointing at the canvas in the corner. "Be my guest. It is a little rich for my blood." And he chuckled knowingly.

Mystified, Morozov hesitated, then turned and stared at the painting on its easel. He walked closer to examine it, and Liz noticed that Greta still had her hand in her shoulder bag. Dimitri had moved and was standing now between Morozov and the door to the hall.

Morozov inspected the picture for a moment, then uttered a caustic laugh. He turned to face the room and his eyes fastened on Greta and Dimitri.

"For this you have brought me to Ireland?" he said, gesturing at the painting. "For this?" he said again, only this time there was an edge to his voice.

He turned and contemplated the picture calmly. Then suddenly he stepped forward and smashed the back of his hand into the canvas. There was a ripping, tearing sound, and a large piece of canvas flopped like a loose shirttail to the floor.

In the brief ensuing silence, Liz could only think that if *Blue Mountain* were authentic, it had just lost most of its £20 million value. But of course, Morozov had done nothing more than destroy fifty pounds' worth of recently bought paint and canvas. Who had painted it? Dimitri quite possibly.

"Why have you brought me to Ireland to show me an obvious fake?" Morozov demanded, turning to glare angrily at Brunovsky. "You thought I was so stupid that I would fall for it?"

"Well, you came!" Brunovsky replied. Some of his self-assurance had returned and his customary grin appeared on his face.

"What is the point of this charade?" asked Morozov angrily, addressing the room in general. "You have taken great trouble and you have spent many thousands of pounds, to do what? Just to fool me? Well, in that you have failed. I am not fooled."

Greta spoke, her voice calm and steely. "The picture was not the point of the exercise."

"What is the point then?" he demanded angrily.

"You are the point, Comrade Morozov."

"I am no comrade of yours, whoever you are. I have a British passport."

"An officer of the KGB does not cease to be a Russian simply because he leaves the Service. He has his oath, his duty."

"What do you mean? Who are you?" demanded Morozov, his voice rising. For the first time Liz saw fear in his eyes.

"You know very well what I mean. *Predatel!*" She spat out the word.

"I am not a traitor," Morozov protested.

"What—are you saying now that you are a German? No true Russian would work for German masters as you did, Grigor Morozov. That is treason. Article 64 of the Soviet Code prescribes the death penalty for such a crime."

Morozov swallowed, seemingly struggling to keep his nerve. "I had no choice. The Germans paid for my son's treatment. Do you know what that costs? How much it meant to me, who was paid as the Soviet state paid its servants?"

Finding no sympathy in Greta's eyes, he changed tack and addressed the room as though it were a business meeting. "There is now no such thing as the Soviet Union. It is history. You have no right to pursue a private citizen. I have a British passport. I am leaving now."

But he did not move. Greta also remained motionless. She said, "What you have done will not go away, Morozov. Treachery is not a crime which expires within seven years, like some others."

Morozov paled suddenly. He asked, "What are you going to do? Kill me?"

"No," Greta said, her voice calm and chilling. "We shall not kill you. We shall put you before a Russian judge. You will have your day in court, as your British friends say. But you know the sentence. The story of your treason will be known to all."

"You are taking me to Moscow?" asked Morozov with disbelief. "How are you going to get me there? You expect me to smile and bow at passport control?"

"No," said Greta. She gestured with her hand and Dimitri moved forward, producing out of nowhere two sets of plastic handcuffs.

At the sight of them Morozov flinched, reflexively holding his arms straight out to his sides. Greta removed the pistol from her bag and pointed it straight at him, saying curtly, "Put your hands down."

He complied reluctantly, and Dimitri cuffed his wrists. Then he roughly pushed Morozov's legs together and, kneeling down, snapped the second set around his ankles. He pushed the helpless Morozov on to a sofa and walked out of the room. Brunovsky stared uneasily out the window, scratching his jaw. No one spoke.

After a minute or two Dimitri returned with Svetlana, who was carrying a syringe and a small bottle containing a clear liquid. She filled the syringe with the fluid. Morozov, on the sofa, moaned and squirmed. Svetlana lifted the syringe and inspected it admiringly. Then she moved towards Morozov.

The Russian flinched and tried to struggle to his feet, twisting his body towards Jerry Simmons. "Help me," he shouted, then seemed to grasp that nothing could or would be done. With an assertive push of one hand, Dimitri shoved him back on to the sofa and, seizing the lapels of Morozov's jacket, opened them out until the jacket's shoulders had slid halfway down his prisoner's arms, encasing him in a home-made straitjacket. Simultaneously, Svetlana leant forward and with one deft move plunged the syringe into the Russian's biceps, piercing the skin through his shirt. Morozov gave a short hoarse cry, and when Svetlana extracted the syringe, a tiny circle of blood appeared on his shirt, spreading like an ink stain.

"What have you done to me?" he demanded, wincing from the jab.

"Don't worry," said Greta. She had relaxed, now that Morozov had been secured. "You won't even go to sleep."

Rohypnol, thought Liz. The date-rape drug. Ten times stronger than Valium. They could walk Morozov through passport control, rather than having to carry him, explaining away his stupor as a vodka-fuelled binge. He wouldn't be able to say much of anything—he'd just nod and smile dozily and before he knew it, he'd be flying at 35,000 feet towards Moscow.

What would happen to him there? A trial, it seemed, though probably little better than a show trial. This one would be designed to show the prying Western media that the Russian state did things the right way. No assassinations, no radiation poisonings, but the punishment meted out would be the same. Death.

Morozov's eyes were growing glassy; already the drug was working. He said something in Russian and shook his head, fighting against the effects of the injection. Then he tried to say something else, but no sound came out.

Greta turned to Dimitri and gave an order. He and

Brunovsky lifted Morozov to his feet and shuffled him out between them. They were going to put him in the car. She turned to Liz and Simmons, silent spectators of the whole drama. "I'm going to put you two in the cellar, along with that old man who answers the door." Then she added with an unpleasant smirk, "Perhaps later on, Miss Cottingham will let you out."

58

A dead squirrel lay flattened on the gravel at the top of the drive, still bleeding. "There's been a car along here recently," said Rodrigues, looking in the mirror at Michael in the back seat.

They were approaching the house that loomed at the end of the double row of lime trees, and a tense silence filled the car. Decay in all around I see, thought Michael as they neared, for though the building was an architectural jewel, it was a damaged one—he noted the missing tiles on the roof and the nest which rooks had made on top of one chimney. There was something spooky about the untended beauty of the place.

Michael broke the silence. "Stop here," he said abruptly,

well short of the terminating semicircle of gravel, where they could see two large black limousines parked. Rodrigues grunted and pulled over. As they got out of the car, both he and Maloney unbuttoned the holsters of their side arms.

The day was unseasonably cold, but the wind had died and a stillness hung like mist in the air. No birds sang, no cars hummed in the distance. They walked silently on the grass at the edge of the gravel drive, aware that the lime-tree avenue gave them little cover as they approached the house. Michael was very conscious of being in charge. This was his operation. But what was the best way to proceed? Ring the doorbell and ask for Miss Falconer? Find their own way in? There must be an open window somewhere.

The answer came when the large front door creaked open and a short dark man came out, moving lithely, almost cockily down the steps. Michael recognised Brunovsky at once. He felt relief—if Brunovsky were still here, then Liz must be as well. And there was no sign that the oligarch was in any danger. Far from it—he was waiting for someone, and a moment later a tall, powerfully built figure in a leather jacket came out, supporting an older man, who looked ill.

What's going on? wondered Michael. Who was this sick man and why was he being helped to the car? Where the hell was Jerry Simmons?

He knew they had to make a move. "Don't let them drive away," he instructed Rodrigues. It was then that they were spotted: as the tall man bundled the invalid into the Mercedes, he straightened up and pointed towards them, speaking urgently to Brunovsky.

"Let's go!" shouted Michael, and Maloney and Rodrigues began to run. By the car, the man in the leather jacket hesitated. For a moment Michael thought he would run for it.

"Garda!" shouted Maloney. Then "Police!"

The man turned to face them and raised his hands in surrender. It was Brunovsky who kept moving, sprinting towards the side of the house.

"Stop," shouted Maloney, but the Russian kept running. You idiot, thought Michael; didn't he understand it was the Garda? Michael was also running now, only a few yards behind the Irish policemen, and as he reached the car he decided to leave Brunovsky to it; he would be easy to find in the grounds later on. Right now his priority was Liz, and he stopped and turned to Maloney. "Leave him," he said, gesturing in the direction of the fleeing Russian. "Come with me."

They ran up the steps and into the house, where they stopped in the cavernous entrance hall and listened. Silence. Then, very faintly, they heard a slow thumping noise towards the rear of the building. Michael turned to Maloney and put a finger to his lips. "Wait here," he whispered, "and don't let anyone leave the house."

Michael moved cautiously along the corridor until he reached an open door. He peered into a sumptuous but faded drawing room, with a view of gardens and, in the distance, a large oval lake. There was a woman in the corner, struggling with one of the French windows. She was trying to open it, he realised, and when she saw him standing in the doorway, she turned back and pushed hard against the lock.

"Where is Jane Falconer?" he demanded, just as the lock gave way and the French window flew open. Instinctively, Michael stepped forward into the room. "Wait," he said, fearing the woman was about to run outside. "Don't move."

She cast a look back at him, openly scornful, and he took two quick steps towards her. This must be Greta. He still expected her to run for it, and was taken by surprise when she suddenly reached into her bag. The next thing he knew she was holding a gun. She said, with the precision of a foreign speaker, "Do not get involved."

She's going to get away, was his initial reaction before he had time to be afraid. "Put it down," he said self-consciously, wondering where the line had come from. A movie? A thriller? He was amazed how calm he felt. "Don't be stupid," he said. "Maloney!" he suddenly shouted. And as he took another step towards her, watching for her to drop the gun, he wondered quite irrationally what Anna would think of him now.

It was the last thought he ever had. Greta fired twice, though only the first shot was needed—it hit Michael two inches above his left eye, and killed him instantly.

Maloney recognised the noise from the practice range, though he wanted it to be something else—a car backfiring, a balloon popped by a child; anything other than a gunshot. He was halfway down the hall when he heard it. Lord Jesus, he thought, then said it to himself, like a mantra, "Lord Jesus."

He was reaching for his holster as he approached the doorway and he stopped momentarily to be sure he had his gun in his hand before he went into the room. He had never, in thirty-seven years on the force, drawn a weapon in anger, and he was relieved to see that his hand was steady. Still, he felt slightly foolish, as his initial panic gave way to doubt—probably he would find nothing more than some people embarrassed by the accidental bang they'd caused.

As he crossed the threshold of the room, his mind registered the body on the floor, crumpled and lying on its back. He realised it was the young lad from London, his eyes staring vacantly towards the high ceiling, a small black hole above one brow. But Maloney took this in only fleetingly, for in the background there was another figure, a woman, dressed smartly.

He would not normally have seen a female as a threat, but he saw the expression on this woman's face, an expression neither of panic nor shock but of determination. She was holding a pistol by her side and something—he was never able to say what—told him in unequivocal terms that she was going to shoot him dead. He held his arm out to its full length, and just as he saw her weapon start to swing up, he squeezed the trigger of his own gun.

The noise and kick of the explosion surprised him, so much that he almost fell backwards. Recovering, he saw the woman drop the pistol, and his eyes watched with perverse fascination as it landed on its metal butt, bounced on the large Oriental rug, freakishly bounced again, then was suddenly smothered by the body of the woman as she collapsed on to the floor.

The first thought that came into his head—though he was to tell no one this, not even his wife—was: that wasn't so hard. But then he fell to his knees, literally knocked down by the realisation of what he had done. Lord Jesus.

59

I vow to thee my country—all earthly things above—
Entire and whole and perfect, the service of my love . . .
The love that never falters, the love that pays the price,
The love that makes undaunted the final sacrifice.

As they sang the hymn Liz noticed the brown-haired girl in the second row of pews. She was crying silently, tears streaming down her face. A university friend of Michael Fane's? Perhaps even a girlfriend. More likely an ex-girlfriend, since she wasn't sitting with members of the family—Geoffrey Fane, his former wife and an elderly woman Liz assumed must be a grandmother—in the front pew. The new French husband of the former Mrs. Fane had thought it politic not to make an appearance. So, less forgivably, had Brian Ackers.

They were in the Chapel of the Order of St. Michael and St. George, located inconspicuously off the long nave of St. Paul's Cathedral, separated by beautiful brass and iron grill doors. It was a small haven in a vast public space, though occasionally noise drifted through from the cathedral, which even on a week-day morning was streaming with tourists.

The chapel seemed to Liz a strange choice for a service for someone as young as Michael. A choice made presumably by Geoffrey Fane, whose CMG, given to him fairly recently for his counter-terrorist work, would have entitled him to have his son's memorial service there. "Call Me God" as the award was known frivolously, given for significant service to the state in the foreign arena. Both the honour and the chapel represented an Establishment Michael Fane would never make his mark on. Liz felt uneasy at the unstated implication that they were mourning the death of a future English leader, when she knew all too well that Michael Fane had not been making the grade. Maybe if he'd lived he would have done well. Certainly his last act had been brave, though also headstrong.

There were two readings—the first from Leviticus given by a school friend of Michael's, who read in a low sonorous voice, like a much older man. Then the girl Liz had spotted crying got up and came forward. She read from Ecclesiastes—"Remember now thy Creator in the days of thy youth"—starting so jerkily that for a moment Liz feared that her emotions would over-whelm her. But the girl seemed to take hold of herself and read simply and movingly to the end of the verse: "Vanity of vanities, saith the Preacher . . . all is vanity."

An image flashed before her, of Michael's body lying on the

drawing-room floor. The woman she knew as Greta also lay dead nearby. Liz had been freed just seconds before, by an Irish policeman who'd been holding a gun, ready to fire.

How easily it could have gone another way. Instead of attending this memorial service Liz would be sitting in her office in Thames House, trying to stay patient with Michael Fane's countless suggestions, becoming mildly amused when Peggy proved less successful in controlling her own irritation with the man. Man? He'd been a boy, really, Liz thought now with sudden sadness.

"If onlys" continued to play a game in her head. If only Brian had agreed to her coming out of the Brunovsky house, though that was not the sole cause of these might-have-beens. If only she had seen through Brunovsky himself, sensed from his carefree, sometimes madcap behaviour that he knew he wasn't in any danger at all. She supposed, too, that her scepticism about a plot had blinded her to Greta, with hindsight clearly not what she pretended to be. They'd been looking for an Illegal, though frankly there had never been any real reason to suspect there was one—and certainly not in Brunovsky's circle.

She stopped the "if only" game. That way led to recrimination and guilt, neither of which would change anything now, least of all the death of Michael Fane. Liz had long ago learnt that if you did your best, that was all you could do—that, and try to learn from your mistakes. A cliché, perhaps, but no less true for it.

You had to hand it to Brunovsky, she thought, as a speaker walked slowly towards the lectern, set in front of the modest altar. The oligarch had managed to flee Ballymurtagh in the most dramatic way—escaping in the same helicopter that had brought Morozov there. Interviewed by the Garda later that evening, the shocked pilot explained how the Russian had come sprinting across the lawn behind the house and jumped straight into the helicopter's passenger seat. When the pilot had protested, this new passenger had stuck a derringer to his head and ordered him to start the engine.

One hour later they had set down in a park on the southern outskirts of Dublin, not far from the Martello tower of Joyce and *Ulysses* fame. Backed by the pistol, Brunovsky had ordered him to take off on his own. As he'd hovered briefly 400 feet up, the pilot had last seen the Russian getting into a large black car waiting at the edge of the park.

It could not have been planned—Liz was certain that Brunovsky had expected to return to England with her, establishing an unbreakable alibi for the kidnapping of Morozov—but there must have been a fallback. He'd have been helped, possibly, by the Russian Embassy in Dublin. Or perhaps by some sympathisers—that seemed unlikely, but then so had the idea of an Illegal until Greta had proved otherwise.

In any case, the oligarch had disappeared without trace. No one resembling his description had gone through any of Ireland's thirty-six airports, despite intensive scrutiny from both the Republic and the Northern Ireland aviation authorities. A search of maritime passenger lists had proved equally barren. Was it possible that the Russian had remained in Ireland, waiting for the situation to calm down before making his move?

Then, four days ago, the MI6 station in Moscow had reported a sighting of Brunovsky, admittedly from a not altogether reliable source. He had been spotted in an expensive restaurant, lunching with a senior official from the state oil company. He had seemed carefree, relaxed.

As for "Greta," she now lay in an unmarked grave in County

Cork—the same Russian Embassy had shown no interest in helping to identify the dead woman, about whom the only thing to be said with certainty was that she was *not* Greta Darnshof.

The eulogy was being given by one of Michael's old schoolmasters, and as he spoke, Liz realised that the man hadn't really known Michael very well—his praise of Michael's promise was unspecific, and he didn't seem to have kept in touch once Michael moved on from university. There was an ineffable pathos about it all.

But then, as the schoolmaster went on to recount Michael's love for cricket, Liz thought, just how well does anyone know another person? She contemplated the strange, rich cast of characters she had come across in this latest and oddest assignment of her career. She thought of the Brunovsky retinue, and their irregular array of secrets. She doubted she would ever see Monica again, unless it was to catch a glimpse of her shopping on New Bond Street in an Hermès scarf, or rushing to lunch at San Lorenzo. She would soon have another rich man in tow.

Mrs. Warburton, the housekeeper, and the cook, Mrs. Grimby, would probably have forgotten about Liz already, and right now Jerry Simmons would have other things on his mind—like the interview with the brigadier about his future employment. Peggy had told her that Harry Forbes was back in New York; long may he stay there, thought Liz.

And Dimitri, of course, who had been held by the Garda for two days, then quietly expelled, along with Svetlana, the planted carer for Miss Cottingham. It would have been difficult to prove either was going to kidnap Morozov, and it had been Greta who had the gun. Henry Pennington had had some explaining to do to his colleagues in the Irish Foreign Affairs Department, but at least his worst nightmare had been avoided and the prime minister's trip to Moscow was going ahead as planned. Morozov had recovered in twenty-four hours from the huge dose of Rohypnol and was back in London, no doubt with reinforced protection.

The schoolmaster finished his eulogy, and the clergyman moved forward for the concluding prayer. Next to Liz, Peggy Kinsolving knelt down on her kneeler, head bowed and hands firmly clasped, while Liz, a non-believer, merely bowed her head as a mark of respect. How young Peggy was, and seemingly such an open book. Yet there were indications of a developing resolve and a mental toughness that held promise for the future. You grew close to people in the shared responsibility of this sort of work. But it was an intimacy forged by a common goal, not by the sense that getting to know each other was a be-all and end-all.

Except. She cast a discreet sideways glance at Charles Wetherby, who like Liz had not knelt but merely bowed his head. Even with him, a close familiar presence at work, there were whole areas of his life she had never even glimpsed. She'd never met his wife, or his sons; she wondered if she'd find him the same man when he was with his family. Now, she wasn't even sure for how long he would be back in Thames House.

Yet increasingly she was aware—and there was no point in fighting it—that she cared for him deeply, and quite independently of work. Did he feel the same? She simply didn't know, and in the circumstances—he was again her boss now, his wife was still terminally ill—Liz couldn't see how she was going to find out any time soon.

They sang a final, familiar hymn, then slowly made their way out of the pews and into the cathedral nave. As she and Wetherby came to the entrance of St. Paul's, Geoffrey Fane was there, standing on the steps outside, greeting the departing mourners. They queued briefly, then Liz found herself shaking his hand.

"Thank you for coming," said Fane. And then, "It has been very unpleasant for you."

"We'll miss him," said Liz, and Fane nodded gratefully. The slightest quiver of his lip belied his cool façade.

Wetherby had tactfully moved on.

Fane said, "I can't help thinking that if only I had told you that Morozov had been turned by the Germans, the whole disaster could have been avoided. You might have seen it was Morozov they were after."

The possible truth of this was undeniable, but Liz shrugged. "I should have suspected Brunovsky. He never seemed worried enough for a man supposed to be in danger."

Fane shook his head. "Not at all. You did very well, with the sketchy information you had." It was clear he was determined to blame only himself.

Fane's thoughts moved on. "You know," he said wistfully, "Michael and I didn't have much of a relationship. My fault, I'm afraid—I suppose I let my quarrels with his mother infect things. But the last time I saw him, he asked if we could have lunch."

"I'm sure you would have become close."

He smiled wryly. "That's just another vanished opportunity I'm going to have to live with."

He looked with resignation at Liz, then turned towards the mourners behind her, who were ready to offer their own condolences. As Liz moved down the steps on to the pavement courtyard, now soaked in the midday sun, she saw Wetherby waiting for her patiently.

ALSO BY STELLA RIMINGTON

AT RISK

A terrorist is targeting Britain. And to make matters worse it's an "invisible"—someone traveling under a British passport and virtually impossible to find before it's too late. The job falls to Liz Carlyle, the most resourceful counter-terror agent in British Intelligence. Tracking down this invisible is a challenge like none she has faced before. It will require all her hard-won experience, to say nothing of her intelligence and courage. Drawing on her own years as Britain's highest-ranking spy, Rimington gives us a story that is smart, tautly drawn, and suspenseful from first to last.

Espionage Fiction/978-1-4000-7981-0

SECRET ASSET

When it appears a "secret asset"—a sleeper spy—has infiltrated British Intelligence, the Director of counter-terrorism assigns Liz Carlyle to dig up the mole. The spy, possibly a former IRA operative now working with British-born Al Qaeda sympathizers, has one thing on his (or her?) mind: total devastation. With a major attack looming, Liz must trust her instincts and move fast. But this assignment is deadly, and suddenly she feels like she has wandered into a "wilderness of mirrors," where nothing is what is seems and no one can be trusted.

Espionage Fiction/978-1-4000-7982-7

VINTAGE CRIME/BLACK LIZARD
Available at your local bookstore, or visit
www.randomhouse.com